Series A
Southold Chronicles #2

discard

To Capture Her Heart

This Large Print Book carries the
Seal of Approval of N.A.V.H.

TO CAPTURE
HER HEART

REBECCA DEMARINO

THORNDIKE PRESS
A part of Gale, Cengage Learning

GALE
CENGAGE Learning·

Farmington Hills, Mich • San Francisco • New York • Waterville, Maine
Meriden, Conn • Mason, Ohio • Chicago

LIBRARY OF CONGRESS CATALOGING-IN-PUBLICATION DATA

DeMarino, Rebecca.
    To capture her heart / by Rebecca DeMarino. — Large print edition.
      pages cm. — (Thorndike Press large print Christian romance) (The southold chronicles ; book 2)
    ISBN 978-1-4104-8157-3 (hardcover) — ISBN 1-4104-8157-3 (hardcover)
    1. Large type books. I. Title.
PS3604.E4544T6 2015b
813'.6—dc23   2015019402

Published in 2015 by arrangement with Revell Books, a division of Baker Publishing Group

Printed in Mexico
1 2 3 4 5 6 7 19 18 17 16 15

To my three sweet daughters,
Jennifer Ann Brashear, Lisa Marie Taylor,
and *Kelly Michelle Adams.*

They are the lights of my life
and the dots that connect the lines
from one generation to the next.

A NOTE FROM THE AUTHOR

As I wrote the second book in *The Southold Chronicles* series, I once again enjoyed being immersed in Southold, Long Island, town history. The village was isolated from English rule in the seventeenth century, but with the Montaukett to the south, the Dutch to the west, and the Narragansett to the north, it was never humdrum.

While Dirk Van Buren is a completely fictitious person, the existence of Heather Flower is somewhat controversial. Many believe she was Quashawam, the daughter of Wyandanch, the Grand Sachem of Montauk. Some say she was a second daughter of Wyandanch, and a few believe she was Catoneras, a native woman who married a Dutchman. Others say she is a legend. Historically there are accounts of the kidnapping of Wyandanch's daughter, with a ransom paid by Lion Gardiner.

The Hortons and Southold provide the

backdrop for *To Capture Her Heart,* with the second generation coming of age and not always seeing the world through their father's eyes. They were looking forever forward, while through my stories I take a look back. My mother, Helen Jean Horton Worley, inspired my first novel, and she remains forever my inspiration.

1

June 21, 1653

The thunder of a thousand hooves pounded in her ears and she buried her head beneath her tethered hands. She muffled the noise with her arms pressed against her ears. Heather Flower sat very still. She remembered the childhood game peekaboo. She'd believed if she could not see her mother, her mother could not see her.

But this was not a game. Her legs, bound at the ankles, were drawn up under her skirt, and her knees trembled as she lowered her covered head till her forehead touched them. A pool of quiet tears soaked the soft, beaded deerskin.

Sudden silence, save for the occasional snort from the winded horses, or the soft swish of their tails, brought intense fear. Her body shook as she tried to draw herself into the smallest mound possible. The restraints dug into her slender wrists, but her lips were sealed together in a thin line and not a cry escaped.

The footfalls approaching were not the tread of her Indian captors. A leather-clad hand lifted her chin, and her heart quaked in her chest. Her throat constricted until it ached as she gathered her courage and lifted her eyes.

"Hallo! You are Heather Flower, the daughter of the Great Sachem, Wyandanch?"

His posture bore no malice but was instead gentle, kind. She dared to hope he would not harm her.

Her chin quivered in the cup of his glove, her moist lashes fluttered, but her voice was strong. "I am Quashawam, the Heather Flower of Montauk." She studied his face and saw kindness.

"We were sent from Lion Gardiner and his friend John Smith to find you and take you to your father, who waits for you." His voice was deep like the sound of the ocean in a conch shell, smooth and comforting. He removed his gloves and drew his knife. With a quick cut he released her ankles. He grasped her arms and lifted her to her feet.

Her legs found no bearing, and he steadied her before taking her hands in his to cut the last tether.

"Thank you, my paleface brother." She looked into eyes the color of the crystal clear bay on a warm summer afternoon.

"Take some water to drink, and when you have had your fill, I have some biscuits and dried berries for you. When did they last give you food?"

"They left me here for many days. I do not remember how many. They might come again soon. We must go. I fear the mean brothers of Connecticut." His face blurred in front of her as she dropped into his arms. The young white brave helped her back to the ground and pressed a cup of water to her lips. She drank deeply, then pushed the cup away. "*Ooneewey*. Thank you."

She knew the accent of his speech. "You are Dutch? What is your name? Why would the Englishman Gardiner send you?"

"I am Lieutenant Dirk Van Buren, from Fort Amsterdam. I serve a different army, but when Gardiner needed men, I asked to be permitted to head the party. These men are English from the Southold Militia, led by Lieutenant Edward Biggs. They are under my command on this mission. We Dutch have our own reasons to hate the fierce Narragansett. And I know their territory intimately."

He dug into his knapsack and offered a

11

biscuit. "You may call me Dirk. Here, eat this before we travel. You need strength."

A thicket of bayberry shrubs directly behind her rustled and she startled, her reply frozen in her throat. A young cottontail scrambled from beneath. Relief rushed through her veins, quickly replaced by a wave of embarrassment. It did not go unnoticed by this man Dirk.

He squatted close beside her and pressed the biscuit in her hand. "Amazing what noise a small creature can make, *ja*? You are safe now. Take this."

She chewed as she stared at the rescue party, now dismounting and rummaging in their own knapsacks for food. She counted twenty-five men. "I heard the running of many hooves — I thought hundreds of horses, thousands of hooves."

"I'm not sure there are that many horses on Long Island." His clear blue eyes penetrated hers. "*Hoe gaat het?* How are you? How were you treated?"

She drew a deep draught of warm air, scented with the bayberry and old pine needles, and calm engulfed her. "They were happy to have the daughter of Wyandanch. They taunted me with thoughts of what my father must endure. And though they did not hurt me with arrows or knives, they cut

12

to my heart with their words. When they received the wampum sent by my father and the paleface Gardiner, they told me they were releasing me, but then left me here to die. Or worse, to fear they would return with their mean ways."

Dirk stood and held out a strong hand. She held tight as he pulled her up and watched as he brought his horse, the color of tanned buckskin with a sooty black mane and tail, to her side. She held out her hand and stroked the horse's muzzle. "She has a name?"

"*Ja,* her name is Button. Miss Button I call her."

Heather Flower nodded.

"I can protect you best if you ride in front," he said simply as he lifted her in one swoop onto pommel of the saddle.

The English lieutenant gave the search party the command to mount their horses and they split to ride fore and aft of the Dutch lieutenant. The long ride around the North Sea began.

The woman captivated Dirk as he guided his horse up a wide deer trail. The Montaukett were a tall, strong people, and she was almost his equal in height. She held herself in a majestic manner that bespoke of

13

the royalty she was born into. Her eyes were fiery like black opals, and her mouth pouty and red like a blossom. Her skin was a creamy copper, and her hair ebony with the sheen of bear grease. Tangles and snarls from weeks without a comb made him want to reach out and smooth her tresses. He made a mental note to give her his military issue comb when they made camp.

He was drawn to her, there was no denying, and he longed to be her hero, to protect her. That he would do, but her heart was tender. Ninigret, the fierce sachem of the Narragansett and enemy of the Long Island natives, had killed her groom on their wedding day. His warriors forced her to watch and then kidnapped her and thirteen other Montaukett women. Dirk would protect her, yes, but that meant to protect her heart as well. He'd have to guard his own to do that.

He urged his steed down a steep embankment toward the bay and kept the reins in, guarding Heather Flower like he would a flickering flame on a windy day. "We will ride west along the bay until we can cross the East River at Manhattan over to Brooklyn. It's a hard seven-day ride to Montauk in good circumstances. You must tell me when you need to rest or when you are hungry. I want you to be strong."

She stared straight ahead, head held high. He knew he would not hear a complaint from her, not even a whimper. It was the way of her people.

Hours passed and the sun became a blazing ball in the west, low on the horizon. Fort Saybrook loomed on the hill and Dirk passed word to the front that Captain Mason expected them. As they rode past the old burned-out portion of the fort, he found it odd to be coming here, a Dutch fort now under English control, and he, surrounded by Englishmen. But there were issues in this wilderness that brought them together on some fronts.

As they entered the palisades, a small contingent of men greeted them, taking their horses to the livery and directing them to headquarters.

Captain Mason stood up from behind his desk and came around to shake Dirk's hand, but his eyes were on Heather Flower. She remained in the open doorway, and with her high cheekbones, large eyes, and lips like Leonardo's Mona Lisa, Dirk was certain the captain was as enchanted as he was. "Sir, I present Heather Flower, daughter of the Grand Sachem Wyandanch of Montauk."

Mason cleared his throat. "We have much regard for your father. It is a privilege to assist Captain Gardiner in your return. You shall sleep here tonight and on the morrow Lieutenant Van Buren shall escort you home. Now in the meantime, you need a hot meal." He took her arm and led her out.

A hearty meal of corn mush and biscuits with a slather of butter was served, and Dirk watched with pleasure as Heather Flower eagerly ate a full portion. The contented but weary party threw their bedrolls down for the night. He spread hers a bit further from the men.

"You are safe here. Men guard the gates and fence line at all hours." He settled himself atop his own bedding, tucking his musket close to his side. The ground was hard and the night alive with cricket chirps. Somewhere an owl hooted. He propped his hands beneath his head and stared at the heavens.

The night was warm and the ink sky a dance of thousands of winking stars. An astral display fell as if the sky had parted. Some Indians believed it to be a sign of travel heroes and he glanced over to the still form of Heather Flower and hoped she'd seen it.

He asked God for travel mercies as sleep

claimed him.

Heather Flower was awake before the sun
rose. The crescent moon had set hours ago,
but the crisp stars still illuminated the sky.
She crept toward the glow of the fire and
sat. She clutched the comb Dirk had given
her the day before and began to pull it
through the tangles in her hair. Strand by
strand the snarls came undone. As the men
began to stir around her, she finished a long
braid over her shoulder.

Cook came out to refresh the fire and fried
yesterday's corn mush for a tasty breakfast.
He put together a dinner packet of salt pork,
biscuits, and dried apples. Dawn was still
new as the small band of men mounted
their horses. Dirk lifted her to the saddle,
then swung up behind and led the party out
of the palisade gate.

The man Dirk was very quiet, but Heather
Flower did not mind. She was safe and she
was going back to her father and mother,
back to her people. "You are brave to rescue
me from the Narragansett. You are clever
too. You did not come across your North
Sea in the great canoes with wings. You
would have been slaughtered by Ninigret.
You came by horse following the land."

"*Ja.* I know the heart and thoughts of

17

Ninigret. I know his land like my own home-country. It is why Captain Gardiner entrusted his best men to my care. It was the wish of your father, as well."

They rode in silence as she thought of her family, her head barely touching Dirk's shoulder. She studied the trail in front of them and listened to the wind in the willows that lined the path. She would know trouble before it could be seen and certainly before any of the rescue party.

At length they entered an open saltmarsh and she relaxed ever so slightly. "They killed my new husband. I saw them. As we celebrated our wedding, Ninigret killed him. My father, mother, and brother were tied up. His warriors held me by my arms and made me watch. My husband looked into my eyes until his last breath. And then Ninigret ordered his men to take me and the other women. They threw us into the bottoms of canoes and rowed swiftly across the black waters."

"You need not tell me this if it hurts you. I know the story. I am sorry for the terrible massacre. I am sorry for your husband and your pain."

"I would die rather than stay with the Narragansett."

"*Ja,* but you don't have to. You are safe,

Heather Flower. Safe with me."

She let her head rock backward until she rested in the hollow of his shoulder. This man she owed her life to. A small smile played at the corner of her mouth — the first smile since she'd smiled at her new husband — as Dirk tried to speak her language with his Dutch accent. It was very different than the English, but she liked the cadence.

They rode long days, with few stops. With the summer solstice only a day behind them, the evening light gave them a long day of travel, and when it faded they bedded down where they could, always with men guarding the night. On the fourth day of travel, Fort Amsterdam was a welcome sight. Heather Flower was given her own quarters that night. The Englishmen slept in their bedrolls by the fire.

At dawn Heather Flower awoke before anyone, as she had each morning. She warmed herself by the fire until the search party joined her. They broke their fast with little cakes the Dutchmen called *poffertjes,* which she found to her liking. She watched Dirk while he ate with gusto. Her brother, Wyancombone, could wolf his food in that way. It would be good to see him again. Soon she would be home.

■ ■ ■ ■

Dirk tied his knapsack and musket to the back of his saddle. Moving to the front of Miss Button, he untied her feedbag and talked low as he patted her neck. The last leg of the journey would be a long one. They could make Wading River in two days, but tonight they would need to find shelter somewhere in Samuel Ketcham's valley. Montauk would be another day's ride.

Button's ears flicked toward excited shouts at the front gate. Dirk turned as Joseph and Benjamin Horton rode through to the livery. He strode toward the brothers. "Hallo there!"

"Good morrow to you, Lieutenant." Joseph swung down from his Great Black and stuck out a hand, his gloves tucked under his arm.

"What brings you to New Amsterdam?" Dirk's brow creased as he gripped the Englishman's hand.

"We've been sent to escort Wyandanch's daughter."

Something of a rock formed in his throat and he swallowed hard before answering. "I am her escort. You may accompany your men home with us. We will make Samuel

20

Ketcham's by dark." Dirk looked from the Horton brothers to Biggs.

Benjamin stepped forward and offered to shake. "Captain Gardiner and my father, Barnabas, send their regard and a hearty thank-you, but we are instructed to bring Heather Flower from here. There will be no need for you to travel with us."

A flock of noisy red hens pecked at the dirt in hopes of a seed or kernel of corn. Dirk watched as they bobbed and then scurried in every direction as Heather Flower approached. How would she feel? She trusted him. He wanted to scoop her up onto his horse and ride fast.

Instead, he waited for her to join them. "These men are here to take you home. They tell me I am to stay here at the fort, and you will be under their jurisdiction. Is that what you would want?"

She nodded to Joseph and Benjamin. "*Aquai,* friends. Dirk, they are like brothers to me. They are the sons of Mary, friend of my aunt Winnie of Southold, Old Yennicott. It would be unkind of me to say no. But I thank you from the heart for what you have done for me. I will never forget you."

Joseph untethered the horse they brought had for her and Dirk stepped forward to brace Heather Flower's foot as she swung

21

to the saddle. He caught her hand as she picked up the reins and gently squeezed. She graced him with her small smile that barely turned the corners of her mouth. Her dark eyes shimmered with dew as she turned away and followed the Horton brothers eastward, away from the fort.

He shielded his eyes against the bright morning sun, watching as the small rescue party rode into the distance. He rubbed his hand across his mouth. He was always so sure of himself. So in control. But in the matter of a moment, from the first they had met, he'd fallen. *Ja.* He'd fallen all right. He'd never loved before, but there could be no mistaking the jagged pain that started in his throat and burned down to his very heart. He wanted her to come back. No, he wanted to get on Miss Button and chase her.

2

June 26, 1653

As the rescuers neared the East River, Heather Flower turned to Benjamin as he pulled up close on Star, his Great Black gelding. Except for her fear of Ninigret and his men returning, this was the most danger-ous part of the journey home. She listened intently.

"We'll be crossing the river where the Dutch run a ferry," Benjamin said, "and then we'll be on Long Island." He pointed to the edge of the river. "There are the rowboats, and I want you to ride in one. I'll go with you, and the horses will swim. Jo-seph will ride across with our mounts on leads behind him. The current is tricky. It changes often, but this is the best time of day to cross and the weather is decent."

They rode up to the river's edge and he helped her into the wooden boat, holding it fast to the shore until his brother and the rest of the party had guided their horses into the river. As their mounts found the current and swam with it to the opposite shore, Benjamin pushed off the bank and the two muscled Dutchmen who operated the ferry began to row. The air was still, the surface water but a ripple, and the little boat scuttled across. Joseph and the men arrived first, wet but safe.

Benjamin climbed out, then held her hands as he helped her out. The earth felt good beneath her feet and comfort settled over her like a soft rabbit fur. *Paumonak.* Long Island. She was home. She gazed at the forest they would ride through. The thick hickory and white oak concealed deer paths known only to her people. They would be watched as they rode toward home, but from a distance by friendly eyes.

Joseph dug two stuyvers from the leather bag he kept on his belt and paid the ferrymen for their service. Their horses' strides hit a rhythm as she rode between the Horton men. How could two blood brothers be so different? Joseph was tall with broad shoulders and the high Horton forehead. He had his father's good looks with a mass of mahogany brown hair worn a bit longer than Barnabas's, and the same mossy green eyes. Mary said Benjamin looked just like his mother, Ann — blond curls and clear blue eyes and the smile of an angel. And the differences between the brothers didn't stop there.

But they both were charmers, and the blond one was in love with her. She'd known that since she was ten. But her heart had belonged to her warrior for as long as she could remember. Sadness filled her. Grateful for the silence, she allowed her thoughts to linger on the last time she had seen him. She needed this quiet interlude.

Keme was the boy who always laughed when they were growing up. Not at her, but with her. Even when ceremonies called for silence she could see laughter in his eyes and she knew where his thoughts lay: tranquil moments chasing butterflies with her — azure beauties flitting through the forest and orange Monarchs, their wings dry, taking flight for the first time from their milkweed home in the meadow. Or running through the birch woods, fascinated as they paused to watch an English bee swallowed within the pink folds of the moccasin flower. They wanted to stop it, but feared its sting. Keme's mother smiled when they'd told her about the poor bee eaten by the flower and assured them it didn't die, but left pollen for the flower and took some more away with it.

As they grew older, the laughter in his eyes was imbued with admiration, and he would pick the pink flowers for her and play his flute by her door. She knew he loved her, and in truth, she could not remember a day when she did not love him. For her she could not imagine a day without Keme, and there had never been a question if she would be his wife.

Her throat closed tight until it ached and her eyes stung as she stared at the ground she traveled with Joseph and Benjamin. Her own people had worn this path many years before, now widened by the white men's horses and frequent travel. They rode for hours as they followed the eastward-flowing Peconic River where they could, with a few wordless stops to water their horses and fill their water pouches.

Joseph pushed up in his saddle, stretching his legs. "We should reach the lake tonight, and tomorrow we will make Montauk before nightfall."

Heather Flower listened, but remained silent. The company of men rode before the trio and behind, and as the trail narrowed, the riding party formed a single line. Joseph moved his mount ahead of her, while Benjamin fell behind. No one would harm her on this journey home. But it would be a bittersweet homecoming. She wiped at the moisture on her lashes, glad the white brothers could not see her tears.

They spread out once again as they rode through bogs and marshes and eventually approached a clearing near the river. Joseph urged his horse to a canter and rode to the front of the group. He pulled up. "We'll camp here tonight. Lieutenant Biggs, give me some of your men to go on a hunt, and send the rest to gather wood for a fire." He watched as a young bald eagle, still a solid dark gray, swooped and nailed its prey with deadly accuracy.

Heather Flower followed his gaze to the sacred bird.

Benjamin swung off of his horse and tethered him to a log. He held the bridle of Heather Flower's mount and offered a hand while she climbed down.

"Thank you," she said. "Would you walk with me down to the river? I must talk with you."

"Of course. Are you all right?"

They walked toward the water in silence. He would wait for her to answer and she appreciated his willingness to let her take the lead. She listened for a moment to the breeze whistling through the tree limbs, the water flowing nearby, and wished they could sit together without words and be still. But as they neared the water's edge he stopped.

"Heather Flower, are you all right?"

"I am not. I will not be if I go home. My husband's blood soaks the ground."

Benjamin's baby blue eyes searched hers.

"Take me to my aunt's home. Let me stay with Winnie."

He lowered himself to a fallen tree and motioned for her to sit next to him. "Your father would be grieved to not have you in Montauk. He may be angry if we do not bring you back as he directed."

"It is my decision to make. He will respect it, Benjamin. We must take the north fork in the morning. We must go to Southold."

"All right then. Let me talk to Joseph. I'm sure he will have the same concerns as I, but I think we need to honor what you wish."

She felt the nearness of him. He would want to hold her hand, to put his arm around her for comfort. But he would keep the space between them out of respect for her dead husband, out of respect for her feelings. He was a good man with a strong belief in the white man's God, the same God her aunt prayed to. Winnie's mother had learned of this God when she lived with the palefaces of Massachusetts.

Heather Flower stood. "You are kind, my brother." She shivered in the coolness of the summer evening and looked up. The sky was a dusky blue above with clouds to the west, now swathed in orange and pink as the sun sank behind them. A purple hue ran the length of the horizon below the sherbet-colored clouds. A few faint stars began to shimmer overhead as she moved up the path toward the crackle of fire.

Benjamin thought he was the first to wake the next morning, but Heather Flower's form near the low embers told him he was not. He sat up and took stock of the other sleeping men, his gaze falling on Joseph who slept with one hand on his musket, the other clenched on top of his chest. No doubt he fought some kind of battle in his sleep.

Heather Flower hummed and he turned his attention back to her. It was not a happy song, but a dirge of sorts. A sorrowful, soft wail. Joseph had said at first they must return her to Chief Wyandanch. They had no choice. But Benjamin stood his ground, and his brother gave in. Taking care of her was a priority now, if she'd let him.

He pulled on his boots. She turned toward

the noise. He smiled as he stood and stretched his stiff limbs, then joined her at the fire. A nudge to the blackened logs woke the embers beneath and sparked a flame. "Did you sleep?"

Her face was solemn, her black opal eyes never leaving him. "I do not sleep, I mourn."

"I understand." He studied her a moment, then looked at the gray, humid sky. "Please take care of yourself. We can make it to Southold by noon if we can get packed up and leave soon. But it's a hard ride. You must eat something. Tonight, at your aunt's, you must sleep." The urge to take her in his arms and rock her to and fro drove him to turn away. He bit back all of the words he wanted to say but knew he could not. She was fragile.

Joseph roused Biggs. He was anxious to be on their way now that they were going straight to Southold. He never liked leaving his sweet wife, Jane.

Benjamin stood and left Heather Flower by the fire to help his brother pack up the camp.

Within half an hour they mounted and crossed the Peconic to head north, into Southold territory. The town green was a good four-hour ride. Benjamin rode in silence and mulled over Heather Flower's wishes. It could be good for her to stay in Southold with Winnie, though it had been a long time since she last visited. She'd been a young girl, a lot had changed.

The royal family had come across the bay from Montauk in canoes when Winnie's eldest daughter, Abigail, had married. Abigail had come to live with the Hortons many years ago, when Benjamin's half brother Caleb was born. She was only fifteen, but she'd helped birth him. His mother, Mary, loved her like a daughter and called her Abbey.

Ten-year-old Heather Flower had looked regal in her beaded and be-feathered robe and matched the beauty of the bride even at her young age. When Benjamin grew up, he fell in love with Anna Budd, but he'd not forgotten the Indian princess who came to Abbey's wedding.

"My brother, the wind has shifted and a storm comes."

Her words brought him to the present and he straightened in the saddle. He sniffed the air. "You smell the rain?"

"*Nuk,* yes. I feel it too. A big storm comes in from the west."

The cloud cover had hung low all morning. He couldn't see anything that looked threatening like thunderclouds. But she knew things in nature the white man could only pretend to know.

"Joseph, a storm's coming in. We'd best move with haste if we are to get home before it hits."

His brother spurred his horse toward the front of the company, and he and Heather Flower pressed their mounts to a canter. The easy gait of the Great Blacks made it comfortable to sustain until the outlying wigwams and longhouse of the Corchaug people came into view.

They crossed Downs Creek as heavy drops of rain began to fall and the wind picked up. They split as Biggs's men rode toward Ester Bayley's boardinghouse in Southold. She would provide a hot meal for the horse troop before they returned to their homes as she did every Saturday after the troop's militia training.

Benjamin and Heather Flower rode ahead of Joseph as they approached the Corchaug village. Wigwams stood outside the fort's palisade and a few women sat outside scraping hides with sharp shells. They watched as the trio rode through the palisade, into the fort.

Heather Flower looked back to Joseph, then turned to him. "I don't remember my aunt's wigwam."

He nodded toward a large, round hut

covered with grass. Smoke poured from a clay-covered opening at the top. Winnie would be inside, perhaps tending to Winheytem. He'd fallen ill before the Horton boys had left on their mission to bring back Heather Flower. "Your aunt won't be expecting us. No doubt she will be overcome to see you. Your uncle wasn't well when we left to get you."

Joseph jumped to the ground and wrapped the reins around a hickory pole. "Mayhap I should go in first?" He looked to her, an eyebrow raised.

He raised both brows when Benjamin answered instead. "You go, we'll wait. Tell Winnie if Winheytem is too sick, we can take her to Father's. Is that all right with you, Heather Flower?"

"Abigail would have me, if my aunt cannot, Benjamin."

Benjamin climbed down from his horse and helped Heather Flower down. "Of course." He tipped his hat to Joseph, who walked up to the wigwam, the doorway covered by a heavy bearskin.

At Joseph's hello, the pelt was pulled back and the low incantations of the medicine man could be heard. He stepped inside.

Within moments Winnie appeared and enveloped her niece in her arms in stoic silence. "You will stay with me, my child. Winheytem prepares to enter the spirit world. I pray to the white man's God, but He calls for my husband. We must send a message to your father and mother. They will understand. They will know I hold you close to me."

Benjamin was torn. He knew Winnie needed Heather Flower as much as she needed Winnie. But he hated to leave her. His heart had been broken by Anna Budd, but the Indian princess made him forget that. When she was ready to love again, he wanted to be there for her — the one she could turn to.

3

June 28, 1653
Mary, obviously with child but determined to get a first look, came out to the flagstone walkway and watched Ben and Jay — she still called them by the nicknames she'd given them when she'd first become their mother — ride up the main road. The horse they'd taken with them for Heather Flower trailed behind on a lead-rope. All three horses were descendants of her beloved Starlight, one of the Old English Great Blacks her papa had bred back in England. There'd been an embargo on the mares when they first came over the pond. Thank goodness Barnabas's brother, Jeremy, had been the shipmaster who brought their family over in *The Swallow.* Eventually he brought Starlight after the embargo was lifted.

Caleb, her firstborn — and the first white child born on eastern Long Island — had brought her the news the rescue party was on their way and joined her on the walkway as the Horton men approached. She put an arm around her thirteen-year-old, who was now taller than she was and possessed his father's sturdy frame. Though his eyes and hair matched hers, he had the Horton smile and chuckle.

"I'm so glad they are back safely. I worry whenever they ride into Dutch territory."

Caleb patted her hand. "They can take care of themselves now, Mama. And we are at peace with the Dutch, are we not?"

"Not according to Ben and Jay. Or Johnny Youngs. And in truth even New Haven hasn't a clue as to what goes on between Holland and England. By the time ships arrive with the latest news, our Parliament has taken a different course." She brushed a loose curl from her forehead.

"We have a welcoming party." Ben smiled as he pulled in Star. He swung down and Caleb took the reins from him. "Hey, thank you." He tousled his brother's hair.

Jay dismounted and Caleb took his horse as well. "Thanks, Cabe." He gave him a soft punch to his shoulder that brought a smile, then turned to Mary and wrapped her in a hug. "Good to see you, Mother. How are you feeling?"

His words warmed her heart. " 'Tis good to see both of you. I'm feeling fine, but you know how I worry." She smiled though tears threatened, and brushed at the lock on her forehead again. Ben gave her a hug too, and the three walked up to the house as Caleb led the horses to the barn.

"How is Heather Flower? I've been sick at heart for her. I'm sure Winnie is too. Did you take her to Montauk?" Her questions tumbled out. "Does she know about Winheytem?"

Ben ran his hand through his hair. "She's at Winnie's. She's going to stay there for the time being, though Winheytem is very sick."

Jay took Mary's hand as he helped her in the door. "It might be actually a good thing she is there with Winnie for a while."

"I offered for her to come here, if need be." Ben looked at her, his brow raised.

"That would be wonderful. I would like that and Abbey would too. But I think Jay's right. Winnie needs someone there. I haven't seen her for a time because I cannot travel and Winheytem has been too sick for her to leave. I've worried so."

Ben nodded. "He is dying, I'm afraid."

Her clutch on Jay's hand tightened. "Oh, no. Do you think so? I knew he was very sick." She stopped for a moment and rested a hand on her stomach. A tear crept down her cheek. "I will attend his funeral, you know. I won't let my condition stop me from going."

Jay and Ben exchanged a look and then helped her into her rocker.

"Don't think about that yet. He might get better. Who knows? But Heather Flower is there for Winnie. She'll take care of them both." Ben rubbed the back of his neck. "And I will check on them from time to time to see how they are doing."

Jay looked at his brother. "Any chance you have your own reasons for wanting to do that, little brother?" His moss-green eyes held a glint.

"Mayhap. But my own reasons will go to the bottom of my list while Winheytem is sick and Heather Flower mourns."

Mary looked from one son to the other. They were grinning so this was good-natured teasing. "Would you like to explain?" She fanned herself with her hand and Jay fetched a wooden fan from the mantel.

"It's nothing, Mother. But you know Benjamin will use any excuse to be around Heather Flower." He looked at his brother. "Right?"

"Like I said, Winnie and Winheytem are

our first concern. And Heather Flower thinks of me only as her friend."

"You've been friends with her a long time, Ben. I think 'tis good you are there for her now."

"Thank you. I hope I can be the kind of friend she needs." He looked at Jay. "Should we go find Father and fill him in on our trip?"

"We should. And if I'm not mistaken, he's over at the meetinghouse with the reverend, right, Mother?"

"He is. They will both be anxious for your report."

Mary gathered loose tendrils and fanned the back of her neck. "Before you go, what of the women that were kidnapped with Heather Flower? What has happened to them?"

Jay shook his head. "We don't know. Heather Flower says she was kept separate from them. She did find out one of the women was killed, though. I know she worries about the rest, but I don't think there's much we can do. We were so lucky to get Heather Flower back."

Mary smiled. "It was an answer to many prayers, rather than luck, to be sure."

Her sons nodded their agreement.

Ben offered to go to the livery to get

39

Biggs, but they didn't get out the door before ten-year-old Joshua and five-year-old Jonathan came bounding in. They made such a noise with their greetings that the littlest Horton, two-year-old Hannah, woke from her nap and squealed when she saw her brothers.

Mary was finally left to rock with Hannah on her lap, such as it was, and gave herself a moment to think about and pray for Heather Flower, Winheytem, and Winnie. Winnie's eldest daughter, Abbey, was grown and married now, but she'd become like a daughter to her and Barney when Caleb was born. Mary taught her to read in addition to teaching English domesticity. She'd lived with them and took care of each of the babies as they were born until she married James and had a baby of her own.

James was a recent arrival from England and employed by Benjamin in his carpentry business. The Corchaug people accepted their marriage in stride, the English people not as much. But the love they had for each other soon won the hearts of the tiny hamlet.

She still came over with little Misha to help take care of the children, and they paid her for her work. Mary had been worried that Winnie needed her more as Winheytem's health began to fail. But with Heather Flower here now, Winnie would be taken care of. Thank heavens for that, because she'd need Abbey more than ever with the new little one coming soon.

Hannah grew restless.

"Sweet one, would you like to go outside and play in the orchard? Mama will sit and you can chase butterflies if you would like. Joshua and Jon are out there. They might help you pick some flowers for me. Come, let's go out and see what there is to do."

She pushed herself up out of the rocker and with Hannah's tiny hand in hers they wandered through the back kitchen. It was late on a hot afternoon and all of the bread and sweets baked early in the morning were sold by mid-day. It meant she had a rare afternoon to herself and the children — a more frequent occurrence as her belly grew, and a welcome one.

She settled in the orchard grass and leaned against the tall corner apple tree, its limbs already laden with tiny fruit. Hannah chased after her brothers, who did not want to be caught.

Heather Flower would be good for Winnie, but would it be a good place for her? She'd lost her husband in a very violent way. And had been kidnapped by those northern

Indians. How terrifying that must have been. And terrifying for the other women — she had been there and it was horrible watching as they were dragged away. Mary's heart was sick. She twisted a stray lock of hair with her finger as she thought of that night and wondered what had happened since. Most likely they were slaves to the Narragansett tribe. But they also could be forced to marry even tortured and killed. Certainly the stories they'd heard suggested that.

She needed to talk to Barney. Perhaps a rescue was planned. And on the morrow she would need to talk to her sister, Lizzie, and Patience Terry about what they could do for Winnie and Heather Flower.

Patience was like a sister to her, and she'd almost missed finding that out. Her first friendship in Southold was with Winnie, a Corchaug native, who wisely pointed out that she was judging Patience without even knowing her. Soon the three were close like sisters, and when Lizzie Fanning and her husband Zeke came over from England, their circle of friendship was complete.

Lizzie worked as a seamstress in her own home, and Patience taught Dame school in her house during the morning hours. She taught little girls mostly, but she had a few of the younger boys, too, and taught them their alphabet, spelling, and a little arithmetic. Both Lizzie and Patience kept two afternoons a week available to meet with Mary and Winnie.

Mary had spent years striving to keep a small ladies support group together in this wild land. Lizzie, Patience, and Winnie were her mainstays. Certainly they could gather around and support Heather Flower and Winnie in their time of loss. But she couldn't just ignore that thirteen women had been dragged from their village, one of them murdered, and perhaps none of them ever to be heard from again.

The next day, with the baking done early, Mary prepared for Lizzie's and Patience's visit. News spread about Heather Flower, and she intended to talk with her sister and friend about the situation. Winnie always liked to come into the village to meet with them but hadn't since Winheytem became ill. She'd taught them how to make the sieves and drying baskets from white oak and ash years ago, and Mary would miss having her with them on this workday.

In preparation for today, Ben had cut the trees the month before, and after quartering each one, he'd split the wood. Each slat was pounded with a mallet and then split again and again until they were thin enough for the baskets. It was Caleb's job to bind them and weight them down before soaking them in the creek.

Mary enjoyed the weaving much more than needlework, though she would never admit that to Lizzie. Her embroidery had improved over the years, but it still took every bit of her concentration for her stitches to be uniform and the underside of her piece to be neat.

She looked in on Hannah — Abbey already had her down for a nap with Misha — and then wandered out to the herb garden. She had built the raised beds with just a little help from Barney. The first flush of lemon balm, pineapple-mint, peppermint, sage, thyme, and tarragon were waving in the gentle breeze, and she plucked some of the peppermint and pineapple-mint to brew teas for her guests.

As soon as she immersed the leaves into the mugs of hot water, the bell above the door tinkled and Patience and Lizzie arrived together. She hugged them both.

"My little sister, the kitchen looks so nice and clean."

"Abbey helped me. It gets so hot these days 'tis better to get it done early. But we did not put away all of the ginger cakes. We need to eat if we are to work, do we not? And I've some peppermint tea. And pineapple-mint, if you'd care for some?"

Patience took off her cap, and her straight blond hair tumbled down. She took the comb from her hair, twisted her hair in a knot, and secured it. She patted the sides of her hair. "I would love some. Did Barney make the ginger cakes or did you, Mary?" Her crystal blue eyes crinkled at the corners when she smiled. She was younger than Mary, but still the years had been kind.

"Barney did — I almost never make them because his are so good." Her smile faded as they settled at the long oak table and took their refreshment before they set to work. "Jay and Ben said Winheytem is dying. I think we should talk about what we can do to help Winnie when the time comes."

Lizzie shook her head and her silky black curls, now laced with silvery strands, danced. Her teary eyes were like violet puddles. "I hate to think Winheytem will not get well. He is such a dear man."

Patience reached out to pat Lizzie's hand. "He has the consumption and that is hard for even us to fight. The Indians don't seem to survive it well at all. And he's older than Winnie, I think. Isn't he, Mary?"

45

"Yes, he is. It may just be his time. God is the one who knows that. But I hate to lose him too. So sad."

"We can take her food, and perhaps she would like to come live with one of us. Zeke and I have room, we'd be willing to have her stay with us."

Mary smiled at her dear sister. "That is good of you, but Heather Flower is here and it sounds like she will be for a time and be able to take care of Winnie. But I do think we should help them both with meals. Heather Flower is mourning too."

She tapped on the tabletop as she thought, then absently ran her fingertip around the heart scratched into the table with the *J*. For a brief moment she thought about how the table was almost left behind in England. The memento of Jay's initial, scratched when he was just learning his letters, and the heart his mother had drawn around it would have been lost forever.

She drew herself back to the present. "There is something else that troubles me. Heather Flower is home now, but the women who were taken with her are not. I just cannot help but think there is something we could do."

Both Lizzie and Patience stared at her.

"I don't know what. And I know it grieves

Wyandanch. Lion Gardiner surely did his best to bring home Heather Flower and would have brought everyone home if he could have. The natives gave much allegiance to the Dutch until Lion came and offered his protection to Wyandanch. The two became great friends." She wrinkled her brow. "I don't know what we could do."

"I don't mean to sound uncaring, but I think it happens much more than we realize with the natives. 'Tis the way of the land here, is it not?" Lizzie's eyes were wide, and she looked from Mary to Patience and back.

"It doesn't sound uncaring." Mary pushed at the lock on her forehead. "There is some truth there, I suppose, but when I think about what those women are going through, even if they are well cared for, it just maddens me. I want somebody to do something."

Patience leaned forward. "What does Barnabas say about it?"

"It upsets him. But I haven't asked him what the men of Southold can do about it yet. I wanted to talk to you two first."

As the three worked on their baskets they talked of different plans, but it only reaffirmed there was likely nothing that could be done. They were curious what Barney and the other men would say.

After they left, and Abbey went home with Misha, Mary confided to Barney her deep concerns, but it was as Lizzie predicted. The men had discussed it, and to send the horse troop out a second time would leave the town vulnerable, whether to the northern tribe or to the Dutch, whose relationship with them was tenuous at best. New Haven had been against the first rescue mission. There would be no second rescue, which would undoubtedly be a bloody confrontation if they tried.

She lay in bed that night in the safety of her home and cried quiet tears for the women who might never see their own beds again.

4

July 19, 1653

Winheytem lingered for three weeks. Dozing on her pallet, Heather Flower had fallen asleep to the shallow breath of her uncle, taken in sporadic gasps, but woke to silence. Without rising she turned to look at her aunt, who sat rigid next to her still husband. She sprang to their side and put her cheek close to her uncle's mouth and nose. Nothing. Slowly she sank to sit beside Winnie, touching her hand.

Sorrow for her uncle and aunt intensified her own loss, but throughout the day she took care of her younger cousins and tended to her aunt. Winnie sat statue-still by the side of her husband and prayed as her mother had taught her. Her quiet strength touched Heather Flower's heart and she wondered at the power of her God.

"My uncle is gone to the Great Spirit, you no longer need to pray."

Winnie rocked back and forth. "I pray for his homecoming. I give thanks that he sings with the angels. I pray God gives me comfort."

Heather Flower moved close to her and touched her aunt's ice-cold hands. Her voice, when it came, was rushed like the wind. "I pray for that too."

The next day, as the sun came up, six young braves entered the wigwam to carry his body to the burial place, already prepared. Smoke signals sent yesterday morning signified Winheytem was no more. Her father and mother would arrive today from Montauk with her brother, Wyancombone.

Heather Flower shuddered at the thought. Her parents would want to take her back with them. But she pushed the thought away and concentrated on her aunt. "Today you must eat, you must regain strength." She tucked a mixture of ground corn and water into several corn husks and pushed them into the embers of the central fire. As the little packets cooked, she drew leathery strips of dried venison from a pouch and placed one in Winnie's hand.

It dropped to her lap.

Food was the last thing she thought of in her own grief as well. She understood. But she remembered the day the Dutchman, Dirk, gave her the hard biscuit and a few dried berries. She swallowed without tasting, but how grateful she was for the nourishment. She was grateful for the Dutchman too. She was grateful for life.

Heather Flower bent to fan the fire with a feathered turkey wing. The hot sun already baked the hut, but there was much to do. "Abigail will come with her brothers and sisters. Barnabas and the children are coming, Aunt. Mary will stay in — it is too close to when the baby comes. And my family will soon be here. There will be many to feed. I'm going out to grind corn for samp."

With no answer, she slipped out the door to gather corn from the bin and hauled it to the scooped-out tree stump that served as a mortar. She poured handfuls into the bottom of the bowl and ground it with a heavy stick. Sweat and tears stung her cheeks, and she brushed at them with her arm as she worked. Her mother's words came to her: "Busy fingers, busy minds." She'd tell her mother she was needed here, to care for Aunt Winnie. The Corchaug fort would be a place of safety where she could heal. To go home would be to languish in her sorrow.

Lost in her thoughts, she was barely aware

51

of the creak of wood and wheels as the wagon pulled up. The Great Blacks, each with a star on its forehead, stamped their feet and tossed their heads at the harness to announce their arrival.

The Hortons, dressed in their Sunday clothes, black and somber, out of respect for the passing of Winheytem, waved to her. Caleb was the first to jump down. Heather Flower remembered the year he was born. It was 1640, the year the small group of English, led by Reverend John Youngs, came to Yennicott and changed its name to Southold. They named it after the seaside town of Southwold, England. Barnabas had just finished the house he'd promised Mary.

She knew the story well. The Hortons had been through much persecution in their homeland and God had sent them here in great white-winged canoes and blessed them greatly. Her father accepted them with open arms, as had Uncle Winheytem and Uncle Momoweta, the sachem of the Corchaug people.

Caleb reached up for Jonathan, and Barnabas climbed out after them. Silver among the mahogany of his thick hair gave Barnabas a distinguished look. And indeed, over the years he'd distinguished himself in this town. He worked side by side with the reverend building houses, farming the land, and forming the foundations of Southold's church and government.

Barnabas reached for Hannah. "Here you are, sweetheart." She was their only daughter after five sons.

With her own babe strapped to her back, Abigail waited for Joshua to jump out and then began to hand down baskets of food to each of the boys. Filling her own arms, she slid down the side. James helped her and gathered the rest of the bundles.

Heather Flower picked up Hannah and turned to Barnabas. "*Aquai,* my friend. It is so good to see you again. And so many new little ones." She glanced at the wagon again. "Joseph and Benjamin, they will be coming?"

"Benjamin stayed behind to help Joseph with a calf. But they will be here, along with the Budds."

"Budds?"

"Jane's family. You know them, but you might not remember them." He walked with her toward the hut. "Winnie, is she all right? Mary wanted to come right away, of course. She was unhappy to be left behind, but it is too dangerous to be out in her condition."

"Mary's time is soon. My aunt needed time to sit alone. She will welcome you now.

She prays to your God and holds on to His strength. Some of that I needed for myself."

Barnabas stopped and turned toward her. "This must be terrible for you too. Heather Flower, please remember that the God who gives Winnie, Mary, and me comfort is the same God who loves you."

"I will remember that, my friend." She said that to appease her aunt's friend. But how could you trust God or man when such terrible things happened? She would not forget the bloody sight of her husband — could she call him husband? — and all the other brave warriors cut down as they celebrated. Celebrated for her.

Before they entered the wigwam, Elizabeth and Ezekiel arrived with their assortment of children and grandchildren. Patience Terry was not far behind. Greetings and food abounded.

Inside, Heather Flower took the towels off the tops of the baskets, revealing a large cured ham and a still-warm roasted turkey. Other baskets held crusty breads, meat pies, corn puddings, and crisp ginger cakes. The smell of beans made savory with onions and sweet with molasses wafted from an iron pot.

Gratitude heaped in her heart. The burden of providing for their many friends would not fall completely on her. In another time, she would have welcomed it and provided with ease, but today she wanted to steal away and let her pain surface. She directed everyone carrying food to the longhouse and awaited the arrival of her parents.

They came with the Corchaug sachem, Momoweta, soon after the first wave of visitors. Everyone hushed as Wyandanch, Grand Sachem of the Montaukett, entered with Heather Flower's mother, Wuchikit-taubut, known to all as Wuchi. Momoweta and Wyancombone, followed.

Wyandanch presented Heather Flower with a deep purple and crisp white wampum belt, six fathoms long, in gratitude of her safe return. Her parents were given a seat of honor next to Winnie amidst the bustle of activity, and she sat close to them. "My place is here with my aunt in her time of grief, Mother. I am hoping you understand her need and mine."

"We grieve for our daughter like my sister grieves for her husband, my child. You will come home with us. I will take care of you."

Wyandanch cleared his throat and a hush fell across the room. "Your mother pines for you, my Flower, but I agree with you. Stay. Take care of our Wauwineta. She needs someone like you, and it will make you stronger."

Wuchi looked at him like he'd gone mad but abided his words. He had spoken. She took a small leather pouch from her neck. Hanging from a leather strap and adorned with tiny colored beads, it held a set of whalebone sewing needles.

Heather Flower's eyes flew open. It was the gift her mother gave her on her wedding day.

"Wyancombone found this by the water the night you were taken. I thought it was all I had left of you from that day. My daughter, wear this and remember you have a mother who waits for you in Montauk."

"I thought of this each day the Narragansett kept me. I didn't know how I lost it or if they had taken it from me. I only knew it was gone. Thank you, Mother. I will wear it and use it and remember the mother who loves me."

The arrival of Joseph with his family and Benjamin brought relief to the tension. To Heather Flower it brought escape. As she slipped out the door, Benjamin followed her.

"I was hoping to have the chance to talk to you," he said. "I was visiting with Mother and she told me you are coping, but I wanted to see for myself. How are you?" His gentle hands held her shoulders at arm's length.

Her face warmed as she met his gaze. His baby blue eyes held something more than concern. There was a pleading in them and she was not ready for this. "Benjamin, my friend, I need to walk."

"I'll go with you."

"No, I need to walk alone. You are the truest friend. But I hurt inside and I want to be alone with my hurt." She pulled away and he let her go. She didn't look back. His sad face would have been more than she could bear.

Miss Button shook her thick black mane as if to urge Dirk forward, but he held her in. He watched from the little hill as Heather Flower broke from Benjamin and walked toward Downs Creek. Just as he'd suspected. When news had come back from the Isle of Wight that the daughter of Wyandanch did not return to Montauk but had proceeded to Southold, he'd been certain it had something to do with the Horton brothers. The younger one in particular.

He had half a mind to go after Benjamin, but instead he followed his heart. Leaving Miss Button tied to a willow, he found the trail she'd taken. Long, thorny arms of blackberry bushes ripe with fruit grabbed at his ankles and long hanging limbs of hickory lashed at his face as he made his way down the little-used trail.

If she wished not to be found, she'd picked the perfect path, but it was too late for him to worry about intruding. There she sat by the water's edge. She'd heard him long before he'd seen her and her look was none too happy.

"I heard you were here. *Hoe gaat het?*"

She did not respond.

"*Ja,* I see, you are not well. Is it Mr. Horton? If it is, I will talk to him directly."

Heather Flower stood. Her eyes were damp, a furrow on her brow, and she clutched her thick braid like a rope. "It is not Benjamin. It is no one." She blinked and he could see a slight tremor of her chin.

"Do you want me to leave?"

"It is not you either. Stay. Sit by me for a moment."

They both sat in the shade on a large boulder that projected out over the water. He was careful not to sit too close. And he hesitated to say anything. He waited for her.

The *klee-klee-klee* of a sparrow hawk as it swooped in on its prey broke through the silence, and he tried to concentrate instead on the movement of the river below, slow and drifting. But he couldn't brush the thoughts of Benjamin away as easily. He'd been hoping after a time he could come to see Heather Flower, and she would be stronger and healed since the death of her husband. Now he wondered if he should have remained close, to protect her from the likes of Horton.

"I have told you little of the day my husband died."

His head jerked up, he chose his words carefully. "You don't have to, if it's too painful."

"It was a very happy day for me. My friends and my nieces surrounded me and we gathered flowers to put on my hair and my dress. My mother decorated my dress with quills and feathers, and the darkest purple shell beads she owned." Her fingers went to the pouch hanging from her neck. "She gave me this and Keme wore a necklace of bear claws."

"Keme? Your husband?"

"He would have been my husband." She looked away.

Immediately he wished he'd not asked. She hid her eyes, but he knew the pain they held. Still, she continued.

"There was fresh deer meat on spears over the fires. Corn, still in their husks, under the burning logs. Fish and clams and mus-

59

sels baked in the earth under hot rocks. Winnie's family came and the Hortons. They brought more food and gifts."

"You don't have to go on."

"There was much dancing and singing. Everyone celebrated. We were about to eat the food prepared. We heard war cries, but it was too late. The Narragansett swarmed in, surrounding us. I saw my Keme fall, his blood spilling, and I knew he would not live. He looked at me. But I could not run to him. Two warriors carried me to their canoe, hidden in the reeds." Her voice shook, but she remained very still, sitting straight and tall.

He ached to hold her, to comfort her, but he sat as still as she. "Why didn't the Hortons do something?"

"What could they do? The Narragansett had me, and my father feared I would be killed. He was tied up, but he gave an order that no one was to fight.

"It was many weeks they held me captive. I tried to count the days in different ways, but they always discovered what I was doing and destroyed my markings. Ninigret taunted me with what they had done to Keme. With what my father must feel to know that he, Ninigret, had me. He told me of plans to kill my father, my mother, and brother. Anything he could tell me to wound my heart, he did.

"And when my father paid with wampum, sent by Captain Gardiner, Ninigret took me and promised me he would return me to my people. The wampum belt was given as a sacred trust that I would come back. Ninigret laughed when he left me in the woods. He left me to die."

Dirk tried to speak but it sounded more like a croak. He cleared his throat and began again. "His men took thirteen other women that night. We still do not know what became of them. Did you see them when you were in captivity?"

The silence was long and the wind in the willows picked up. She ran her hands along her arms as if she were chilled. Finally, she answered. "I was kept in a wigwam, away from everyone except the warriors who guarded me. But I heard them talk. The other women were given to men to be their wives. There was one who would not cooperate. They killed her. Her name was Nashan, my close friend, like a sister. Strong and beautiful." Her eyes closed.

"There was nothing you could do, you know that, *ja*?" His finger drew her chin toward him. He searched her black opal eyes for understanding. He saw fire.

61

"I would have. I would have traded my place for hers."

He thought of the day he found her. Of holding her close while they rode toward safety. He hoped the day would come when he could hold her again. But it would not be this day. He stood and offered his hand. "May I walk you back?"

"My friend, Dirk. I hear many things from Mary and my aunt. You are well beyond the truce boundary."

"There is no truce. Our countries are at war, for over a year. Your father trusts me, Heather Flower."

"He does, I think, but my people's loyalties are to the English."

"That may be changing. In the meantime, I will heed your thoughts. Let me walk you to the trailhead and I'll be gone."

The path opened to a small vale and he left her, the hardest thing he'd done in eons. Before he urged Miss Button on, he turned one last time to see her standing with just the hint of a smile as she waved. He'd hold that image in his thoughts until they could meet again.

5

Later that day Heather Flower joined her family and friends as they surrounded Winnie and moved out of the fort, up to the burying grounds in a long procession. Winheytem already sat upright in the deep grave the braves dug for him that morning, a black wampum belt draped across one shoulder. The ceremonial goodbyes were said and Wyandanch stepped forward to set a bow and quiver full of arrows beside Winheytem.

Winnie lowered her husband's bearskin into the grave as a final farewell. She left before the young warriors filled the dirt around her beloved. Her mourning, in many ways, was just beginning. Now she could cry the tears of a widow.

Followed by Wuchi, Abigail, Patience, and Lizzie, Heather Flower led her aunt to the riverbank and the wailing commenced. Every woman had tears to cry, but her own wails mingled with Winnie's — not only for her dear uncle, but for the young warrior who should be by her side. He was too young to die.

And for what? Because her father was friend to the *wonnux,* the white man? That he refused to aid in ambush against his white brothers? More likely it was the wampum the Narragansett had been able to extract from the Long Island tribes in the form of annual tributes. When the English had come, Wyandanch had stopped the payments. She admired her father for his convictions, but at what price?

Such thoughts fueled her determination to rise above the grief the fierce nation to the north had inflicted. But where was the Great Spirit? Had He abandoned her? Was He the God of her people or the white man's God? Maybe if she knew, she would know how to speak to Him.

Her wails calmed to sniffles and she looked about the small gathering of women. Wuchi sat on the other side of Winnie, rocking and moaning a soft chant. Abigail, Patience, and Lizzie sat with their hands clasped firm and prayed with their eyes clamped closed and reddened cheeks damp with tears.

Heather Flower rested her chin on her

knees as she encircled them with her arms. She remembered the stories about how Mary came to Yennicott, and she and Aunt Winnie had become friends, but Mary and Patience had not.

After a time a tranquility settled over the women, and Patience looked up and met her gaze with a smile. "You are like sisters," Heather Flower said as she nodded toward Winnie.

"Yes, we are. I am rich in family here in Southold, am I not?" She looked around the small group of women. "God has taught me many things since I came here."

"He taught?"

"To be thankful for what you do have instead of longing for what you don't." She grinned at Lizzie.

Lizzie knew the story of Mary and Patience. "Had it not been for Winnie, Mary would have missed one of God's biggest lessons in her life."

"What was that?" Heather Flower asked.

"That we should look for the good instead of expecting the bad in someone we do not know. Mary thought Patience's admiration of Barnabas was a threat to her marriage, and she kept her as far away as she could. But Winnie pointed out that Mary didn't even know her, and that perhaps Patience needed a friend."

Winnie's sad mouth spread into a smile. "Mary kept talking about a women's group that supported each other. And she missed Lizzie so much. Patience didn't have a sister and she seemed to need a women's group as much as Mary needed to arrange one. They needed each other."

Lizzie looked at Winnie. "She learned to put her trust in God, and not in herself. 'Tis something we all must learn. Burdens are lifted when you learn to depend on His strength."

Heather Flower listened to the music of the crickets and bullfrogs. The chill of night air, hurried along by a breeze, made her shiver. "You tell me that too, Aunt."

Patience stood. "If the trust is not there, you must set it in motion, Heather Flower. Listen for God's prompt. He will teach you to trust. Come now, shall we go in and see how the little ones are doing?" She looked toward Lizzie. "Your daughters have had their hands full, have they not?"

Lizzie, gently rounded by the years and as beautiful as ever, got up and offered Winnie her hand. "Jane stayed to help Rachel and Ruth with the young ones."

The small band of women moved up the path toward the wigwam. They would put the wailing behind and bear their sorrow in silence.

Inside the smoky hut, a hodgepodge of the earlier feast bubbled over the fire. The families crammed together until everyone could sit and eat their fill. Afterward, Wyandanch stood and regaled them with stories of the quiet Winheytem in their younger days. The tales brought smiles, not tears, as they celebrated the man they loved.

Benjamin sat across the room and the firelight played across his dimpled cheeks when he smiled at Heather Flower, kindness in his eyes. She smiled back, a small reassurance, she hoped, that all was well between them.

Winnie sat next to her and leaned in. "Benjamin looks at you. His heart has always been full for you."

"I see, but I do not have anything to give to him. I am lost and empty. What do I tell him?"

"You do not need to say anything, my child. He understands your heart. It doesn't change his."

Heather Flower looked back. His eyes were now on the fire, watching it dance while her father talked on. "I am happy my father says I may stay with you. When everyone leaves to go to their wigwams, you will be alone for the first time in hundreds of moons. It will be good to have me near, to comfort you. It will be good for me, for I will find my comfort with you."

Winnie lowered her head to rest on Heather Flower's shoulder, and she put an arm around her aunt. Eventually the light of the fire died down to embers, and the Hortons and Fannings prepared to leave. Patience helped Abigail get the children into the wagon and Caleb offered to escort her home.

Benjamin left with Joseph and Jane. He gave his condolences all around but saved her for last and pulled her into a brief hug. His closeness yielded a longing, but for her Keme, not for Benjamin.

With only her family left, Heather Flower settled on her pallet. She closed her eyes and saw him. Her handsome Keme.

Benjamin rode alongside Joseph's wagon, vaguely aware of the chatter between his brother and sister-in-law.

At length Joseph turned to him. "You're very quiet. Any chance Heather Flower is on your mind?"

"You read me like a book, but what's new? Aye, that she is."

Joseph rolled his eyes. "You set yourself

up for a wagonload of hurt, brother. You did the same with Anna. You knew she would marry Charles Tucker. You ought not to let yourself go there."

Benjamin looked at Jane, a half smile twitched on his lips. "Anna couldn't help herself, falling in love with old Charlie, could she, Jane?" Joseph's words were true, but the truth hurt. Anna was Jane's younger sister and grew up right next door. She'd always been there. He loved her then, and he loved her now. He wasn't sure why she'd married Tucker. But she had. It was one part of his heart he didn't like to open up, and Heather Flower helped him forget it. And it was different with her, was it not? She might not be ready to love again, but she'd been his friend since they were children. When she was ready, he'd be there.

"Anna has always had a soft spot for you, dear Benjamin. I know how sad you were when she married Charles, but she admires you and cares for you so very much. Do not listen to your brother. And don't give up on Heather Flower. Just give her time. You are a good man and any woman would be blessed to be your wife."

He touched his hat like a salute and nodded at her. But his throat tightened and he looked away so she could not see his pain.

They rode up Town Street, crossing a shallow spot at Dickerson's Creek and passing the tanner's house on the right. His brother's house came up first on the left and Joseph pulled in the reins. "Friends, brother?"

"Aye. Nothing changes that. And for what it's worth, you might be right. But I will remember what you said, Jane." He said his goodbyes. A few feet up the road, he glanced toward Charles and Anna's house and spurred Star on past Tucker's Lane to the Horton homestead.

He'd built the house with his father and Joseph when they first came to Southold. He was twelve years old and his father let him work like a man. He loved it. And he loved the home they'd created. It was the first timber-framed house completed on eastern Long Island, and then they worked to help the Terrys and the Budds finish their homes.

The light still glowed from the diamond-paned glass windows as he put his horse away and walked up the flagstone path. Inside he found his father sitting with the old family Bible, reading silently while Caleb and Joshua were climbing up to the loft.

Mother was putting little Jonathan and Hannah to bed in the room they shared with him. Two good reasons to be looking to build his own home. He sat down in the chair next to his father.

Barnabas looked up and set the Bible aside. "It was a difficult day."

"Yes, sir. I'm glad it's over. I'm sure Winnie is too."

"Certes. It will be good for her to have Heather Flower with her for a time. I was pleased to see her parents agreed."

Benjamin shifted at her name and leaned to study the fire, mute.

"Joseph seems to think you may be too preoccupied with her." His father raised an eyebrow.

"Well, Joseph should be talking to me about it then, not you — sir." The last was added quickly.

"I see. I just would like to say be careful, son. She's been through much and I imagine feeling very tender."

"I know, Father, I'm keeping that in mind. It doesn't make it easier for me, though. I do love her."

His father paused before he spoke. "Be patient, son. You know not what the Lord has in store for you."

Mary came in, her face gently lined with the years, still pretty with crinkles around her wide, hazel eyes and a smile that lent

71

encouragement. Her auburn hair, now mostly gray, was in a thick braid down her back.

Benjamin stood and gave her a hug as she eased into the chair. "Are the poppets asleep yet?"

"You've spoilt them, Ben. They wait for your bedtime stories." She settled back and closed her eyes with a smile.

"Ah, at least there is someone I enchant. Well, good night then." He bowed and retreated to the bedroom he used to share with Joseph.

But when he entered the darkened room, his siblings were tucked beneath the worn quilt, sleeping like two little bear cubs in winter. He climbed into his own bed and let his thoughts drift.

He could wait for Heather Flower as Jane suggested. But he could see that he must take care and not let her — or anyone else, for that matter — know that he waited for her. He would frighten her away, and Joseph would not pass up a chance to make him the object of his jests. He was a Horton, after all.

He got up and took his Bible to the glow of the hearth. The one thing he'd learned growing up from his parents was to bring your troubles to the Lord first, and He would answer you in His time.

6

August 31, 1653

Mary was in her confinement, but on this Tuesday Barney and the children went to church to give thanks for the first harvest of wheat. The celebration was called Lammis Day, and Reverend Youngs consecrated the loaves.

Abbey had the day off for the celebration, so after church Patience came over with armloads of leeks, carrots, and dill from her garden to help Barnabas with dinner.

Mary stopped rocking and put her needlework down on her rounded belly. "Look what you have — those are beautiful! I've missed working in the garden."

"Have you forgotten how hot being in that sun is?" She set her baskets on the floor and took her cap off. As she hung it on the peg near the fireplace, her straight blond hair slipped from her combs, and she reached to secure them.

Mary pushed her foot at the floor to continue rocking. "To be cooped up like a hen is not my idea of healthy. The Corchaug women work in the fields with only a pause to have their babes, and it seems to me they have a much easier time, do you not think so, Patience?"

"That they do, I must agree. But other than that, how are you?"

"I could go on and on about all my aches and pains, or is that simply a polite greeting?" Her laughter tinkled.

"Why, of course I mean that, Mary. You may go on and on if you like, but I was really wondering if you had some peace whilst the family was at church?" The clatter of dishes and children erupted from the kitchen, and their eyes teared with laughter.

"I suppose I did, but I must confess I miss the noise and the children when everyone is gone from the house. I love the commotion of our big family."

Patience sat down in the chair opposite Mary. "Remember when it was just you and me and Winnie? Your boys were old enough to pretty much look after themselves, and Lizzie and her family hadn't come across the pond yet. Jeremy brought your horses and you taught us to ride. We felt like there wasn't anything we couldn't do." She smiled at the memory.

"Abbey was old enough to watch her younger brothers and sisters. Winnie had so many. I thought I'd never even have one." She wished she hadn't said it the moment the words were out. She suspended her rocking. "I'm sorry, Patience. I know that hurts you. I didn't mean to say it."

"Oh look at you, so big and round with child and so worried about me who has none. 'Tis all right. I love your children like they were my own, and truly they fill any maternal need I have. And I don't have to stay up all night with them when they are sick, the dears. I long ago decided the good Lord did not intend to give me my own. Instead I teach the little ones, and I do believe it's my calling."

"I don't know what we would do without you."

A shout outside brought Patience to her feet. "What could that be?"

Mary pushed herself out of her rocker and moved toward the door. It swung wide before she got there, and Joshua rushed in. "Mother, you will not guess who is coming — Uncle Jeremy! He's here."

He stood back and in walked Jeremy. His Horton presence filled the room. He was tanned and dark blond hair fell across his forehead. Except for some additional crinkles around his mouth and eyes, the years had not changed him. Mary almost lost her balance. Patience and Jeremy both dashed to her side to steady her.

"Why, Jeremy, you smell of the sea."

He chortled as they helped her to her rocker. "I should. I've just arrived from Barbados. And I've some molasses and sugar for you. Some for you too, Patience. Trading was good this trip. Where's old Barn?"

"He's in the kitchen preparing dinner. It will be a feast you will enjoy. Patience came to help him."

He turned to Patience and her cheeks turned crimson. Her confidence about her spinster state a few moments ago seemed to have disappeared. She scooped up the baskets and hurried toward the kitchen, blond hair tumbling down her back. She stopped just before leaving the room and bit her lip. "I'll see what I can do to hurry things along. You must be starving, Jeremy." Then she was gone.

Mary turned back to her brother-in-law. "I think Patience always finds herself feeling awkward around you, Jeremy."

His tanned face held a hint of a flush too. "I don't know why. I've always found her to be a pleasant respite from my ocean-going ways. Someone to talk to if she but takes a moment to spend with me."

"Patience has always worked hard. She needs someone like you to slow her down, find the goodness in life." Did she say that for Jeremy's benefit or Patience's? Surely they both seemed to have found goodness in life on their own, without anyone else. Perhaps for some people that was how it was meant to be.

But she hoped not. She and Barnabas, though they'd had a rough beginning, were perfectly matched, facing their joys and sorrows together — each other's rock. People needed a helpmeet, did they not? She looked at Jeremy. Did he think she meddled?

"Patience loves the children in her care. She doesn't have time to think on affairs of the heart like you do, Mary." His eyes danced.

He was teasing her, but it was her turn to feel her cheeks flame. "I do not have time for such things either and you know that well. But I worry about her. And you, Jeremy. You cannot be sailing the seas forever, can you?"

"I can very well try, can I not?"

"And Patience is not the only woman who can run the Dame School."

"Have we had this conversation before, Mary?" He was chortling at his comment when Barney bounded through the kitchen doorway.

"Jeremy, so good to see you. We were concerned you'd lost that ship."

"You are concerned every time I make the voyage, Barn. Good to see you." They clasped each other in a bear hug and pounded each other's backs.

"Well, Mary is too. The whole town is, for that matter. Dinner will be ready shortly, so your timing is impeccable."

Mary smiled. "You always arrive in time for a good meal." She giggled. "We are so glad to have you here. I hope you stay a good long while. Joseph and Benjamin will want to know right away that you are here."

Jeremy nodded toward the door. "Joshua went to get them."

Barney disappeared into the kitchen.

"Sit, Jeremy. There's so much to bring you up to date with."

He took the chair opposite her, and she told him the story of Heather Flower's kidnapping and how Lion Gardiner had paid a ransom for her and Ninigret left her in the woods to die. When she told him of the Dutch lieutenant, Dirk Van Buren, finding her and bringing her to safety, he found it amazing that the English and Dutch had joined together to accomplish her rescue.

"She and Benjamin grew up playing together?"

"Yes, Ben has always been fond of her, and now it seems Lieutenant Van Buren is as well."

"What about Anna Budd?"

"She married the Tucker boy. She broke Ben's heart, but he would never admit it."

Jeremy smiled. "A man's got to protect his image, you know." He winked at her. "And Heather Flower? She is back in Montauk?"

"No. Winheytem died, Jeremy. Winnie is in mourning. Heather Flower is staying with her to make sure she eats and to keep her company. But Joseph says that the Dutchman has been spotted near the Indian fort."

"That sounds like trouble."

"Yes, it is. Jay and Ben would like to see the Dutch off Long Island altogether, of course. Reverend Youngs's son is behind that, I think. He constantly talks of training the horse troop, and not just for protection."

"Well, being ready to defend the town is one thing, but these young rousers need to realize it is peace that Parliament wants."

"Is it, Jeremy? 'Tis so hard to know because we are so far away. We get conflicting reports with no way to verify anything."

"Aye, I know. And it doesn't help that Parliament changes with the wind."

"Heather Flower's parents are worried about her. They are upset she is not home with them and they are embarrassed that she might have romantic notions about the Dutchman."

"I would think Lion Gardiner and Reverend Youngs would be as well."

Joshua ran through the door. Jay and Ben were not far behind and had Jane in tow.

"Uncle Jeremy, it's so great you're here."

"It has been too long. We've much to talk about." He turned to Mary. "Mayhap on the morrow we can sit and I'll tell you and Barn the news from home and how Mother is doing." He turned back to the boys. "And I've a trunk or two that needs to be fetched with a few trinkets from England. A book or two as well. We'll do that in the morn."

The younger children came down the stairs and more bear hugs were exchanged before Patience came out to call them for dinner.

Soon they were seated at the two long tables, with Hannah insisting she sit next to Uncle Jeremy. Muffkin, Barney's cat and a little ball of gray, would not be ignored either and jumped up on the bench between them. They all joined hands and Barney led them in prayer.

Mary looked at her family as they all said "Amen." She rubbed the strain in the small of her back before she began to eat. She was worn out and ready to retire as soon as they were finished eating and the kitchen was cleaned. But for now she was content to sit back and enjoy their family, friends, and bountiful food. She was thankful for what they shared, and hopeful for what the morrow would bring.

7

September 1, 1653

Mary woke with a sharp twinge low in her belly. It was brief, but the next one was sure to come. She lay still, counting off the seconds, then minutes. Each stab lasted a bit longer. She writhed while she held her breath and ground her teeth as she remembered the births of her sweet baby boys and little Hannah. All would be well, she prayed. She waited to waken Barney. His beloved Ann had died in childbirth. Now he worried with each birth, and Mary wanted to savor her anticipation of this new life.

She looked to the window and saw a black sky scattered with crystal chips. Her breath caught as she thought of God the Creator, and she whispered a prayer for a safe birth. Dim memories of her mother embraced her like a gentle hug.

Her fingers brushed the soft gray fur of

the little cat curled at her side. Muffkin stretched with a purr. Her dainty, pink tongue gently licked her thumb, and Mary fluffed her fur between her ears. "There, there, little Muffy. Everything will be all right."

She prayed, rather timidly, for a little girl. Truly she'd be thankful for boy or girl, but the memory of Rachel, Ruthie, and Hannah playing together as little girls made her want a little sister for their daughter. They'd named her after Lizzie's youngest and she was the sweetness in this brood of boys. Lizzie's Hannah grew up and married well in Mowsley, and when the Fannings made the decision to come to Long Island, Hannah and her husband remained in England. Joshua — Lizzie and Zeke's only son — also stayed in Mowsley, much to Lizzie and Mary's sadness.

The sky lightened to gray, and she continued to count the minutes as the darkness dissolved to pink on the eastern horizon. She clenched her fingers into a fist, and Barney's hand reached out to cover hers. She tried to roll over to him, but her stomach was rigid and all she could do was squeeze his hand.

The bedcovers flew, and Barney hovered over her. "It is time? Our babe is coming?"

His gentle hand skimmed her belly as her muscles relaxed and the pain receded. He reached to smooth her hair back and bent down to kiss her forehead. She thrashed as the next wave began.

"Caleb! Caleb, go get Abigail. Your mother needs Abigail!"

She was only half aware of Caleb entering the chamber, stuffing his nightshirt into his breeches. She listened to him clamor down the stairs, then pain peaked and she concentrated as it subsided. Her skin was damp with pinpricks of sweat. She heard Barnabas and knew he was talking to her, but he seemed far away.

"Mary, I'm going to build up the fire and fetch some cloths. I filled the pot with water last night. I'll get the Bible and read to you whilst we wait for Abigail. God be with us." He scooped up Muffkin and pounded down the stairs.

Alone, she tried to remember to keep breathing. She'd rather hold her breath, but Abbey would tell her to breathe. She didn't want to moan and wake the little ones, so she bit her lip and turned her face toward the pillow. Her back arched with the knifing pain that was stronger and longer than the previous one. Where was Abbey? Where was Barney? She strained to hear them below.

Did they not know this little babe wouldn't wait for them?

At length she heard Barney enter and she forced her eyes to open a crack and watched him bring in a stack of cloths, several wet. He placed a cold one across her brow and for a blessed moment it soothed her. "Abigail should be here soon. I told Caleb to go get Patience and Elizabeth after he talked to her and I told him to have James ride out to the fort and fetch Winnie."

"It seems to be taking so long for Abbey." She spoke through gritted teeth.

"Aye, it seems that, but truly it's been only a short while since he left. She'll be here soon."

He fussed about her, rearranging her pillow and wiping her brow. Finally he sat and opened the Horton Bible and turned to the page marked with the frayed blue ribbon. Ann's. When she'd died in childbirth so many years ago, he'd thought he couldn't go on. Anything and everything reminded him of her and tossed him into a black pit of despair. But Mary's love changed that and any other day he could touch the ribbon and remember Ann tying her hair up and smile. But Ann died giving birth to their baby girl and now he was terrified.

His hand was gentle on Mary's as he said a silent prayer for God's help and strength. Then he began to read to her from his Bible. Jonathan crept into the room and climbed into his father's lap and not too long after little Hannah was crawling into the big bed to snuggle with her mother.

"Come, Hannah, sit with me. Your mother will have a brother or sister for you today."

Mary reached for her little girl. "Nay, stay with me. 'Tis all right for a moment. I love you." The last was said in a whisper, and Hannah looked at her papa with a question in her big hazel eyes.

"She will be all right. Give your mother a kiss and sit still for her."

Hannah snuggled her face into Mary's neck, her little arms hugged tight. Mary kissed her daughter's soft brown hair. "Good girl." She settled back, eyes closed, her little girl's soft breath warm on her neck.

But the next moment pain gripped Mary again. Barnabas stood quickly and with Jonathan in one arm, scooped up Hannah and took them down to the front parlor. He set them in the chairs before the fire and poked the logs to give the flames new life. A sleepy Joshua shuffled down the stairs. "Be a good boy and stay with your sister and brother. Mother will have her babe today and Aunt Patience will be here soon to take care of you."

Joshua went to sit with Hannah. "Do you think it's a boy?"

A groan came from the upper chamber, and all the children's eyes grew wide. Barnabas started for the stairs, but said over his shoulder, "We won't know until it's born. But if I have my guesses, it will be a big boy."

Before he could reach her, the front door flew open and in hurried Abigail and Lizzie with Patience close behind them.

He bounded back down the stairs in two long strides. "You're here. We need you now."

Lizzie's violet-blue eyes flew open and she hurried past him, up to Mary.

Abigail stayed but a moment. Her hand touched his arm with a gentle pat. "Mother will be here soon. James left right away to get her. He took the horse."

"Ah, that's good, Abigail. Mary needs you. She's been asking."

She glanced at the children huddled in the parlor as she hastened to the stairs and stopped. "Do the neighbor ladies know it's time? Did anyone hit the skillet outside with the mallet?"

Blank faces stared back.

Patience removed her hat and hung it on a peg near the front door. "Ah, I shall tend to that at once, Abigail. She leaned down to the little Hortons. "And how are you three? Are you excited about a baby?"

The boys jumped up and down with smiles, but Hannah pouted. Patience bent and drew her close. "Shall we go find some porridge and perhaps a bit of cheese, sweet one?" She winked at Barnabas and he nodded. "I shall ring the news with the skillet too." She gave Hannah a gentle squeeze. "You may help me if you like."

Hannah's face brightened and Patience led the siblings toward the kitchen.

Barnabas called to her. "Aye, that's a good idea. When Caleb gets back, I shall take him and Joshua to visit with Zeke. Mayhap you or Winnie would come fetch us when the babe arrives?"

"Yes, of course. You should go say goodbye to Mary now, before things get too exciting. We'll be just fine here, won't we, sweet one?" Hannah clung to her neck and she carried her to the small, front kitchen, trailed by the two boys.

He entered the bedchamber quietly. Mary's face twisted with agony, droplets of sweat — tears? — trickled to the bolster beneath her neck. She clenched and pulled the sheet. He grabbed her hands and brought them to his lips as Abigail talked his wife through another pain. As it subsided, Abigail turned to Barnabas. "Give her a kiss and leave now. I am going to prepare her for the birth."

He slipped his hand beneath her damp head and bent over her. Her glassy eyes, wide with fear, had a gray cast as she tried to focus on him. Her mouth was pulled back in a grimace that showed her teeth. His stomach knotted and he wondered if he should leave her at all. She threw her hands up toward him and he thought she would hit him, but instead her arms wrapped around his neck tight, clinging with a strength he thought not possible.

He attempted to rock her, and spoke low, soothing. "Mary, my sweet, you are going to have our babe. Soon we will all be rejoicing over our beautiful child. Be strong. Be brave. Abigail is here. All is well. God be with you, my love."

With that he pried her arms away and held them tenderly across her chest as he kissed her cheek. "I shall return soon."

He left the room without looking back, for if he did he would surely stay.

Heather Flower arrived with Winnie and

Caleb. After Barnabas left with the two older boys, Winnie went up to Mary's chamber to help Abigail.

She followed Patience back to the large back kitchen, added to the original house to accommodate the bakeshop. "We should put together dinner for everyone. Mary will be hungry once the babe is born."

Patience nodded to Heather Flower. "She has a ham that I thought would be good, and last night I put some beans to soak and I brought them with me." A weary smile formed on her lips. "I'm making a turkey pie too. And a pippin."

"I'll make a corn pudding like Winnie does. She said it is Mary's favorite." Heather Flower set to work cutting fresh kernels from cobs of corn. Her mother mostly dried the corn and she was intrigued by the fresh corn pudding Winnie had learned from Mary. "Do Benjamin and Joseph know?"

Patience looked up from the ham she sliced. "Everything has been happening so quickly, I don't think anyone has told them. Unless Barnabas stops by on his way to Zeke's. And Jeremy stayed the night with Joseph and Jane. I suppose they will all know soon." She raised her arm to brush back a wisp of blond hair with her sleeve. "I did ring the skillet, but who knows if anyone heard it."

Heather Flower continued to chop without replying.

"How are things with you and Benjamin? We all know he is sweet on you." Patience smiled as she said it.

"There are no things. Only friendship." She looked up to make her point.

"Mary hopes that is not so. She is fond of you, and she knows her son's heart. She hopes you will return his affection. I know things have been hard for you, but do you ever think you will?" She kept her eyes on the ham as she spoke, turned it this way and that as if she were trying to be casual about the conversation, but she didn't conceal her curiosity well.

"Will what?"

Patience giggled. "Return his affection."

She could not help but laugh too. "He means much to me, Patience. He has been my friend forever. I do not have a heart to give him now. Maybe never. I don't know. I don't want to lose him as my friend. That would be too sad."

"Someone thought they saw the Dutchman hanging around the fort. Did he come to see you?"

Heather Flower looked up. She weighed Patience's words before she answered. In no way did she want to endanger Dirk. If only he wouldn't endanger himself, then she wouldn't have to answer questions like this. "He came once, to see if I was all right. He found out I did not go home and he wanted to be sure that is what I wanted."

"Why would he care?"

"Lion Gardiner instructed him to bring me back to my parents. It was his duty."

"Did you tell him that you were the one who decided to stay at Winnie's?"

"Yes, *nuk.* I told him not to be worried and that Lion Gardiner knew he had done what was needed."

Mary's shrill wail reverberated through the house, followed by a moment of silence. They paused to listen. A baby's first jagged cry broke into the world.

Their eyes met, smiles spreading.

Tears sprung in Patience's eyes. "He is here. The babe is born." She hurried over to Jonathan and Hannah and hugged them both. "He's here!"

Winnie rushed halfway down the stairs just as Jane arrived, a pot of stew in hand. "She has a baby girl! Children, you have a little sister! Heather Flower, go to Elizabeth's and tell Barnabas and Zeke they must come."

"How is Mary?"

"She is fine, she is wonderful! Now go!"

Heather Flower left quickly and ran down the road to the Fannings'. Breathing hard, she pounded on the door. It swung open and there stood Benjamin. Words escaped her.

"My mother? The baby's here?" A smile broke loose.

"Yes, Benjamin. You must get your father and Zeke and come."

Barnabas came to the door. "And Mary? Mary is all right?"

She nodded. "I think she is very happy for everything to be over with."

Barnabas was already pushing past Benjamin on his way out the door. "Heather Flower, what is it? A boy, yes?"

"No, you have a girl."

"Heigh-ho! A girl!" Barnabas started out in a brisk pace with Zeke, Joseph, and Jeremy. Caleb and Joshua ran out ahead of them toward home, and Heather Flower and Benjamin took up the rear.

She smiled as she watched them rush back to the house. "The men. You all came to Zeke's house to wait?"

A whisper of a breeze rustled the leaves of the maples, showing their silvery undersides. Dappled sunlight fell across Benjamin's handsome face as they walked the main street. "That's what we do. We stay out of the way and when the women have done their work, we come when we are called. Yes, we do." A smile spread across his face, a dimple punctuating his cheek. Anticipation shone in his eyes, but Heather Flower sensed his contentment at being with her too.

As they entered the house, she left Benjamin and Joseph behind with their younger brothers and followed Barnabas into the bedroom.

Mary gave her husband a tired smile. "She's a loud one, and look at her. Not one hour old and she looks around like she wants to tell us everything she knows. Which is much, I think."

Winnie had the newborn at the foot of the bed, wrapped snugly in a blanket. She picked her up and lowered her to Mary's waiting arms. "Good morrow, my little one. Your papa said we would name you Sarah. Are you telling the world you are here?" Her wails stopped and she squirmed in Mary's arms. "Oh, look, she likes her name. Sarah it is." She looked up to her husband. "She is so beautiful, is she not, Barney?" She ran her finger over her light peach-colored hair.

"She is. She looks like you, yes?"

"She has my hair, I think, but her eyes are

yours." She counted ten tiny fingers, then unwrapped spindly little toes.

Patience came in carrying a steaming bowl of corn pudding, with Hannah right behind. "Heather Flower made this for you, Mary. We knew you would be ravenous." She set the bowl down carefully and peeked at the new baby. "She's precious. And so beautiful. She has your eyes, Mary."

Mary laughed. "I suppose 'tis too soon to know." She sniffed the savory aroma of the pudding and turned to Winnie. "Mmmm. That smells so good. You would think food would be far from my thoughts, though." She hugged her babe close.

"I know the hunger a woman has after birthing. It must be from God as you will need your strength. You must eat." Winnie lifted the tiny babe and placed her in her father's arms. "Sarah. Does Sarah have meaning?"

Barney bent his head to his child. "Yes. Princess. It means princess."

"How blessed you are this day, Barnabas. I am so happy for you."

"I am." He looked at Mary. "We are, yes, my sweet?"

"Yes, she is perfect."

"God gives good things to those who wait." He smiled at his daughter and gently

96

tucked the blanket around her. "We waited a long time for you, little Sarah. You have five brothers and a sister, and we all waited just for you."

Mary ate a spoonful of corn pudding as Lizzie, Winnie, and Patience crowded about, peering at the tiny bundle in Barnabas's arms. "You are like sisters to me. And Abbey — you may be Winnie's daughter, but to me you'll always be my first daughter." Tears began to gather on her lashes, and Abbey rushed to her side and blotted them with a soft handkerchief.

Sarah began to cry in earnest.

"Heigh-ho, little one, what is that? Methinks she is hungry too, Mary." Barnabas nodded to Winnie to take the bowl from her and he gently placed the babe in her waiting arms. "Abigail, when she's had her fill, you will bring her to see her brothers?"

"Yes."

He nodded and made his way to the stairs and the menfolk below.

"We will have the men feast downstairs." Winnie nodded to Lizzie and Patience. "The we'll bring food up here and celebrate with Mary."

"Mama, Mama." Hannah begged to climb on the bed, but Patience lifted the little girl to her hip. "Come with me, my poppet. We shall let your mother rest whilst we gather the meal." She swooped her out of the room, followed by Lizzie and Winnie.

Heather Flower hung back. She watched as Abbey settled next to Mary, humming a lullaby, and a yearning put an ache in her heart that surprised her. The pain wasn't the same as when she mourned the loss of her husband. It was more an achy emptiness. Two men wanted a place in her heart and each would wait for her. One was kind and patient. The other, kind but eager.

8

In the midst of Sarah's birth, Jeremy's trunks were forgotten. But not for long. The following day, Benjamin hitched up Star, and he and Jeremy rode down to the dock to retrieve the two trunks.

"Grandmother Horton is doing all right since Grandfather died?"

"Well, yes and no. She is healthy and very much able to get around on the estate. But she misses him, of course. She hasn't been the same."

"Does she ever think about coming out here with you and living with us? I know we would love to have her here."

"Nay. She's too old, for one thing. The trip would be too hard for her. But she wouldn't feel right leaving Mowsley. It's where she and your grandfather lived all of those years. It wouldn't seem right to her, I know."

The Swallow came into view at the end of the long pier and Benjamin pulled the reins in on Star. When they first came to Long Island, they had to ride in a small shallop just to get to shore. And even then they waded through the surf the last several yards. But now they had a long, sturdy pier where almost all of the big ships docked.

He tethered Star to a log — not that she'd be going anywhere with that wagon behind her, but they wanted time to wander about the ship. Benjamin was ten years old when they made the trip over, and it had seemed huge to him. Now walking up the plank with his uncle, the ship didn't look all that big.

They went to the shipmaster's cabin where Benjamin had stayed with his parents and Joseph for the journey. "I don't even remember where you slept when we stayed in here."

Jeremy chuckled. "That doesn't surprise me. Let's go up to the scuttle hatch and I'll show you. It's not so bad — it's where my ship's first officers sleep."

He walked up the creaking stairs with his uncle, and as they came out into the open of the upper deck, the smell of the sea was fresh and invigorating. "I could almost like this kind of life, Uncle Jeremy."

"Of course you could." He clapped him on the back. "But it was Joseph that I thought would want to come out with me at least for a season. He loved the astronomy and he had a head for it."

"But he met Jane."

"Women will do that to you. If you think you'd like to sail with me, Benjamin, you best not fall for one." He winked.

"Too late. I fall for them all." He laughed at his own joke, but it was almost true. He loved Anna, and he loved Heather Flower. Mayhap he only fell in love with the ones he couldn't have.

They watched the gulls swoop down for fish. Jeremy leaned on the rail. "Did you know there is an island of sand right at the mouth of the Hudson River? The natives called it Gull Island because of all the birds, but the Dutch call it Oyster Island now. I guess because of all the oysters."

"I was going to say it's not right for the Dutch to change the name, but I guess we do that too."

"Oh yes, we do. But why change a name when it is fitting like Gull Island? But speaking of Indian names, tell me more about Heather Flower." He kept his eyes out on the ocean, but Benjamin knew his ears were on him.

"There's not much to tell. I think I've been in love with her for a long time, and it took Anna marrying Charles for me to see that."

The gulls were squawking overhead and they looked up just in time to see an eagle soaring high with a fuzzy baby in the clutch of its claws. A gull chased after but was no match for the eagle's speed.

Jeremy shook his head. "She's been through a terrible time, has she not?"

"Yes. I fear too much. And it was that Dutchman, Dirk Van Buren, who found her and was bringing her home until Joseph and I went and got her from Fort Amsterdam. He played quite the hero."

"Aye. He was to her, I imagine."

"He doesn't know her like I know her, though. And her feelings are raw."

"Well, she's with her aunt and I suspect she will heal in time."

"True. How long will you be here?"

"Not much longer. I'm headed back to Barbados. I'm here just long enough to load up some pelts and get a few repairs on my sails. Then I'm off. Want to come with me?"

Benjamin's face lit up and his dimples deepened. "Yes, of course. But I'd be stuck because you don't come back this way."

"Aye, you'd have to be in it for the long

haul. But think of it, you can go home to England and see your birthplace."

They walked down the stairs and picked up a trunk on either end and started for the wagon. "I couldn't leave. I guess my heart's here." They set it down and headed back for another one. "You should move here, Uncle Jeremy."

"Well, someone has to check in on your grandmother from time to time and go over the books for her and make sure the mill is still running."

They settled the second trunk in the wagon and climbed up. Benjamin gave a gentle slap with the reins and Star clip-clopped down the road alongside Town Creek.

The latch was ajar and Benjamin shoved the door open with his shoulder. He and Uncle Jeremy hauled the trunks into the parlor.

Patience and Lizzie brought food to share and enjoyed a good visit with Jeremy. Joseph and Jane came over after the meal and the evening was spent going through Uncle Jeremy's trunks. Mary stayed upstairs with little Sarah.

Benjamin smiled at his brothers and little Hannah and remembered how excited he and Joseph were when their uncle came with surprises. It was still exciting.

For Mary, Lizzie, Jane, and Patience, Jeremy brought bolts of silk and brocade, along with silk thread and French lace. He presented Patience with a set of ivory combs in a tortoiseshell box and told her it was for the birthday he'd missed. Pink tinged her cheeks.

After all the gifts were given, Lizzie and Patience took Mary's gifts up to her room. The men down below could hear their murmurs and giggles.

Benjamin settled in a chair and listened to Jeremy tell Barnabas, Joseph, and Zeke about his planned trip to Barbados. His uncle would be leaving on the morrow. He let himself dream a little about leaving with him. It could be good to get away and see something new. A new land with different possibilities.

He couldn't help but allow himself to imagine telling Heather Flower. Would she be sad? Or relieved? He shook his head. What was he thinking? He no more wanted to make her feel bad than he wanted to push her into something she didn't want. But what did she want?

9

September 4, 1653

Heather Flower rose early to prepare for the church service and put on a regal deerskin dress, adorned with shell beads of deep purple and fringed on the sleeves and hem. She tied her purple-and-white wampum belt around her waist and slipped the leather pouch from her mother over her head, along with her necklace of multi-stranded jingle shells and polished stones. She undid her braid and pulled the ivory comb Dirk had given her through her glossy black hair. She sat while Winnie redid the braid for her, working witch hazel blossoms in here and there.

Little Sarah's baptism was today. She was curious about the ceremony. She'd never seen a baptism or church service, most likely it would be like a *pau-wau.*

Her aunt was dressed in deerskin too, though not as elaborate, with shell beads of blue and white. Heather Flower helped her tuck stems of the yellow witch hazel and tiny pink bleeding heart flowers into the stitching of her dress, securing them with more thread.

She picked up the comb and began working it through Winnie's long black hair, salted with white strands. "You have seen a baptism, Aunt?"

"I've been baptized, child. Many years ago. Before the Hortons and Terrys came here to live, there were explorers from across the ocean. They took my mother when she was little and kept her. She learned English from them and they baptized her and taught her of Jesus. My mother had much faith and she passed that on to me."

"That is terrible they took her. Like the mean Narragansett."

"No, her parents had died. White men killed them, it is true. But not the ones who took her. They were kind, and they saved her. And many years later, they helped her come back to her people, to the Corchaug."

"You still feel sorrow for Winheytem. Does your God not give you release from your pain?"

"Oh my dear, yes, I miss him. But without God my heart would have been pulled from my chest. I would die too. God is my strength."

Heather Flower closed her eyes and imagined her heart pulled from her chest. Yes, it seemed it was, with just a hollow place where it should be. "Come, Aunt. Let's go to the church. I want to see a baptism." She took Winnie's hand and they walked the path into town.

The clapboard edifice was the tallest in town, with two stories and a bell tower on top. It was the first structure the men built when they arrived in Southold, called Yennicott by the natives. On this Sunday morning, the men hung their weapons on the wall as they took their pew. Four men stood guard at the entrance and kept long wax-coated reeds lit to fire off their muskets if need be. The Southold militia had been in place from the start, and the recent attack on Heather Flower's family reinforced the need to be ever ready.

The bell pealed as they approached. Heather Flower led Winnie to a place on the women's side, toward the back. She watched as Abigail entered with baby Sarah. Lizzie followed with Hannah on her hip, and Caleb, Joshua, and Jonathan behind her. Barnabas already sat in his front pew, with Joseph and Benjamin beside him.

Mary, still in her confinement, remained at home.

The baptism was held first. Abigail unwrapped the blanket, and Sarah looked so tiny and pink in her little linen dress with thread-lace hem and delicate embroidery. She squirmed and Abigail lifted her and patted her back. "There, there. Nothing to fear, sweet babe."

Reverend Youngs summoned Abigail and Barnabas to come forward, and she laid the baby in her father's arms. She stepped back as Lizzie and Zeke, Patience, and Winnie came forward as sponsors. Reverend Youngs asked Barnabas the name of the child and proceeded to dribble drops of cold water down Sarah's wrinkled forehead. She squeezed her eyes shut, waved her little arms, and began a furious wail of protest. Laughter rippled through the congregation as Abigail came forward quickly to claim the infant. She wrapped her in the blanket, and whisked her away home.

Heather Flower leaned in to Winnie as her aunt took her seat. She laid her hand on her arm. "Is that it? The baptism?"

"Shhh. Yes, that was it."

They rose to sing a hymn, but she could not take her mind off the baptism. It left more questions than answers. She glanced at the pew across from them and noticed for the first time Grissell and Nathaniel Sylvester. Grissell nodded toward her with a smile. The two young women had become friends on Shelter Island, the island between the two forks, but Heather Flower was surprised to see her at the Southold First Church.

Benjamin listened to Reverend Youngs, but thoughts of Heather Flower popped into the pauses no matter how he concentrated on the reverend's words. As the sermon ended, he was glad to stand with the congregation for the final hymn.

His tenor blended with his father's rich baritone, as they sang from the Psalms, "Teach me Thy way, O Lord." At the "amen," he could not help but turn to catch a glimpse of her at the back.

The reverend moved to the door of the church and shook hands as Heather Flower and her aunt departed. Duty prevented Benjamin from chasing after her, and he remained at his father's side. The more he prayed about her, the more he knew he needed to give her time.

He followed his father as they filed out. Someone tapped his shoulder. The younger John Youngs — Captain Youngs, or Johnny as they called him — fell in beside him, his betrothed, Margaret, on his arm. "I hear Winnie is feeling better. I think it helps to have Heather Flower with her, don't you think?"

"I do. Winnie has a strong faith. She'd heal regardless, but I think having Heather Flower's company is a blessing to her."

"And to you, Ben?"

Benjamin grinned and nodded. "Well, yes. You know me too well. I like having her here. But I have to say, nothing has changed between her and me. I still feel like a lost puppy and she still gives me a pat and sends me on my way."

"She's been through a lot. She can't even face going home is what I hear."

They picked up their muskets and headed for the door.

Reverend Youngs stretched out a hand to Benjamin. "Good morrow, Ben, good to see you."

He tucked his Bible under his arm and shook the reverend's hand. "Good morn, sir. Enjoyed your sermon."

"Thank you. Good morrow, dear." He bowed to Margaret.

She curtsied back with a smile. "Good morrow to you, Reverend Youngs. Mother has been ill, and I mustn't tarry. She did tell me to give you her regards."

"Why, sorry to hear that, dear. Tell your mother I will call on her this evening after services." He turned to his son. "You boys will be back this afternoon for more, of course." Reverend Youngs grasped his hands in front.

Johnny towered over his father. "We always are, Father."

"Aye, you are — when you are home." A smile swept his face. "You know I'm not happy with you out scouting around in Connecticut trying to stir up trouble with the Dutch."

"There's trouble with the Dutch anyway, Father, and Cromwell would well like it if we chased them out of New Amsterdam."

He sought agreement from Benjamin, who was happy to oblige, as they were like-minded on this. "True. New Haven may set the policies, but we've always been isolated enough from them to handle things our own way. They are behind the times in seeking peace with the Dutch. England's at war with Holland and we won't have peace here with the Dutch living on half the island."

Reverend Youngs shook his head. "We keep with New Haven's policies. And son, if you keep going up to Connecticut and rousing around with Captain Scott, you will cause trouble for yourself and us." He held Johnny's shoulder with his hand and gave him a light pat before he turned to the next parishioner.

Barnabas clapped both young men on the shoulders as they stepped into the bright sunlight. "Winnie and Heather Flower are coming to our house for dinner between services. Then they will continue home. Johnny, would you care to join us?"

Johnny pummeled his flat stomach with his fist. "I would never turn down a meal at your house, Mr. Horton."

Benjamin chuckled. "With Mother in confinement, he's been baking every spare minute. Patience and Lizzie have helped with most of the cooking, though, so we've been eating well."

"Aye, and I heard Winnie will put together her samp. It gets better every year." The smell of bacon fat wafted in the air and Barnabas inhaled deeply. "She's already fixing it."

The three ambled toward the Horton home and bakeshop across the road.

Inside the house they stacked their muskets against the chimney. Barnabas trotted up the narrow stairs to Mary's bedchamber. Johnny settled into the parlor on the right, but Benjamin could not resist wandering back to the kitchen. He stopped at the doorway. Heather Flower jabbed at thick slices of bacon that sizzled in a heavy skillet over the fire. Winnie chopped wild onions and corn from the cob. Lizzie, with the help of Patience, had prepared much of the meal the day before to preserve the Sabbath. Now she stirred the pudding she'd made, as it warmed in a pot. Only Heather Flower looked up and caught his eye. A rosy copper flooded her cheeks and she gave him a warm smile.

"We could smell that bacon clear across to the church. How long until it's ready?"

Winnie looked up. "Soon, my friend. And if you cannot wait, take a few ginger cakes and go out to the parlor. We've no room in here for hungry men."

Benjamin grinned and snuck one last look at Heather Flower, who nodded at the crisp little cakes and turned back to her frying.

He entered the front parlor, a large, well-appointed room with a fireplace in the middle that connected to the central chimney. Johnny stood by the library shelves on the far wall, perusing navigation books. He handed him a crisp cake.

Johnny popped the little cake into his mouth and chewed thoughtfully. He swallowed the tasty morsel and brushed a crumb from the book's leather cover. "I am always amazed at your father's books. And I like these old volumes on celestial navigation. Quite the collection."

"Those were Uncle Jeremy's. At one time Joseph was very much intrigued with learning to sail. You both were. My uncle gave him those books. But millwork is as much in our blood as sailing." He walked over to the casement window and pushed open the diamond-paned sash. "I think the air is fresher out there than in here."

"It's a beautiful day, though no wind for sailing." Johnny set the book back on the shelf and glanced out the window. "Is that Joseph and Jane I see coming up the road?"

Benjamin spread his hands on the sill and leaned out with a grin. "Well, good morrow to you, brother! Come to see the new sister?" He hurried to the door.

Joseph stood back and allowed Jane to enter first. Benjamin kissed her cheek. "The women are split between the kitchen and Mother upstairs, so take your pick." He turned to his brother and they clapped each other's back. "Good to see you. Father's upstairs too. And Captain Youngs is in the parlor, if you'd like to join us."

Joseph looked at Jane with a raised eyebrow. "What say you? Shall I come up

114

with you?"

"Nay, stay here. Join us when you're ready."

Her skirts swished as she climbed the stairs. He watched her go before he joined the men in the parlor.

Benjamin turned a hand toward a chair and nodded to Johnny. He pulled up a third chair. "Sit awhile, Joseph."

"I will. So what do you gather from your friends in New Amsterdam, Johnny? Are we at peace with the Dutch or not? To listen to Underhill, they claim one thing but plan another."

"Cromwell wants the Dutch out of there, and I think he's right."

Benjamin scooted forward on his chair, his hands on his knees. "But New Haven and Stuyvesant both have worked toward peace. The Hartford Treaty is alive and well, is it not?"

"Don't think for a minute that guarantees a whit. Given the chance, Stuyvesant's army would advance on us. He gives guns to the Indians as fast as we take them away. He does not understand that after the attack on Montauk, the Indians here know we will defend them against the Narragansett, and they have no need for weapons. Montauk will not happen again." Johnny turned to

115

Joseph. "What say you?"

He eyed his father's musket, the old quart pot, hanging above the fireplace. "Agreed we won't let an attack like we had on Montauk happen again. In England, Parliament has been talking of peace as far as we know, but we continue to get news of battles. We were very successful in the Battle of Portland. But attacking New Amsterdam would be in direct violation of New Haven."

Johnny ran his hand down the back of his hair. "We don't follow New Haven in everything and you know it. They know it. They pretty much leave us be, with only an occasional cranky comment about how late our youth stay out." He chuckled.

Patience entered from the kitchen, wiping her hands on her apron. "Lizzie says we are all to gather at the long table in the bakeshop to eat. Abbey's preparing a tray to take up to Mary and will send everyone down. After we eat, she'll bring down the babe Sarah."

The men stood and Benjamin looked past her in hopes of a glimpse of Heather Flower.

Joseph noticed, he could tell by the gleam in his eyes, but his brother turned to John without comment. "We could talk all day about the Dutch and not solve a thing."

"No, it's action we need. That's why

Captain Scott and I will be sailing up to Connecticut to see who we can convince to take steps against New Amsterdam."

Benjamin's thoughts turned to Dirk. He'd like to kick him off the island, but was that right? Probably not. "Whoa. Those are strong words. And I think whether we like it or not, we are bound by the laws of New Haven."

Patience smiled, but fixed her hands on her hips. "Are you coming?"

They followed her to the kitchen where the table was laden with platters of turkey, ham, and rabbit, surrounded by steaming bowls of vegetables, and apples from the orchard, baked whole with cinnamon. Loaves of fresh bread and crocks of butter were laid out on the sideboard along with pots of fruit preserves. Stacks of crisp little ginger cakes and apple tartlets sat behind them.

Barnabas was the last to join them, and they all clasped hands as he gave thanks for Sarah, Mary, family, good food, and good companions. Winnie set a heaped trencher in front of him.

He savored a bite of Winnie's samp. "Why is a meal always better when someone else cooks it?"

The women all looked at him, smiling

their appreciation. Heather Flower passed the samp to Benjamin and nodded toward Winnie. "My aunt tells me that Lizzie's and Mary's cooking is only surpassed by yours, Mr. Horton."

Lizzie giggled and smoothed her curls. "If that be true, 'tis only because we have been cooking longer than anyone else here." She glanced at Winnie and she nodded in agreement.

Joseph ran his fingers through his thick brown hair, ruffing it a bit. "Seems to me, Father, you finally conceded to Mother that she was your equal in the bakeshop, did you not?"

Everyone stopped mid-fork to listen to his reply. "Aye, that would be true. But I would have to admit that since then I do believe she's got the best of me. Eh, Elizabeth?"

She smiled, the purple of her silk dress accenting the hint of violet in her eyes. "Our Mary is a fine cook, Barnabas. I never would have thought I could say that when I remember all the days of explaining to her the difference between a simmer and a boil."

Barnabas chortled and pushed his chair back. "I've fond memories as well of teaching your sister to cook."

Abigail entered with the sweet bundle of Sarah in her arms, and everyone rose to take a peek at the sleeping baby. She carefully pulled the blanket back, and Sarah scrunched her face without opening an eye.

"She looks like you, Benjamin, poor little poppet." Joseph looked pleased with himself.

"Only because of her hair. Really, she looks like you, Hannah." He scooped up his sister and let her peer into the babe's face. He took her hand and helped her feel the auburn fuzz on her sister's head.

Hannah smiled. "I love her."

Barnabas moved close. "Aye. You finally have a sister. You will be close to her, Hannah, just like your aunt Lizzie and your mother." He kissed the top of Hannah's head.

The meal was finished and the women wiped the plates and utensils, and set the pots of leftovers at the back of the fire to keep warm for a light supper at the end of the day. Heather Flower offered her help to the ladies and Benjamin wandered out to the apple orchard with the men to finish their earlier discussion and to talk of family, both present and far away.

He put his hand on his father's arm. "Times like this, I miss Grandmother and Grandfather Horton."

"Aye, Benjamin. They loved being with

you and Joseph when you were little. I think it tore your grandmother's heart when we left. She would have liked to hold all of her grandchildren."

Joseph moved toward the corner apple tree, the oldest and tallest of the lot, its branches reaching up to a large dome, filled with ruby-red fruit. "And Mary's father. He would have liked to see her poppets. Hard to believe he and Grandfather are gone."

Barnabas reached up and plucked an apple. "They must be singing hallelujahs right now along with your mother. And sending their light down through God's little windows."

"Windows?"

"Aye, Caleb. You know how your mother calls the stars 'God's little windows.' "

A horse stomped and snorted, bringing all eyes to the side of the house. Benjamin's heart thudded an extra beat, and he glanced toward the back of the house as he stepped forward. "Van Buren. What would you be doing out here? Did no one tell you there's a war going on?"

Dirk swung from the back of Miss Button, dropping the reins and pulling off a glove. "I'm here on orders of Director-General Stuyvesant." He extended his ungloved hand.

Benjamin grasped it with a rough shake. "That has no meaning to us. What's your business?" Wrinkles crossed his brow and his blue-eyed glare matched Dirk's, whose bay blues flicked to the house and back to Benjamin.

Barnabas, Joseph, and Captain John Youngs stepped in to back up Benjamin. The four faced the Dutchman. Dirk nodded without a flinch and fixed his gaze on Barnabas. "Hallo. We've numerous reports that your countrymen, despite the fact they've been granted considerable territory to the east of Oyster Bay, continue to encroach. If they continue to inhabit the town, they fall under the Dutch provincial rule. And if they do not pay the taxes or submit to the laws, they will be arrested."

Barnabas shook his head with a grin. "No, they purchased that land straight out and fair from Sachem Mohannes. You'd best be on your way. We have laws here too, and you are in violation of the treaty."

"Mohannes has no authority to sell the land. It is Wyandanch who is the Grand Sachem, and it is he who sold the tract to deVries. *Ja.* It is Dutch. Pure and simple."

Joseph took a quick step forward, but all eyes shot to the house as Heather Flower stepped out and gasped. Benjamin hurried over as she stood still, holding a large pot of dirty wash water on her hip.

"You'd best go inside, I would not want you to listen to the words being exchanged."

"Words, Benjamin? Or are you and your brother about to fight Dirk? Do you forget he saved my life?"

Dirk strode over and Benjamin stepped in front of him. "You'll leave now."

"The lady can decide that." He looked to Heather Flower and her dark opal eyes grew wide.

"I do not wish harm, Dirk. You should leave. I am well. Now go."

Every tense muscle in Benjamin relaxed and he nodded to Dirk. "She is fine with us, now do as she requests."

Dirk gave a long look at Heather Flower as she dumped the dirty water to the side of the porch and stomped back into the house. He turned and in a few quick steps was at Miss Button's side, swinging up into the saddle. He reined her to the west, gave a quick salute, and urged her to a full gallop.

The men traipsed inside. Benjamin exchanged a look with his father and brother before facing Heather Flower. He'd protected her from that no-good. But why did looking at her now make him feel so low?

10

September 19, 1653

The morning broke glorious and Benjamin's plans were to forget Heather Flower for a day and take his younger brothers out trapping. September, greeted by cooler weather, now gave way to a warm Indian summer. The haze from the fires the natives built to flush out game gave a lazy effect to the long afternoons.

School lessons would soon begin. But the lessons of the wild were taught during September more than any other month. Armed with only his musket, a sling and a bag of agates for each boy, some flint, and rope, Benjamin led Caleb, Joshua, and Jonathan deep into the forest. They found a stream to camp by, and he demonstrated to the boys with a rare white hair from Star's tail how to loop it through the drilled hole in a hook made from fish bone and fish with it.

They worked throughout the day. They built snares with bent trees and nooses, identified berries to eat, and caught fish. Before the sun set, they'd built a fire to roast the squirrels and fish they'd caught day. As they sat fireside, Joseph hiked in to join them for the night, and the younger boys were entertained by their brothers' stories of coming over from England on the ship called *The Swallow* with Uncle Jeremy.

Jonathan's hazel eyes grew big and he glanced at the trees that surrounded them. "Were you afraid when you got off the ship and there were just dark woods, nothing else?"

Benjamin chuckled. "No, we were glad to see land. We were sick of the ship by then and wanted some good food to eat and soil beneath our feet. Right, Joseph?"

Joseph sat with his knife, carving on a thick stick he found along the way. "That's right. And Father was brave so we thought we should be too." He wiggled his eyebrows at Jonathan. "You are a brave lad, are you not?"

Joshua laughed and pushed at Jonathan's shoulder. "You're a lily-liver, aren't you?"

"Am not!"

Joseph's look was stern, just like his father's. "There will be none of that, especially out here in the wilderness." He held up his stick that had grown legs and a head. "Can you guess what I'm carving?"

Caleb answered a split second before Joshua. "A horse — it's Star I bet."

Benjamin leaned close to the fire, the flames flickering on his dimpled cheeks. "Grandfather Horton used to carve horses for me and Joseph. We used to watch him sit by the hearth after supper and whittle. It was fun to see a block of wood become a beautiful horse. Sometimes he would make a cat, but the horses he always made for us."

Joseph nodded.

The flames died down and finally they brought out their blankets and settled under the starry sky. Benjamin and Joseph kept their muskets close by their sides with the boys between them.

They lay watching the stars as more of the twinkling lights filled the dark. "I miss our grandparents," said Benjamin.

"I do too. I miss our mother too."

Jonathan's small voice could barely be heard. "We'll see Mother tomorrow, won't we?"

Benjamin chuckled. "Of course we will. Joseph and I have another mother too. She died, Jonathan, when I was too young to remember her much — but Joseph does."

Joseph propped himself on his elbow. "I do remember her. And Mary says that's a good thing. She said she never wants me to forget."

Benjamin's eyes were closing. "That's good, because by you remembering I won't forget either." He tried to picture his mother in his mind. He liked Mary's story about the stars and wondered if every generation that passed there were more and more new stars. Then sleep engulfed him.

They woke up with a start to movement in the bayberry bushes.

"Who goes there?" Joseph called as he and Benjamin grabbed their muskets.

Nothing but quiet for a moment, and then a man stepped into the clearing. "It's me, Lieutenant Van Buren. I'm on official business so put down your weapons."

Benjamin stood, barrel trained on Dirk. "What kind of official business? We just got rid of you and you're back? You know, you're mighty near the Indian fort right now. Who is your business with?"

"I have an official complaint against Captain John Youngs for illegal trade in our port. If he continues his activities, he's subject to arrest. I'll be delivering my documents to your father and Mr. Wells tomorrow."

Joseph gestured with his musket toward the fire, which was but low embers now. "Put your weapon down and sit. You'll come in with us as our prisoner actually. And explain yourself once again at our town meeting."

"What's your authority?"

"As a member of our town militia, I have all the authority I need, right, Benjamin?"

Benjamin glanced at his three younger brothers huddled together, eyes wide. "That's true, Van Buren. You'll be treated well as our prisoner, but it's time you Dutch learn that the treaty we have with you does not include riding into our territory whenever you like. There's a war going on at home."

With their prisoner's hands behind his back, and the sun up, a hasty breakfast was served, with the three younger complaining that cold meat was not that appetizing at the break of dawn. Dirk nodded his head toward his knapsack. "There's biscuits in there."

Benjamin smiled at the sad faces when he said no to the offer. "It would not be much of a lesson of survival in the wilderness if we ate what was packed in, now would it?"

He nodded at Dirk. "But I will fetch you one. We don't starve our prisoners."

After their meal, they made Dirk walk with them and led his horse back into town. In the meetinghouse Benjamin found it hard to concentrate while the men convened to discuss the lieutenant.

He watched out the window as Caleb, Joshua, and Jonathan joined the other town boys for a game of hoop war. The three, with their hoops in hand, charged the other boys, with each fallen hoop a casualty. He glanced out after a time and noticed they had tired of the hoops, and settled for a game of marbles. He grinned as he watched the young Hortons hit marble after marble — as well they should, growing up with two big brothers to practice with. Caleb could almost beat him and Joseph, but Uncle Jeremy remained the champion. When it came to arm wrestling, no one yet had whipped their father.

He closed his eyes and imagined how Heather Flower might react to him and Joseph taking Dirk prisoner. So he welcomed the decision, when it came, to release him and send him on his way. No use in starting a small war here. And no use in distancing himself from Heather Flower any more than he already was. But would Van Buren go home? Or was his intention to find her?

Dirk was escorted to the livery and Miss Button was brought out, saddled and well brushed. At least they'd treated her well. He didn't like that Biggs and a couple of his men from the militia were escorting him out of English territory. He'd have no chance to stop and talk with Heather Flower. But he'd had some satisfaction in delivering the papers in regard to the activities of Captain Youngs, though he admired the captain's gumption. Mission of the Cavalry accomplished, mission of the heart not even close.

They cut through Indian Neck, and he searched the face of every woman he saw for her to no avail. Soon they were once again in deep woods and he turned his attention to matters at home. Nicholas Visscher would arrive from New Amsterdam sometime in the future, and his orders were to accompany him through the wilds of Connecticut as the famous mapmaker took notes and studied the land.

It was a good assignment. The job boiled down to scouting, which he liked doing. And it would be good to get his mind off of Heather Flower and the English for a while. It would take him a couple of months of planning and he looked forward to that as much as the trek back into Narragansett territory.

The day he had rescued Heather Flower was not luck. He knew that land like his own back lot. But a strategy to avoid contact with the likes of Ninigret and his men would take some thought. The tribe moved with the seasons, but he could almost predict where they would be on a given week.

Biggs turned him loose just past Wading River, and he urged Miss Button on toward Flushing. He'd stop there for the night and gather his thoughts before riding into Fort Amsterdam. There was one last thing he could do for Heather Flower, whether the Hortons liked it or not — and he loved her enough to give it a try.

11

September 25, 1653

Two hot pippin pies sat on Mary's windowsill to cool. The apple harvest had just begun, but she did not wait to bake the first fresh pies of the season. She'd picked one basket, brought them in, and sliced them up for the pies. And if she promised the boys a slice, they'd help harvest the bumper crop without much complaint. It was the same every year.

Between now and Christmastide the demand for her pippin pies would exceed everything else in the bakeshop, even Barney's little ginger cakes. Lizzie and Patience helped her each year with the baking and in return she sent them home with baskets of apples and all the bread they needed for the week.

Winnie usually made new apple baskets for her, but this year Lizzie and Patience helped her make them. Still, she'd send some apples and baked goods to Winnie and Heather Flower. Friendship meant not needing to be paid back. She remembered so many times that Winnie had given to her in just that spirit.

This year Lizzie suggested Mary put together a recipe book filled with treats from the bakeshop, and she decided she might as well start now, with little Sarah still asleep and the pippin pie recipe fresh in her mind.

She found an empty journal that was just right for this project. She wiped her hands on her apron, picked up a pen, and dipped the nib into the ink bottle.

To Make a Pippin Pie

Take 6 medium pippins or any apples, peel them and mince or slice them very fine. Stir 3/4 cup sugar, 1/4 cup flour, 1/2 teaspoon cinnamon, 1/2 teaspoon ginger, and a pinch of salt in apples to coat. Put your best pie pastry into a 9-inch pie pan. Pile apple mixture into pastry and dot with 2 tablespoons cold butter. Top with second pastry round, cut slits, and crimp edges. Bake in hot oven until crust is browned and juice bubbles. Halfway through baking, brush with rosewater and sprinkle with sugar.

There, she'd started it. If she wrote a recipe down each time she baked, it would probably be done in no time at all.

After supper, Caleb, Joshua, and Jonathan went out to the orchard with her and, with the promise of pippin pie, climbed the trees to reach the apples she could not. Together they picked enough apples to fill fifteen baskets while Hannah played next to Sarah, telling her baby sister all about pippins and poppets.

Mary was worn out by the time they gathered with Barney and Ben, but with Sarah in her cradle and Hannah already in bed, she sat with her redware bowl on her lap, paring and slicing apples as she listened to Barney read from the Bible. Each perfect slice fell into the drying basket next to her feet and would provide for good eating through the long winter.

She finished one basket that evening, and on the morrow, between baking, she would work her way through more. Even after all the baking, drying, and sharing the bounty with neighbors, there would be plenty to trade for sugar when the ship came in from Barbados.

Caleb took Joshua and Jonathan off to bed, and Mary finally set her knife and bowl down, rubbing her sore fingers. Sarah would wake up soon for another feeding. When she did, she'd take her up to their room for the night. But for now she had a moment to visit with Ben.

"There will be a harvest moon on the morrow."

Ben and Barney both looked up from their books and smiled.

"I imagine Jay and Jane will come over to help us bring in the pumpkins. Zeke and Lizzie too. We have a big crop this year. It must be the honeybees. They're thriving."

"Yes, Mother. I was checking the pumpkins today — they're ready for picking and we could have an early frost this year so we need to get them in." Ben glanced at her hands. "Your fingers look raw from cutting apples. At least the pumpkin needs to cure awhile before you do anything with them."

Barney nodded and looked back to his book for a moment, then looked up again. "I'll have Caleb and Joshua help you with slicing apples tomorrow. And you should have Abbey help too. You take a nap when Hannah and Sarah nap and let Abbey work on the apples."

Mary gave him a warm smile. "That is sweet, my husband, but as much as I or Abbey plan their naps, Sarah is not inclined to oblige and sleep when Hannah does. And

Hannah is turning three. Her naps are shorter and shorter."

He shook his head. "They grow up too soon, those poppets." He raised his brow at Ben. "You did."

"Ah, Father, and you're not rid of me yet, are you?"

Mary's eyes flew open. "We don't wish to be rid of you, Ben. But we do wish for you to be happily settled with a good wife to keep you company. You must tire of sitting with us old folks, eh?"

"Not so much. I rather enjoy your company."

She rocked for a minute. "You should go fetch Heather Flower and have her help us bring in the pumpkins. She could take some home for Winnie."

"I could do that, although I imagine they have plenty of squash." He winked and closed his book. "And now I am off to bed." He kissed her good night and bade his father good night as well.

Sarah wiggled and sighed in her cradle, and Mary got up with her bowl of peels and apple seeds. "I'm going to dump these in the barrel and then take Sarah up. She'll be ready to eat soon."

Barney jumped up. "Let me get that for you. You take Sarah up and I'll be along shortly."

He gave her a hug and she picked up their little girl and headed for the stairs. She was blessed. But she wanted Ben to be blessed too. Barney was fond of saying "in God's own time." She hoped God's time would be Ben's time soon.

Benjamin hitched Star and started down the main town road toward the Corchaug fort. He was glad Mary suggested he ride out. As much as he'd tried to not think about Heather Flower, he did wonder if Van Buren had managed to stop and see her.

He also wondered what she would think about what he and Joseph had done. He didn't have to defend their actions, but he'd like the chance to warn her that the man kept lurking and he didn't like it. She probably didn't regard it as lurking at all. Fudge.

Last he'd heard about Winnie, she was feeling better, so mayhap she'd come with Heather Flower and pick pumpkins with them. It would do them both good to get away and visit.

He shifted his weight on the bench. It'd been a long day. He and James finished building the town's one-room schoolhouse, and he'd tried to help with harvest through most of the construction. Today he'd built a desk with the new schoolmaster, Mr. Howell. He leaned forward to stretch his achy back.

He entered the palisade and pulled up close to Winnie's wigwam. Heather Flower worked outside, under the shelter of a lean-to, stitching a pair of moccasins with white cylindrical beads. She didn't notice him as he walked up.

"You are hard at work this afternoon."

She looked up with a smile. "You thought I did not see you. But my ears hear."

Her glad-to-see-you smile made him forget what he intended to say and his face warmed. He collected his thoughts. "Mother told me I should come and ask you to help with our pumpkin harvest. It's the harvest moon tonight. It should be beautiful. You could stay with Jane and Joseph."

She looked toward the wigwam. "I don't know if I should leave my aunt. I thought she did better after we came to Sarah's baptism, but now she weeps and sits."

"Well, she should come with us then. It will be good for her to see Mother. And it's good to be busy, especially when you're hurting."

Her small smile spread. "Do you speak of me too, Benjamin?"

Surely she heard the commotion his heart

made in his chest, but he would not miss this chance. "Mayhap. Come on, gather your things and let's go get Winnie." He followed her inside the hut.

Winnie refused, and after much persuasion, Heather Flower finally came with him. They rode mostly in silence back to the Hortons.

The family moved out to the pumpkin patch situated west of the orchard. Sarah was in a sling around Mary's neck and even Hannah was out to pick pumpkins. She ran ahead of everyone to find the biggest. A gleeful shriek announced her find and she tried to lift it. Benjamin took his knife out to cut the vine, then lifted Hannah's pumpkin for her. He lugged it to the cart as Heather Flower helped her choose a smaller one.

As the sun went down in the west, the full harvest moon rose in the east — a big sugar-cake moon — and they worked in its ethereal beauty until midnight.

Benjamin took her home, The night was still, save for Star's footfalls, and Heather Flower was quiet.

"Has Van Buren come to see you?" He could feel her eyes on him.

"When?"

"Well, anytime I guess. But in the last

couple of weeks?" He looked over at her as Star followed the well-known path.

The moon lit fire in her eyes. "I have not seen Dirk in the last few days, Benjamin, but that should not matter to you, should it?"

"I'm only asking because Joseph and I had a run-in with him. I took my brothers out into the woods to spend the night and hunt. Van Buren was there, and we believe he was spying. We took him in, and he was interrogated and then released. I wanted you to know, in case you hear about it somewhere else. He was well treated."

Now her eyes glittered. "I will see Dirk as I choose, and I will not tell you, my friend. I've no desire to hurt you, but there is nothing to be hurt over. I've told you both I need you as my friends. But that was not acting like a friend."

He slowed the wagon as they came to the fort.

"Heather Flower, it had nothing to do with you. And I only told you about what happened because you will find out about it one way or another. I'm not trying to pry." But as she climbed down from the wagon without waiting for him to assist her, he wondered if his words were true.

12

October 3, 1653

Barnabas arrived early with his three youngest sons as Mr. Micah Howell prepared for his first day as the new schoolmaster. He had been instrumental in procuring the teacher and had pushed hard for the township to move forward with plans for a grammar school.

When he and Mary first came to Long Island, he schooled Joseph and Benjamin himself. One of the earliest laws he and the founding fathers enacted was the requirement of parents to teach their children to read. He taught them with the Bible and a copy of *Aesop's Fables.*

When Patience's parents died of the fever, Mary and Lizzie convinced her to open a Dame School for young girls, and she had even taught Caleb, Joshua, and Jonathan their alphabet and little rhymes she remembered learning at her mother's knee in England. "Thirty days hath September" was her favorite.

After the church, education was the highest priority for the men of Southold, and they soon put together the funding for the first full-time teacher. They hired Mr. Griffing and provided him with a house where he both lived and taught. His classes for boys were the basic reading, spelling, writing, and arithmetic.

But for Mr. Howell they approved funds for a schoolhouse, and Benjamin had been hired to build it. Now Barnabas looked around the room with its neat rows of benches for the boys, a hearth and chimney in the center, and a desk and chair for Mr. Howell. Benjamin had mentioned he was particularly happy at how the bookshelves he'd built looked, and Barnabas was pleased to see Mr. Howell had brought a box of books to fill them.

They despaired of finding a gentleman who could teach their boys the Latin and ciphers needed to prepare them for college. The hope of the next generation lay with education, so Barnabas sent letters as far away as London in search of the right candidate.

But he'd found him straight out of the graduating class of Harvard College, and now the boys of the town filed in for their first day of instruction with Mr. Howell.

The Indian summer would not last much longer, and each student brought a log so that when it was time to light a fire for warmth, the teacher would have a supply. The students brought their own ink as well and reams of parchment.

As class began promptly at seven o'clock, Barnabas gave one last lecture on the importance of school and reminded his sons they must not waste a minute of their opportunity to learn as he bid them goodbye. He chuckled as he told Mary when he got home about their serious faces as he left them in the schoolroom with their quills, ink, and hornbooks.

Caleb and Joshua brought the hornbooks that had belonged to Joseph and Benjamin when they were little. The wooden boards were trimmed in leather and had a transparent sheet of horn over the front that held parchment paper. On the backs were written The Lord's Prayer. Jonathan had a brand-new one, and his was made to match the first two.

The boys came home for dinner. After they returned to their classroom, Abbey gathered Misha, Hannah, and Sarah up for their naps, and Mary and Barnabas spent a rare afternoon together in the bakeshop. Mary sighed as she checked her pies in the oven. Two more were on the oak table waiting to be baked.

He watched as she sprinkled the tops of her baking pies with rosewater. "We have done the right thing in hiring Mr. Howell, I believe. He is well read and his collection of books is impressive. He'll teach our sons well."

" 'Tis good to know. Mr. Griffing was certainly excellent until he went back to England. Do you think Southold attracts the best because it's such a lovely place?"

"No doubt." He took a couple of slices of apples from the basket and ignored the look Mary gave him as he took a bite. "Benjamin did a good job with the bookshelves."

"I'm not surprised. I hear the whole schoolhouse is very nice. He learned from you, did he not?" She smiled as she crimped the edges of her pies.

"That he did."

Mary straightened from the table, her ear toward the front of the house. "What was that? The boys? Why are they home so early?"

Barnabas strode toward the parlor and Mary followed, wiping her hands on her apron. One look at Jonathan's and Joshua's face told her something tragic had happened at school.

"What's the matter? What has happened?" Barnabas looked from one boy to the other. "Joshua, speak. Tell me."

"Mr. Howell didn't look so well. He told us to practice writing the list of words with one syllable he posted on his desk. I couldn't see them so I raised my hand like he told us to do. He said, 'You may come up to the desk and read it, Master Horton.' But he didn't sound very good."

Mary grasped his shoulders. "What happened? Is he all right? Tell us, Joshua."

His voice trembled. "I got up and walked to his desk and then Mr. Howell made a funny noise. Mr. Howell's face was red and sweaty and he started to stand up, but then he just fell over."

Jonathan started to cry.

"We ran as fast as we could."

Mary went pale. "Oh no. I hope it's not fever."

Barnabas hoped not too, but most likely it was. They'd heard there'd been a big outbreak up in Cambridge, but Mr. Howell had assured them of his health and he seemed very hardy and full of vigor. Certainly he did not look sick this morning.

"We need to get the doctor. Joshua, go.

I'll go to the schoolhouse. Have Doctor Smith meet me there." He turned to Mary. "Here now, sit. Are you all right?"

"I think so, Barney."

"I must go." He took out the door quickly, but decided to first go to the meetinghouse to fetch Reverend Youngs. The two ran next door and found Mr. Howell lying on the floor. He appeared in a faint. The reverend sent the class home and Barnabas went out to the well to get a bucket of fresh water.

The doctor arrived and, after examining him, diagnosed the measles. Mr. Howell would need to be quarantined and the children in the classroom as well, until they knew if any of them would become ill. He asked the reverend and Barnabas if anyone else had been close to the schoolmaster.

"Benjamin. He helped him do some work in here on Saturday. Would Mr. Howell have been communicable then, Russell?"

Doc rubbed his forehead. "Could be. Hard to know. You and your boys, including Benjamin, need to stay away from Mary and those little girls until we figure out if this is going any further."

Barnabas's heart beat like it was in his throat. He could not bear the thought of any of his children or Mary getting this sick.

Doctor Smith scratched his head. "You

ought to take the boys and stay at Joseph's until this is over, and have him and Jane stay with Mary. I'll take Mr. Howell here with me. We need to get word to the other parents that their children need to be isolated."

Reverend Youngs volunteered to notify everyone. They helped the doctor carry poor Mr. Howell to his house and then Barnabas walked home. The doctor said they would have to be on the watch for any illness for two weeks, and he dreaded telling Mary.

She took the news calmly but made him wait outside while she gathered nightshirts and clothes for him and the boys. She told him that with harvest almost finished, she looked forward to spending a little more time with Jane and Jay anyway. He knew she was in a panic. He could see it in her eyes. But he allowed her to be brave, because to take her in his arms for comfort might make her sick. And he could not risk that.

13

October 17, 1653

Mr. Howell survived the measles under the care of Doc Smith. The fever that raged the first week subsided, and the red rash that began on his forehead and worked its way throughout his body began to recede. Of the boys quarantined in their homes — five had the measles previously and did not require quarantine — only three came down with the measles, and the Horton men and boys were not affected. Doc tended his young patients and they survived too, thanks in part, he said, to their age and hardiness.

The scare of an epidemic shook the little hamlet, but Benjamin knew it put more fear into the people at the Corchaug fort than anyone else. For some reason, when the native people contracted the white man's illnesses, they were much more likely to die. Entire Indian villages were dying from sickness the inhabitants never knew existed before.

He wanted to see Heather Flower. They had not parted on good terms the last time. Doc Smith said after two weeks he would be in the clear, but he decided to wait another week to be sure. He couldn't risk bringing illness and suffering to her or her people.

School resumed with Mr. Howell, and Benjamin enjoyed watching his little brothers trudging off to school with their hornbooks. They had their future ahead, but what of him? Was he happy where he was in the grand order of things?

He walked out to the Town Road and looked at the elm-lined street. He remembered the day they had waded ashore. There'd been nothing but deer paths when they'd arrived.

He and Joseph had worked hard with their father to build their house. He'd learned much about carpentry and it was a good trade. He was thankful for the good life he had here, but it seemed empty to him unless he had someone to share it with. If it were to be Heather Flower, he would be honored. But if she would not have him, he wasn't sure he wanted to stay here. John Budd talked of moving out west. Joseph and

Jane wanted to go with him.

His uncle's words echoed in his mind and he laughed at himself. His brother was always the dreamer. Even Uncle Jeremy said he'd thought Joseph would be the one to sail the seas with him. Yet he could be sailing right now if he'd said yes when Uncle Jeremy had invited him.

Mary called. He turned as she hurried toward him. He'd never leave here. It would hurt her too much, and that he couldn't bear.

"Oh, Ben, there you are. I was going to cut one of the pies and I wanted to know if you'd like a piece."

"You have to ask? I'm coming right in." He followed her up the wooden steps and eyed the table. "I'll take that one." He chuckled.

"Oh, no you don't." She tapped his hand as he reached toward the nearest golden pie. "How unlike you, Ben." She smiled as she tsked. "You are always my one to have some manners."

He stared at her thoughtfully. "Maybe I'm tired of being so predictable."

"Whatever do you mean? What has that to do with manners?"

"I'm just thinking I'm always the obedient one, the one to do what everyone expects of me. It might just be time to do what I want to do, even if on a whim."

She picked up a knife and inserted the tip into the center of the pie. As she lifted a wedge, the syrupy apples oozed and she quickly transferred it to a plate. Ben watched as a glob fell back into the pie pan and he quickly scooped it up and popped it into his mouth, licking his fingers.

"Was that a whim? Really, Ben. Here." She handed him a fork — from a set Uncle Jeremy had brought from France — with his plate of pie.

He stabbed a bite and took his time to answer. He let the flakey pastry crumble in his mouth, releasing the sweet apple and cinnamon he loved. His fork toyed with the next chunk. "Everyone always thought Joseph would take off with Jeremy sometime, but he got married instead. Everyone has always thought I would be the one to marry and settle down. What if I took to sailing? What would you think?"

She stopped the knife mid-slice, her eyes a troubled gray. "You wouldn't do that."

"That is my point. Mayhap I would."

"Oh no, Ben. You mustn't think like that. You cannot put yourself at risk just to make a point. There's nothing to prove. We all love you just as you are. And what about

Heather Flower? How could you leave when you know she needs you?"

She was the reason he'd thought of this to begin with, if he were honest with himself. "I don't know. I was talking with Uncle Jeremy. He's led quite a life when you think about it. Always full of stories about pirates and storms, shipwrecks and treasures." He forked the pippin pie into his mouth and chewed while he thought of the tales Uncle Jeremy told him and Joseph as they grew up.

"But at what expense? He's never had a family."

"We are his family. And he has God. He's happy with that."

She sat down next to him and pushed at her pie with her fork. "Would you be happy with that?"

The sunshine through the window caught the light in her hair, giving her a rosy halo. He ought not to lie. "Not completely."

"I'm not so sure Jeremy is either. God is enough for all of us and should come first. It doesn't mean we don't long for someone to share this life with though. I don't believe running from Heather Flower is the answer."

"Do you think Uncle Jeremy is running?" He watched her as she twisted a lock of hair and then pushed it from her brow.

"No, I think the sea has been in his blood since he was a very young lad. Ben, you are much like your mother, but you are a little like me too. Your calling is more in people. Family. Community. Being the light on the hill people come to when the fog rolls in. You must never think it wrong to be predictable. That means you are dependable."

"But what does that have to do with Heather Flower? She doesn't want me to be her light. She doesn't even know what she wants. Mayhap never will."

"Oh, she will. She just needs time. Just be there when she is ready to turn from her grief." She patted his hand and he wished it were that easy. "When Jay was little, he wore his heart on his sleeve. It wasn't easy for me, but at least I knew what he was feeling. You might not have known this, but I worried more about you when you boys were little. You were careful not to show your hurts and disappointments — always more concerned about everyone else."

He took a deep breath. "Then it would be all right with you if I did what I want for a change."

She shook her head. "Do you mean sailing off with Jeremy? That is not what I mean at all. I don't believe that is what you really want. My point was, you are afraid to show your hurt. To spare Heather Flower the discomfort of disappointing you, you would go off and sail the high seas with your uncle."

With both hands, he ran his fingers through the sides of his hair. "You might be right, Mother." He grinned at her and was certain there was a merriment in her eyes not there a moment ago.

"The chance to go sailing is always there. The chance to fall in love comes so seldom."

He ran his fork along the crumbs on the plate and nodded. "Agreed. I am convinced. But in the end, Heather Flower might not be convinced, and I would wager her parents would not be either. Her people are our friends, but they are a proud people. I've heard Wyancombone say his parents fear they are a vanishing tribe. I think they would be against our marriage."

"Lizzie and Papa were against my marriage to your father. It didn't stop us, and they came around. Trust your heart."

He stood up, arms folded. "She's not so happy with me right now."

"I think 'tis best you think about your work and give her the time she needs. You did an amazing thing with that schoolhouse, Ben. There's a lot of building to be done out toward the Corchaug fort. There is so much to do here. Stay, work hard, and ask for God's blessings. You know what your father says: 'In God's own time.' "

He laughed. "It's our family motto, is it not?"

"Why yes, it is. And I had the hardest time learning it. Even now I get anxious. I suppose we wouldn't be human if we didn't. But it is so comforting to take things to God in prayer and put my worries in His care."

"But you know, Mother, God doesn't always give us what we want. Look at Patience. I think she always thought she would get married and have children."

"God knows our hearts. In our imperfect way, we think we know what we want, but sometimes God has something better."

A baby's cry interrupted and they looked toward the stairs. "Abbey is with the girls, but Sarah will be hungry. It was good to have this conversation, Ben." She got up and hugged him.

"And you're right, I suppose. If I joined Uncle Jeremy, it would be running away from finding my purpose, not discovering it."

She smiled and he watched her hurry to tend to his sisters.

But if his purpose was here, he hoped

Heather Flower was a part of it. A man could hope.

14

October 19, 1653

Dawn's pink light spread across the bottoms of the bunchy gray clouds as Heather Flower picked her way through reeds and marsh to the water's edge at dawn. Shivering, she pulled her thick woven blanket tight about her shoulders. It was three months to the day that her uncle passed to the hunting grounds beyond. Almost six months since her husband had been slain by the ferocious Narragansett.

In the days after her uncle died, her aunt sat in silence, until the time came she could allow herself to weep. They'd walked to the bank of Downs Creek together, arm in arm, their women friends behind them. The wails of grief let loose the pain that gripped their hearts. Now Heather Flower sank to the ground alone, into the cold, wet grass. She pushed away a sharp blackberry vine that bit at her ankles and listened to the hungry fish jumping for their breakfast in the water below.

Her aunt remained in the wigwam, unaware of her requests to take some food or hold her arm to walk with her. Winnie had responded to Sarah's birth and participated in the feast the day of her christening. But once home she lapsed back into a dazed state.

Heather Flower sat for a while and pulled grass seed from stems, tossing them into the water and watching as they spread out and then bumped about like little boats over the gentle current. A memory of making little leaf boats with her brother came to mind, and she yearned for simpler times. She pulled the leather pouch from beneath the yoke of her dress and looked at the beadwork her mother had stitched.

A longing to return to her home in Montauk set in. She missed her mother and father. Wyancombone came across the bay often to visit. He brought gifts from their parents and always a message from their mother to come home. But she could not admit to him, or her mother, that she wanted to. To return would be to face the death of Keme. She'd rather hide from it.

Her friends who were taken on that awful day would never return home. If they could

not, why should she? It was almost shame-
ful that she was safe and they were not. Her
skin prickled with contempt at the horrors
they must face at the hands of Ninigret and
his men.

She ran her hands over her arms and
shook the thought from her mind. She must
focus on Aunt Winnie. Today she would go
into town and visit Abigail. Perhaps she
would have advice, something to help bring
her aunt out of her grief.

She looked in on Aunt Winnie before leaving and found her sitting by the fire just as
before. She pressed her cheek to her aunt's
and tiptoed out. A half-grown litter of wolf
pups, descendants of Winnie's old Smoke,
surrounded her, tails a-wag with eagerness
to follow. She admonished them to stay,
then shooed them into the wigwam. Their
ears flattened and they whined as they
looked at her with sad dark eyes. She almost
relented but knew they'd curl about
Winnie's feet and keep her company, so she
repeated her command.

The bright yellow of the weeping willows
caught her attention as she started up the
path. They, along with the red sugar maples,
marked the beginning of the next season
when Mother Earth, cloaked in finery,
prepared to bed down for the winter to

come. This year it would be a welcomed change. To hide away and sleep through the winter appealed to her as much as she figured it appealed to Winnie. Now that was a frightening thought.

She left the forest and crossed the small meadow leading to Town Street. She passed the Horton house on the left, the small cemetery on the right. The meetinghouse loomed tall and foreboding, and she hurried past.

She came up to Abigail's hut and called to her cousin. Her cousin's whisper invited her to enter. Inside it was dark and smoky but she found her near the fire, nursing her babe. Heather Flower lowered herself to the ground beside her.

"*Aquai,* Abigail." Winnie's firstborn had been named after the Christian woman who raised her. When James and Abigail's little girl was born they picked a native name for her. Misha, or Little Rain, named for the drizzly day she was born, rolled off the English tongue with ease.

"Aye, how are you?" Abigail's voice was quiet.

"I will be good someday, but perhaps not today," she said simply.

"And my mother?"

"That is why I have come. To talk to you.

I worry for your mother. She does not eat. She pines and wastes away. She doesn't let me take care of her."

"She has spent many years taking care of her children. They have grown and now her husband is gone. I think she does not know how to let others take care of her."

"You think she has abandoned this life?"

"No, she is like the willow by the river. It is the season for her branches to be bare, but her roots run deep and wide. She will survive. Her faith is strong."

"While my uncle was sick, we sat for long hours and she told me many stories of when the English first came to Yennicott. She told me the story of Mary and Patience."

"Yes, I was fourteen, so I remember it well. She loves them like sisters. Elizabeth too, though she came later." She put the squirming Misha on her lap, tummy side down, and patted her back. Soon the babe was lulled to sleep.

"Do you think I should take Winnie to visit at the Horton house again? Benjamin wanted me to. She did seem better the day Sarah was born, and for the week until she was baptized. Should I make her leave her hut and visit again?"

"There was illness in Southold, but now all is well. The new schoolteacher had the measles on the first day of school. They had to cancel it, and because the boys and even Barnabas and Benjamin were near him when he was sick, they had to stay at Joseph's house — away from Mary and the babies until they knew they were not sick."

"I did not hear from Benjamin and I worried." Perhaps he was not still mad at her.

"You should take my mother to visit. It has been too long since she has come."

"What do they do at Mary's?"

"They mostly sew, but they talk too. It is their time together. They work on breeches, or shirts, and Elizabeth will teach them new stitches too. Sometimes she makes hats."

Heather Flower's hand went to her own black hair arranged in a thick braid. A decorated band of soft leather encircled her head. "My mother brought me many headdresses when she came for the funeral. I like this one." She fingered the beautiful beads and traced the ruffled edge of the single eagle feather that hung downward to the side of her head.

"It is lovely." Abigail's own headdress was a simple wreath of porcupine quills, the points carefully tucked in and laid flat with a single jingle shell centered over her forehead. "Mary and Elizabeth's father sold his wool and felt to a milliner in London.

161

Elizabeth always liked to sew, and when she settled here, she thought she would make hats. She's very good."

"Do they have no time for Winnie?"

She stopped rubbing Misha's back and looked up, sable-brown eyes wide. "Oh, no. I didn't mean that. They know she is in sorrow. They wait for her. You should take Mother. I will be at Mary's later today and can tell her you come."

Heather Flower stood. "*Nuk.* Tell her we come soon."

Mary watched with Sarah on her shoulder and Hannah clung to her skirt as Heather Flower and Winnie walked up the flagstone path. She welcomed them into the parlor, then led them back to the large, warm kitchen. When Barney first built their house, he built a fine kitchen, much like they had left behind in Mowsley, but over the years he added an addition along the back of the house with its own entrance. It had a full wall of brick hearth with an oven built in to the side. Two long tables were set across the room, one of which was piled with loaves of warm bread, sweet ginger cakes, and tarts brimming with just-picked apples and cherries.

Barnabas was the town baker, but he was

involved with the duties of the township, so much of the baking fell to Mary. Lizzie, Patience, and Caleb all helped when Jonathan, Hannah, and Sarah were born.

Heather Flower's stomach rumbled. "Everything smells so good, Mary. Aunt Winnie, does this not make you want to eat?" Hope laced the question.

Winnie's color already looked better and there was a light — a tiny little spark — in her eyes that glimmered when they walked in. "Yes. Mary, you amaze me what you do, even with the little ones."

Mary smiled and lowered the sleeping babe into a basket padded with blankets. She lifted Hannah into a chair. "Patience and Lizzie have worked all morning with me. Abigail has been here too, to churn the butter and make a corn pudding."

Lizzie cut a large slice of savory meat pie and set it on one of the red Staffordshire plates she had brought for Mary from England. Tender bites of rabbit, English peas, and chunks of carrot and wild onions in a thick white sauce filled the pastry. She smiled at Winnie and beckoned her to sit while she dished up a plate for her friend.

Patience wiped her face and hands with her apron and stepped away from a pot of steaming clams and mussels. "So very glad to see you. Heather Flower, sit here. I'll put these in a bowl and then I think we are all ready to sit down." She looked at Mary for confirmation.

"Yes, 'tis time, I think." She swallowed hard. A lump formed in her throat as she looked at Winnie and the ladies gathered in her home. For a brief moment she thought back to the first ladies she'd ministered to coming on their voyage from England. She'd brought them lemons to freshen the air and sweeten their breath. How she wished she could have done more. But during those long-ago yesterdays, she needed to be thankful for the lemons, and today thankful for the many blessings God had bestowed on her.

She picked out a crusty loaf of bread and set it on the oak table. She reached out and the women held hands around the table. Their heads bowed, she gave thanks for good food, dear friends, and the many blessings they enjoyed.

After the meal, Mary took Heather Flower around the house and pointed out the original part of the home and what Barney had added since they first began living in it. The tour concluded with a walk in the kitchen garden and the orchard with the rows of English apple trees.

Mary pulled some apples off the cornerstone tree and filled her apron. "I'll send you and Winnie home with these. This tree was this high when Jeremy brought it over from my papa's orchard." She held her hand down to show Heather Flower, and blinked in hopes that she wouldn't notice her eyes stung with tears.

Heather Flower admired the cellar door that led beneath the house.

"Ben built that. I store most of my root vegetables down there and the fruit too." She saw something in her friend's face at the mention of his name.

"Where are the men today? Do they come home to eat dinner? Or do you pack them a meal?"

"They are eating with Zeke today. They took the boys, and Rach and Ruthie cooked for them. We had quite a fright with a case of the measles. The teacher Barnabas hired became ill the first day of class. He is well now, but we had to isolate everyone. Even Barney and Ben. But everything is all right. Now they are finishing up in the fields. Jay and Caleb are helping them. Even Joshua. And Jonathan stayed the day with Ruthie."

Heather Flower's face fell a bit.

"Did you hope to see Ben?"

"I thought I might. It has been awhile."

She helped Mary carry the fruit and they walked back to the house.

The apples rolled on the table as they set them down. Mary pointed to a basket high on a shelf and Heather Flower stretched to retrieve it for her. They filled it with fruit and some of the leftovers. "He is fond of you, perhaps too fond, if that can be. I think he hurts when he sees you, and I know he wishes to be more than friends with you. Perhaps you could, in God's own time?" A grin flickered on her face at the last part.

"He makes me smile and gives me comfort. I don't know what I can promise for tomorrow. I don't know if I can promise anything. It makes me sad my white brother stays away. But it would make me worse to know he is the sad one. Do you understand my words?" She shook her head slightly as if she didn't believe Mary could.

"Yes, I do know what you mean. But I think Ben waits in hope that someday you will feel strong and ready for promises. 'Tis how it seems to me."

Mary and Heather Flower went out to the front parlor to join the rest of the ladies, but it was clear that Winnie was tired and needed to go home. They gathered capes and food baskets and bid everyone goodbye.

Mary thought of Ben, sweet as sugar and

thinking of everyone else but himself. She ached for him. She prayed for a change in Heather Flower's heart, that she could be tender to her dear boy. Or if not Heather Flower, some sweet girl to take care of him. Someone to adore him in the manner he deserved. She reminded herself to not be impatient, that God would answer. But she could let God know this was urgent, could she not?

Heather Flower and Aunt Winnie made their way along the Indian Neck trail. The day was crisp in the sunshine and cold in the shade of the wooded section they walked through. Tall chestnut and hickory trees blocked the warmth autumn rays might have delivered. They stopped to readjust their capes when, with whoops and pounding feet, a young boy came racing from the direction of Fort Corchaug.

"Whoa, *muckachuck.* Where do you go like that?" Heather Flower threw out her arm to prevent him from colliding with her aunt.

"To find you. A man gave me a message to tell you." He panted and looked at Winnie, then back at her. "He said alone."

Winnie stepped closer to Heather Flower.

"He was one of the Dutch. He said you

would know."

"You must tell me then. No mind to my aunt. She may hear what he has to say."

The little boy's brow wrinkled like an old man's, but he continued. "He said you are to meet him by the tulip tree tomorrow as the sun goes down. He said you would know the tree."

Winnie gasped. "You can't meet him. Your father would be upset if I let you."

"It is all right. He means well. Nothing will happen to me." She touched the boy's sleeve. "Go and tell him, yes, I will be there."

Winnie shook her head. "But he is Dutch. This is disloyal to our friends. They consider us family. Heather Flower, don't do this."

The boy hesitated, looking from one woman to the other.

"This man I owe my life to. Even Captain Gardiner trusted him. I will meet with him and see what he has to say." She looked at the young messenger. "Go, boy." She flicked her hands toward him and he ran back along the trail.

"Aunt, this man does not care for the English, just as they do not care for him. But he does not come to spy. He comes to see me. He has been a friend to me. I will see him, but you should not tell anyone. It would only cause trouble for him."

That night she climbed onto her pallet as Winnie brushed sooty ash back into the fire. Her aunt had enjoyed the afternoon and tonight she tended to small chores she'd forgotten of late. The outing had been good.

Her eyelids were heavy and through half-closed eyes she watched the embers glow from blackened wood. Her aunt agreed in the end that she could meet the Dutchman with the sincere, bay-blue eyes. But trouble played on her heart and mind. His presence would rile not only their friends but her people as well. And put him in danger. So why did she agree to meet with him?

15

October 21, 1653

The tulip tree towered, clad in yellow, its leaves luminous in the slanting sun. Hidden within the edge of the forest of hickory and oak, Dirk kept watch for her. He'd waited most of the afternoon, with the hope Heather Flower might find her way there early. Now he listened as the katydids began their nightly rendition and the evening grew dusky. He strained to listen for footfalls as he pulled the food he'd packed for them from his knapsack.

Maybe she wouldn't chance a meeting. Or she simply decided she did not want to see him again. He could be sad if thoughts of Benjamin Horton didn't clench his stomach at the moment. He tried to imagine if Horton won her heart, how would he feel? How would he cope? Not good thoughts.

He bit into the crisp little *koekje* without tasting, stared at the man-hand-sized leaves of the tulip tree as they drifted to the ground, one by one. She came so silently — one moment he was alone, the next she was there beside him, her large, dark eyes even more fiery than he remembered them, the hint of a tiny smile played on her pouty lips.

He stood. "I thought you wouldn't come."

"*Aquai,* Dirk."

"*Ja,* hallo. How goes it with you? Your aunt, she is well?"

"Yes, she does not forget her husband, but she is learning to be with the living."

"And you? You are ready to be with the living?" He stepped closer. She stood tall and proud, but sadness draped her like a veil. How he'd like to take her in his arms, to soothe her hurt.

"My tears are kept in a tiny place now. I only bid them when I want them."

He took her hand and placed a *koekje* in it. "I suspect that is often. Here, I brought you this. It's like the ginger cakes you eat, but with almonds." Should he ask about her family? The Hortons?

"*Nuk.* Thank you." She walked to the tulip tree and lowered herself against the dark gray furrowed trunk. Its roughness caught at her buckskin dress, and Dirk retrieved a blanket from his pack and tucked it behind her. He sat next to her.

"So tell me about you, Heather Flower. You grew up a princess, *ja*?"

She chewed the sweet morsel and swallowed before she answered. "Princess is the white man's word. But yes, my father is a leader of men, our sachem. Our king, in the white man's way. So yes, I am a princess, daughter of the king." The little smile played on her lips.

"Was your life happy? I mean —"

She gave him no chance to say what he meant. "I treasure my memories of growing up. I was allowed to run and play with my brother and our friend Keme. We chased through the forests without care, we played in the waves of the ocean on the beach. I helped our mother gather berries and shells and learned to dry the venison my father and brother brought home from the great hunts." She took the bone needles from her pouch. "Mother taught me to sew. We made beautiful clothing with beads and quills and the feathers of eagles."

He stretched his fingers toward the pointed needles and she playfully poked at him. "Do you miss your mother, then?"

The meadow grew dark and a pond far across the meadow was suddenly astir with a large flock of geese taking flight. They watched them form a V as they continued on a southerly migration. Heather Flower shivered and Dirk helped her wrap the blanket about her shoulders.

"I do. But I am happy to be with my aunt. I think she has needed me there and I have needed to be there. She grows strong and has good friends in Mary and Patience and Lizzie. I know she will find herself once more and not need me. But I want to stay. I like it among Winnie's people."

He nodded. "And Horton? Benjamin? Do you want to stay for him?" Urgency crept into his voice so he looked away and hoped she didn't notice.

"My brother used to bring me across the bay in a canoe to Yennicott. I played with Abigail, and my aunt would make us dolls. My uncle made Wyancombone and Joseph and Benjamin little wooden canoes. Sometimes Benjamin would teach me and Abigail to ride his horse. He was good to us."

"Is. He still is good to you, *ja*?"

"*Nuk.* The last time I came to Southold I was ten years old. Abigail married James. After that, Benjamin would come to Montauk to visit me and my brother. He has always been very good to me. But he would not be happy to know I am here with you."

The hair prickled on the back of his neck

and he ran his hand over it. "Why would he care?"

A flash of light danced in her eyes. "It's not what you are thinking, my friend Dirk. It is the trouble between the English and Dutch. You don't seem to fear that you are on English soil." Her pretty eyes got rounder. "And Benjamin said your people took a ship by force in an English port. Is that true? He said the treaty between you is not good."

"The news we hear is not good. The loss at Scheveningen was severe for both sides. There's talk of a new treaty. No one really wants that. We want to finish what we started. At least in New Netherlands. The ship we took was our own. It should not have been trading in an English port."

"That is why I say you are unsafe."

"I think Horton must be filling your mind with all manner of ill will toward me."

"No, that is not true. Benjamin is a good man."

He ignored her last comment. "The fact is we are much more tolerant of the English than they are of us. We were here on Long Island first. We claimed this land. The English kept camping out here on the east end, and we finally gave it to them."

Heather Flower peered into the darkness

of the forest. "The land belongs to no one. She is everyone's. But the white man wars with his white brothers as the red man wars with his. If it is not over land, it is over wampum. Winnie tells me the only thing we should war about is God."

"How so?"

"She means we should be willing to fight for our belief in God."

"Does she believe in God or the Great Spirit?"

"She says they are the same with one difference."

"What is that?"

"God sent Jesus."

"*Ja.* That is so." He grew up with the Bible stories, but he preferred not to dwell on them. He didn't need anyone but himself. God was all right for his parents and anyone else who chose to believe. In fact, it wasn't that he didn't believe — he just didn't need the encumbrance. "Do you believe in Winnie's God and Jesus?"

"I don't know. My aunt's faith is strong, but she has been so very lost without my uncle. I see her getting better. But why does God let her suffer?"

Dirk stared at her a long time, recollecting what he'd learned as a youth. "It is not that God lets her suffer. He waits for her with open arms. It is our decision where we put our faith and trust."

A smile played on her lips. "I am surprised you speak in that way, my friend."

"*Ja*. I know. It's just that much I know to be true."

"Then —" She turned even before Miss Button raised her head, ears forward and nickered.

Dirk reached out and placed a warning hand on Heather Flower's arm. "Hush."

They hovered toward each other, heads cocked toward the noise. A herd of deer moved through the clearing in the evening dusk, carefully placing each step, heads dodging in different directions as they made their way to the other side and into the woods again.

Her nearness was palpable and a ragged sigh escaped him as he offered his hand to help her up. Icy rain began to patter their faces and he looked to the west at the mushrooming thunderclouds. He bent over to pick up the blanket, spreading it about her shoulders. "I should take you home." He walked to Miss Button and retrieved her reins.

"You cannot come with me. It is too dangerous. If anyone sees me with you, it will be difficult for me and deadly for you."

"I won't go all the way, but I can't let you walk. I will take you as far as the Broadfield, and then I can easily retreat." He didn't wait for her answer. He led his horse to her and put his hand out for her to step into. He swung her up and climbed behind her. His heart thumped. Could she hear it? How could he ride with her so near and not tell her he loved her and he wanted to take her away? Wanted her to say yes and be his bride?

They rode in silence as the rain began in earnest, pelting his back as he tried to shelter her. "I should not come to see you again."

"*Chawgwan?* What?"

"This is wrong. It causes you worry and puts you in danger."

She twisted, tilting her face so very close to his. "I worry because it puts you in danger, my friend."

He lowered his lips till they met hers, and for a long moment the only thing that mattered was she was here now, in his arms. The rain, the danger, time and space, all fled his consciousness. And he knew as she first returned his kiss and then drew away, he did not want to leave her. But he must.

They neared the clearing and he reined Miss Button to a halt. He swung off and reached for Heather Flower. As she landed on her feet in front of him, he held her close and kissed the top of her head.

"Dirk." Her voice was raspy. "I want you to be my friend."

"I am your friend, Heather Flower. To let you go right now is the hardest thing I've ever done." He held her from him and watched for a long moment, considering everything he might tell her. "I could not bear it, though, if you give your affections to a Horton." She stiffened. "That was foolish of me. I have no right to tell you how to handle your affairs. Forgive me."

She stood quietly, not moving.

"Go now. There's lightning in the distance and it's moving this way."

She looked up. "But you will be riding into it."

"*Ja,* but I know how to take care of myself. Now go." He gave her a nudge, but wanted to grab her close. Why was he leaving when all he wanted to do was stay?

She didn't look up. She just started walking. He watched until he couldn't see her anymore, as she faded into the dimness. Maybe if he just stood there, her image would be frozen in time. If he didn't move, would he never forget her face, never forget

how warm her breath had felt on his cheek,
how sweet her lips?

16

November 10, 1653

The scent of fallen leaves spiced the autumn air. Mary put little Sarah in a sling and carried her against her chest as she went bayberry picking. Abbey had the day off and Mary didn't want to wait another day to pick the silver-gray berries. They were plump and ripe — ready to be picked — and she anticipated the scent that would fill their house at Christmastime. She brought a basket with her, and while she sang a childhood song about little lambs and goats to Sarah, she made several trips back and forth to the house until her babe was asleep and her fingers stained and her back ached.

She laid Sarah into her cradle and carried a bucket out to the well. Caleb had hauled water the night before, but with ten baskets of berries, she'd need more. After three trips, she'd filled one of her large cauldrons. She added logs to the fire and gave a nudge with her boot to one that tumbled. She poked it with her fire iron to make it stay. Orange flames licked upward, and while she waited for the water to come to a boil, she spread her berries out across the worn oak table and began to pull the stems off.

This was her favorite time of year. Most of the harvest was done, save some of the pumpkins still on the vines, and the hogs had been slaughtered and preserved for the winter. The labors still to be accomplished before winter's icy grip included soap and candle making. The candles she enjoyed as much as her baking.

The next month all three would keep her busy, but by mid-December the bakeshop would be filled with Barney's crisp little ginger cakes, her fruited cakes, bayberry candles, and bars of soap infused with lavender. She decorated each year with pine boughs and cones and the ladies of the town loved coming to the shop and purchasing her goodies.

It was about as close to celebrating Christmastide as she could come, and it brought back fond memories of the Anglican Christmases she'd enjoyed as a little girl with Lizzie, Mother, and Papa. Even after her mother died and Lizzie got married, her papa had tried hard to keep the traditions a part of their Christmas. Although the colonists to the north of Long Island were firm in not observing holidays, the residents of Southold held less of an ardent view, and certainly Barney had always been more on the indulgent side.

A bell tinkled as Jay and Jane came in.

"I thought I saw you out earlier with your basket and Sarah. Mmm, it smells good in here already." Jay bent to give her a kiss on her cheek.

"Does it? I hadn't noticed, but I'm glad. You're in time to help me get these to the pot. While they boil, we can set up the candle molds. Sarah will only sleep so long. I have two skimmers so we can skim the wax quickly."

Jay looked at Jane. "Methinks we are being put to work before we are even bid good morrow."

Her daughter-in-law grinned. "I'd love to help you, Mother Horton. I love your candles."

"And you'll have one to take with you for your work." She patted Jane's shoulder as she handed her a mold. She nudged Jay. "And as for you, good morrow to you," she teased.

He gave her a hug. "Let's get this done

before that demanding little Sarah wakes up."

"I did not say that. Your sister is not a demanding baby. You were a demanding child, so I know what demanding is." She hugged him back. How she loved him. He'd been difficult, but she treasured their relationship all the more.

Jane smiled at them. "It will serve him right when he has his own to listen to."

Mary straightened the last of the molds and handed Jane a skimmer. "Is that soon?" She wished she hadn't asked. Was it not the question she dreaded as a young wife? But Jane seemed to take it in stride.

"Most likely not soon, but one day, Mother Horton. I want to be the first to give you a grandchild." She beamed.

"My goodness, I'm too young to be a grandmother, don't you agree? I'm still having babies myself."

Jay scooped bayberries into the boiling water. "You are and we have plenty of time to be the first to make you a grandmother. Benjamin provides no threat, and the other siblings have a long way to go."

Mary smiled but held back her thoughts about Ben. He might surprise his big brother and be closer to matrimony than

Jay knew. Or perhaps she was just too hopeful.

Jay put the wicks spun from milkweed into each mold while she and Jane skimmed the top of the water and dripped the waxy substance into them. He adjusted the wicks each time they added more. By the time Sarah awoke, the candles were setting outside in the cold and Barney was home.

"You'll stay for supper?"

Jane was quick to accept. "We would love to."

"Of course, tomorrow I'll be making tallow candles and you're welcome back for that."

They slaughtered only two sheep a year, and every bit was used. The sheep fat was cut into cubes with hog fat and then rendered. It was a stinky job. No one looked forward to it.

"Is Ben helping?"

Barney took Sarah from Mary. She stirred the pot of stew that simmered in the corner of the hearth. "Yes, he is. And Abbey will be here to watch Sarah and Hannah, so I expect all the boys to help." She sipped some of the gravy from a wooden spoon, and added some crushed, dried tarragon, stirring again.

Jane took a loaf of bread from the

sideboard and began to slice it for their supper. Jay brought out a crock of butter and a loaf of Mary's prized cheese before he went to call in Caleb, Joshua, and Jon. "Where is Benjamin, by the way?" he asked as his brothers filed in and took a seat.

"He's been working over at the tanner's for a couple of days, building a shed for him. We shouldn't wait on him. He could be late."

They all joined hands and Barney led them in a blessing for their food. As Mary ladled the meal into bowls, he passed them to the table. After everyone was served, they sat and enjoyed their meal.

Jay and Jane were gone when Ben walked in. Barney sat by the fire reading and Mary had settled across from him in her rocker after she'd put the children to bed.

Ben looked tired.

She put her needlework in her lap. "I'm glad you're home."

"I met up with Johnny on my way home."

Barney looked up. "What is he up to these days?"

"The usual. He's heading up to Connecticut and wants me to come with him."

Mary pushed a stray curl from her forehead. "Oh, Ben, no. Don't go."

He chuckled. "Of course I won't go, but I

185

did talk to him about what he's doing. Sometimes I think there is a thread of sense there. If we are ever going to get the Dutch off the west end of the island, we're going to need the support of a few Connecticut towns." He sniffed. "Not to change the subject, but it sure smells like Christmas here."

Mary smiled. "You missed making bayberry candles today, but I pray you are available on the morrow to help with the tallow candles."

"Ugh. Now I think I'll go with Johnny." He stood up.

She studied him with a frown.

He gave her the Horton chortle and sounded like his father. "I suppose I'll just make stinky candles. Now, I think I will call it a day. Good night." He nodded to his father and gave Mary a kiss on the cheek before he headed for his room. She watched him go.

"You cannot protect him forever, you know." Barnabas's tender tone eased his admonition. "We all go through the fire to some degree. It makes us better people."

He was right, of course. But Ben was so sweet and vulnerable. She didn't want him to be hurt again. She put him at the top of

her prayer list that night. And Heather
Flower too.

17

December 24, 1653

Barnabas hitched Star to the wagon and all of the Horton children piled in, save Sarah. Mary and the newest little Horton stayed in the house, filled with the warm scent of ginger cakes and fruited breads.

It was a snowy day and everyone had their topcoats, neck cloths, and muffs, for the mission to cut the perfect tree could not be deterred by the weather. Each Christmas Eve — except for their first Christmastide in Southold which was devoid of celebration — and with more and more children, they journeyed out to the point on the North Sea. They found the perfect tree to cut and gathered as many boughs as the wagon would hold. The tradition was for Barnabas to drive the wagon back, and Benjamin and Joseph to walk back to the house with the younger ones. This year Jane walked with them and held Hannah's hand.

The forest was draped with thick snow, and Caleb, Joshua, and Jonathan pelted snowballs back and forth as they followed the wagon. Occasionally they lobbed one at Benjamin's back and he chased after them. At the house Jane took the children in while Barnabas had Benjamin and Joseph help him unhitch Star and haul the tree into the front parlor.

Mary had hot milk and platters of ginger cakes waiting. As the children ate, the men took the boughs and draped them across the mantels and down the center of every table in the house while Mary and Jane lit bayberry candles. Little Sarah's button eyes moved about the room taking in the sights and lights, and she delighted everyone with giggles and coos.

Mary dug through her trunks and pulled out every red ribbon and scrap of red fabric she could find to decorate the boughs. Tomorrow Barnabas would tramp out to the woods again and find her some holly berries.

Barnabas watched his family and a gladness welled from deep within. He led them in his deep baritone, singing "God rest ye merry gentlemen, let nothing you dismay." He finished the evening with a reading from Luke.

On the morrow they would begin gift giving. They would exchange little gifts each day for the twelve days of Christmas, ending on Twelfth Night with their final and best gift. He loved watching Mary help their small children make surprises for their siblings. Most often the gifts were made from sticks or jingle shells or pretty agates.

She made marchpane candy to surprise the youngest children, in special molds Joseph carved for her, and she bought oranges from the ships to stud with cloves for the older ones.

Barnabas's gift to her this year was a cast-iron Dutch oven with legs so that it could stand inside the hearth. He planned to give that to her on Twelfth Night.

Joseph took Jane home and Benjamin put Hannah and Jonathan to bed while Mary tucked Sarah in her cradle. She had drifted off hours before and slept like an angel in her mother's arms. Barnabas came up the stairs and met Mary at their door. He took her in his arms. "Ah, my sweet. Have I told you lately how much I love you?"

She tilted her pretty face up to him, her green eyes wide. "Why no, Mr. Horton. But have I told you lately how much I adore you?"

His laugh escaped before he could think

of the sleeping children, and she put her finger to his lips.

January's snow continued and by mid-month a harsh winter storm hit. Benjamin counted two sheep dead and spent most of the day searching for a lost calf. He found it, limp and half frozen, and brought it to the barn. Mary gave him an old quilt and he bundled the little fellow and fed it warm milk through an old glove with a hole punched into a finger.

Mary worried about Patience, and his father sent him out to check on her. He made it there and found her warm and safe. Mary had sent him with loaves of bread and sugar, and after he freed her cellar door from a tall bank of snow and brought up a ham, he headed for home.

He was trudging up the flagstone, almost to the door with the wind blowing sleet full into his face when he heard a cry. Or was it a wolf howl? He stopped, frozen snow pelting his mouth and eyes. The sound carried to him once again on the edge of the wind. It was a woman's cry and not from his house.

With great effort, he turned back around and walked to the road to try to gain perspective on the direction. He heard it again and knew immediately it came from the Tuckers' house. Anna. There was something wrong with Anna.

He tried to run but the force of the wind and sleet made it impossible. He could barely see their house. Finally he found his way to their door and pushed it open. Anna was on the floor, bent over Charles who lay there motionless. She looked up with terror in her huge eyes. "I think he's dying, Benjamin. We need the doctor. Can you go get him?"

He rushed out the door and fought through the storm. He plunged his way toward Dickerson Creek. The doctor had to be there or they wouldn't make it back in time. Thankfully Doc Smith threw open his door as he pounded. He grabbed his bag and followed him back to the Tuckers' through the violent snowstorm.

When they came inside, they found Charles sitting halfway up in his wife's lap. After a thorough examination, Doctor Smith told him his heart was weak and he'd need to take care, limiting his activities. He prescribed a cordial and helped Anna get him into bed. She cried when they left, but the doctor squeezed her hands and reassured her Charles would be fine if he would but take care of himself.

Benjamin feared that was not the whole story, and he worried for Charles in a way he never would have imagined. Anna needed Charles and he prayed for God to watch over the Tuckers that night. He wondered about Heather Flower and Winnie and prayed for their safety in this storm, but they'd been through weather like this before, and as long as they stayed safe in their wigwam they would be fine. But Anna and Charles's troubles were a different kind of storm — one that would not melt or go away.

Barnabas shoveled through five-foot drifts as he cleared a path to the meeting house. As soon as the storm abated, Reverend Youngs had called the meeting. Barnabas and William Wells sat up front with the reverend. Joseph and Benjamin sat in the Horton pew as the rest of the men filed in to their own designated seats.

The first order of business was to account for the livestock dead or missing from the storm and the fences to be fixed. Fines would be assessed if repairs were not made, so Barnabas wanted to be sure that the owners were made aware of those that needed tending.

The toll was high from the storm, but

mayhap the damage was not as great as that to the heart of Charles Tucker. He would live, but Doctor Smith advised he would not be able to work. There were some in the town who, with that diagnosis, were put in the poorhouse, but John Budd offered assurance his daughter and son-in-law would be taken care of.

Barnabas moved the discussion to the annual spring burning of the woods next to the North Sea, to control the rattlesnakes that infested the area. Every year it seemed to be a problem to keep the fires under control and the loss of trees to that purpose could not continue. A fire brigade to stand guard was appointed.

William Wells brought up his litigation against the Town Fathers for property out at Indian Neck he claimed belonged to him as restitution for oxen that disappeared, which he claimed the Indians took.

John Budd Jr. stood up and asked for permission to speak. Barnabas granted his request and the younger Budd spoke from his heart regarding the treatment of Quakers in their town. He reminded his elders that most of them had fled religious persecution and that to prohibit those who professed to be Quakers the right to buy land or participate in their government seemed to be repeating past sins.

Barnabas nodded. "Young man, I understand your question. But in fact this is how I view the situation. We left because we wanted to worship in the manner we knew to be right in our hearts and minds, without interference or persecution. We sacrificed much to come here and we toiled long and hard to build our church and our town. If there be anyone who would like to profess to worship as we do, we welcome them. But those that come to preach other ways, or to condemn what we preach, we do not want here. The forest to our west is vast. Let them go find their own paradise to build and teach the way they see fit."

He hit the gavel to the table and gave the nod to move on, but John Budd Sr. cleared his throat. "Now Barnabas, we've been friends a long time. I cannot sit here and listen to you say what you did when I know your heart. We've had many discussions on this." His thick-lidded eyes were kind as he looked at Barnabas. "I've heard you say we are all God's children. He loves us all."

"No one believes that more than I do nor has more compassion for those who suffer because of their beliefs. But we are under the rule and jurisdiction of New Haven. A man must be a member of the church before he may be a citizen of our township. The penalty for living here and preaching a different doctrine is severe. That is why I say, the forest is vast if you cannot live here and abide by the laws of our township and doctrines of our church. Go and seek another place to build your town and worship as you desire. I do not wish to see anyone harmed or mistreated. The Friends are continually in my prayers." Barnabas picked up the papers in front of him and tapped them on the table. The issue would not be resolved tonight. Mayhap not even with his generation.

A discussion ensued about clearing the road down to Dickerson's so the trappers could bring their pelts to the tanner without getting mired down in the mud as they maneuvered around the stumps and rocks. A work party was assigned for a day in April.

The matter of trade took up the remainder of the meeting. Salt pork and apples had been their most successful exports to the West Indies and they received molasses and sugar in return. With the growing cattle herds, leather was produced to the point that they could begin selling it to old England, and furs were shipped there as well. Flax remained their most important crop as the ladies produced linen that clothed the entire village. Crops of wheat and barley were in abundance and shipped across the North Sea to New England for a pretty price.

Barnabas looked about the meeting hall. The Lord had taught him much the year they founded Southold. All those years he thought he knew what God expected of him, and if he worked hard enough, the Lord would bless him. He'd tried to prove himself worthy and it was the most exhausting thing he'd ever done.

But he learned that it was by God's grace he was blessed, and nothing he did on his own. There were times he wondered if he would have learned that lesson if Ann had not died, that mayhap that journey was necessary. But no matter. He was in the place God intended, spiritually as well as in the world, this he knew. And God had given him Mary to share it with and to share his heart. God was faithful.

18

February 14, 1654

A frigid dawn spread gray light beneath heavy clouds. But it was the fussy murmurs of Sarah as she tried to suck on her thumb and kicked at her blankets that woke Mary. She leaned over and scooped the babe into her arms. Dropping the shoulder of her sleeping chemise, she brought Sarah to her breast. Such a good baby. She rarely cried outright and never in an angry sort of way like Hannah and Jon had done.

Today was the anniversary of the day she and Barney were married. He was gone from the bed already, probably for two or three hours now, like every anniversary. He would have embers refreshed in the great kitchen hearth with dry logs and his morning devotions completed before baking a beautiful cake for her. And she loved him much for that.

Twenty-four years ago on this day he'd

told her she would have wedding cake every year, and he'd kept his promise. Some years it was not much of a cake — and the first ten years had been childless, tense years — but once they arrived in Yennicott they'd been blessed tenfold. Barney built the house he'd promised, and they'd filled it with babes. And each year he baked a bigger and prettier cake. She smiled at the thought of red sugar roses and candied posies.

She ran her fingers over Sarah's soft auburn hair and watched her slumber. Feeling dreamy, she closed her eyes with a prayer of thanksgiving. Hannah burst through the doorway and scrambled up next to her, and she wrapped her free arm around her little girl.

"What say you we put Sarah back in her cradle and go see what Father is doing, Hanny?"

"He's baking us a cake. He gave me some cheese and told me to come see you."

"Oh, did he now? Well, I think we should go down and I will put a bit of porridge on for you and your brothers. Does that sound like a good idea?" She laid Sarah down, then took Hannah's hand. "Come on, sweetheart."

Hannah's little feet padded down the stairs next to hers, and they entered the large, warm kitchen.

Barney looked up from his creation. "Good morning, my bride."

"Good morning to you, husband." She stretched on her tiptoes and kissed his cheek. "The cake is beautiful, Barney!"

He gave her a pleased nod. "Just so you know, we are having a feast today, but you will not lift a finger. Elizabeth and Patience have planned the whole meal, and Winnie and Heather Flower will be coming with their own contributions."

"And Jay and Jane? Ben?"

"Of course. They would not miss it, to be sure."

She smiled with satisfaction. "I love having everybody here, in this house. 'Tis more than I could have ever hoped for." She eyed the stacks of bread loaves, ready for their patrons. "But as far as not lifting a finger today, I think I shall have to. And I shall start with a proper breakfast for Hannah and her brothers."

"Aye. But I will manage the cake and help Elizabeth and Patience when they arrive. Not you. Understood?" He smiled as he dabbed some flour on her nose.

Her giggle was like a young girl's. "Oh, yes! I understand, Mr. Horton." She dipped her fingers in the pot of flour and flung a bit at his apron.

Hannah's mouth was agape, but joined in her parents' laughter.

"It's all right, my little one, it is how we play. And I can be thankful she isn't throwing the whole crock at me."

Caleb, Joshua, and Jon came down the stairs together, and after they ate, Lizzie and Zeke arrived with Patience not far behind. Everyone set to work. Mary sat with Sarah and watched Hannah play with the dolly Aunt Lizzie had made for her. A day of leisure was unheard of in Southold, and she cherished it. How many times had she and the other women prayed for a moment's rest?

As more guests arrived, large lacy snowflakes began to drift down. Barney stood at the casement window staring. Mary slipped into his arms and he whispered, "Angels are rejoicing with us, my sweet."

A smile wreathed her face and she clung to him for a moment. "Yes, Barney. Angel happy tears."

He hugged her close.

A pounding brought both to the door, and James, Abbey, Misha, and Winnie entered.

Mary peered down the road. "Where is Heather Flower?"

"She will be here," Winnie said. "James

brought the wagon out to get us, but Heather Flower said she would walk."

Mary helped her with her cape as James helped unbundle Misha.

"Come into the kitchen. 'Tis warm in there, and it smells so good."

Before they could leave the front hall, Jay, Jane, and Ben arrived. Ben brushed the snow from his shoulders, and Jay helped Jane with her cloak. He handed it to Abbey, who collected the wraps.

Jay bent to kiss Mary on the cheek. "You are looking fine, Mother."

She wrapped her arms around him in a hug. "Thank you." She turned to Jane and gave her a warm hug.

Ben gave her a bear hug. He'd spent a couple of days with Jay and Jane, working on their pole barn. "You do look wonderful, Mother. Is everybody here? Are we the last to arrive?" He glanced back toward the kitchen.

Mary knew his real question. "You are the last except for Heather Flower." The sorry in her eyes could not be helped.

He ignored her look. "But she is coming?"

"I think so. At least Winnie said she would." She watched his face cloud and her throat constricted. "Let the others get the meal ready. Come sit with me by Sarah."

He settled near Sarah and bent over, watching her sleep. "She's a quiet one, isn't she?"

"That she is, but who knows for how long. Let us talk."

"You have something on your mind." His blue eyes bore sadness, but his smile invited her to continue.

"I know you have always loved Heather Flower, Ben. I am worried for you."

"Worried? Why worry?"

"I will give you the same advice Lizzie gave me years ago when I met your father. I hope you listen. I didn't." She smiled at him and shook her head. "Give her time and warmth."

"I have, Mother. How much time am I supposed to give her when there is someone like Lieutenant Van Buren lurking in the woods?"

"Lurking in the woods? He rode right up here and had words with you last harvest."

He rolled his eyes like Jay was prone to do. "True, but I've heard rumors that he seeks Heather Flower out."

"Times are difficult, you know that. I worry for your safety as much as I worry for your heart. We have the Narragansett to the north and the Dutch to our west. And Heather Flower and her people right in the middle. And now the lieutenant."

He stood and walked to the casement window. "Mother, you need not be concerned. She doesn't return my affection beyond offering her friendship. I wish it were not so."

"But you hope, do you not, that her heart will change?"

"Yes, I do."

She pushed herself to her feet and took his hands in hers. "I do so believe that with love we should follow our heart. But Ben, this is one time that all I see is danger. I cannot bear to think of something happening to you."

His strong hands held hers tight. "It is the Dutch to fear, not the natives."

Tears glistened on her lashes. "I know that Lieutenant Van Buren has a flame that burns for Heather Flower too. I heard him when he was here at harvest. Perhaps if you both gave her the time she needs —"

"If there be a problem, Mother, he is it. But do not worry on my account. I promise you, I shall guard my heart. But I will guard Heather Flower's too."

Sarah began to whimper, and Mary lifted the babe to her shoulder. "There, my little girl. I thought you slept too long. Shall we go up and see to some dry wrappings?" She stepped close to Ben. "I know you will do the right thing. But if you need someone to talk to, I'm here. Always. I love you."

"I know, Mother." He kissed her forehead and then his sister's downy head.

She climbed the stairs with a heavy heart. She hadn't accomplished anything. He would fall headlong into the thick of it like she did when she was young. But there was a difference. He'd been raised to depend on the Lord and not himself. She just wished he could give Heather Flower more time to know her heart. And not feel so responsible for guarding it.

Benjamin stared down the road through the diamond-paned glass, pushed it open despite the cold, and leaned out. Heather Flower should be arriving soon. Unless she stayed behind for a reason. Mayhap she had plans to see Van Buren.

He pulled the window shut, shivered, and poked at the fire with a rod. He sat down. He'd rather not join the family just yet in the kitchen, his mind too much in turmoil. He picked up the well-worn Bible.

He paged through to the blue frayed ribbon, curious to see what his father had read that morning. His eyes fell on 2 Timothy chapter 1, verse 7: "For God hath not given to us the Spirit of fear, but of power, and of love, and of a sound mind." He grinned. A sound mind in all of this is what he needed. Love would not be a bad thing either.

A small knock on the door brought him to his feet. He strode the distance to the door in an instant and pulled it open. "Heather Flower, come in, get warm." With a woven blanket of many colors wrapped around her, she still looked half frozen. But beautiful with her creamy copper cheeks tinged with pink and her opal eyes bright. He pulled her near the fire.

"*Aquai,* Benjamin. How are you, my friend?" A smile played on her lips.

"I'm better now that you are here. I was worried about you. Why didn't you come in the wagon with Winnie and Abigail?"

"I like walking the paths, spending time with myself."

"You were alone?"

"Yes."

He stepped back and ran his hand through his hair. She looked at him as if she knew what he was thinking.

"Do you believe me?"

"Yes, I do. But are you in love with Van Buren, Heather Flower? Have you been seeing him?"

"You should not ask me such things. You

promised."

His throat tightened and he reached for her hand. "Yes, I did. I know you will not forget Keme, but I worry your heart will turn —"

He regretted what he'd almost said the moment the words began to leave his mouth.

Her eyes closed and her jaw clenched. "I am not done."

"Done?"

"Done mourning. I hurt. I do not want to say goodbye to Keme."

"Forgive my impatience. May I say, though, I do not want to lose you." He studied her face for her reaction. His mother was right. She needed time. Why could he not give it to her?

She sighed. "You will never lose me, my friend."

Joseph stepped out from the kitchen. He smiled at Heather Flower and it broadened as he took Benjamin in. "Father wants everyone back here. Dinner is ready and Mother will be coming down soon. He wants us all present for that."

"Right." Benjamin offered her his arm. It comforted him that she took it warmly, pulling him close as they followed Joseph to the kitchen.

They assembled themselves around the table just in time to watch Mary enter for the feast. She had changed into her best gown, a green brocade Lizzie had sewn for her. She looked lovely, with a falling band fastened with a brooch about her neck and her gray-streaked auburn hair, pulled up into two buns, one on each side of her head.

Muffkin padded after Barnabas as he joined Mary at the front of the kitchen and wrapped her in his arms. "On this day I thee wed."

"Yes you did, Barney. And I love you just as much today as on that day." Her green eyes sparkled with contentment.

Lizzie shook her head, her eyes shimmered. "When I think of those days back in Mowsley, I cannot believe all we have been through." Muffkin rubbed her side against Lizzie's skirt. She picked up the little round ball of fluff. "Oh, here, Muffy, do you want attention too?"

Barnabas chortled and patted the cat's head. "Aye, Elizabeth. It's been much. But my Mary is a feisty sort and puts up with much." He winked at his wife. "Thank the Lord for that." He slid his hand from her shoulder to her hand and grasped tightly. "And let us give thanks to the Lord for food, family, and friends."

They all linked hands and Barnabas led them in a prayer.

Benjamin held tightly to Heather Flower's hand. She had not answered him about Van Buren. He said his own prayer that she might come to know how much he loved her. His "amen" sounded louder than everyone else's and he released her hand quickly. Did he put too much pressure on her? Because if he drove her away, he could not forgive himself.

The discussion turned to the end of the farm year. The big cast-iron soup pot needed to be taken down and scrubbed. A perpetual stew or pottage simmered continuously for the large family, but once a year it came down for a thorough cleaning.

Mary reminded Barnabas that the mattresses needed to be hauled out for re-stuffing before he began preparations for sugaring the maple trees.

Benjamin listened as his mother discussed closing out the accounts for the previous year and doing the inventory like she did every year. His parents made the whole business of living appear easy, but in truth there was hardly a moment when they did not work toward the comforts of their home.

And he was no stranger to the work

himself. He and Joseph had worked beside their father since they came to Southold as young lads. Soon there would be a flush of color in the trees and bushes as buds began to open. The seasons would begin afresh, and he hoped Heather Flower would be by his side. But while the farm year was new, the old problems with the Dutch still lingered.

19

March 7, 1654

Heather Flower sat next to the fire and watched Winnie carve a sumac branch into a spout for collecting *sinzibuckwud,* the maple syrup that flowed from the trees.

Her people had collected the sap since the beginning of time. She knew the art well. It could be done simply by cutting a V into the trunk with a tomahawk and then fitting a sturdy reed into the gash to let the sap run into a birch bucket. But Winnie liked to carve what the English called a *spile* and took pride in fashioning her tools. Most of the winter afternoons had been spent getting ready for the maple drawing season while Heather Flower turned shells into beads and wampum.

Her aunt shaved one end to a point, and on the other end she split the stick in half, removing the top part. She lit a dry twig and carefully burnt the inner core, as the men did in building a canoe, and scraped the ash with a stone. Hollowing out the tapered end was a bit trickier, but she worked diligently until she had bored a hole completely through.

Heather Flower listened as her aunt hummed a song her own mother had taught her and she thought about her youth and how simple it had been. No going back to it though. Time was not like the seasons. Seasons move in a circle. Time only moves forward, as does life.

When would the pain of losing Keme ease? With Benjamin and Dirk both anxious to be by her side, why could she not let them be a comfort to her?

Benjamin was safe and caring and had been there since she was little. He had always treated her with respect and honor. She knew he loved her. He was comfortable, like wrapping a thick blanket about your shoulders and sitting near the fire on a cold March day.

Dirk was in love with her too, but could he really have fallen so quickly for her? He told her he'd never loved before. Did he know what it felt like? Still, he put her safety above his own and he listened to her as she told of her deepest fears, of her deepest longings. Her fears were the nightmares of the past, her longing a dream to live safe and happy, and to share her life with someone, but not lose control of it. She'd never felt more secure or cared for than when she rode with him on Miss Button.

Both men were blessed with rugged good looks. Both were strong and protective of her. But there was no hope for either of them. Not while her heart was bound to Keme.

"Look what you have done." Her aunt's face was graced with a rare smile.

Heather Flower looked down at a shell she held and found it split in two. She looked up at Winnie and their laugh blended like ripples in a lake. "How forgetful of me."

"You know, my niece, I think it is time you go back to your mother. To your father. They miss you and it is where you belong."

Her aunt's face had begun to regain fullness of cheek and a happy crinkle surrounded her eyes. Her voice was stronger than even a few days before. "I can see you getting better every day, Aunt Winnie. I know you are strong and will be fine if I leave. But I do not believe I will be fine. Not there. Not at home."

"You cannot run from your sadness, my young one. You cannot stay away forever. You must accept what has happened. You must move forward."

Heather Flower's eyes widened and she rested her fingers on Winnie's arm. "Those were just my thoughts. But I don't know how to move forward. I look at Benjamin and Dirk. I know each would like me to walk with them. I do not know how to decide. I do not know how to choose."

"Don't choose. Go. Go home. But put away your mourning. Be happy. Live again. You will find love someday. It does not have to be now. Dirk is dangerous for you. The English will never live with the Dutch in peace. It would be like you living with the Narragansett."

"And Benjamin?"

Winnie turned to the fire and Heather Flower could not see her face. Did she not want her to see? Everyone in the village loved Benjamin, and her aunt did too.

"He would be good for you, this I know. He loves you and would treat you well. But my child, you do not know your own thoughts. You must go home. When Wyancombone visits next, you must leave with him."

Heather Flower's eyes stung, but she held her head high. "Yes, my aunt. I will do as you say." How could she go home? It did not seem possible. But Winnie was her elder, and family, and she would do her bidding. It would be another two weeks before her brother would arrive. Something could happen to change things by then, at least she could hope. But what?

Miss Button picked her way through the icy salt marsh. The days were warming, but nights brought a freeze. Dirk wasn't in a hurry and he leaned back in the saddle. The last time he saw Heather Flower, he'd let her walk away. He wouldn't do that this time.

But he'd pretty much decided if she stayed here in Southold he'd never win her heart. Something needed to change, but the how would need to be left to the Almighty because he couldn't figure it out. Now that was a thought. Depending on the Almighty. He hadn't done that since he was a wee one. He hadn't needed God. He depended on no one but himself. But what was that verse? It kept nagging at him, scratching him under the skin. *Raise up a child in the Lord and he will not depart from it?* Something like that.

He entered the woods that surrounded the Indian fort and dappled light scattered from the canopy above. He glanced about, much more aware of what could be concealed in the forest than the open expanse of the marsh.

He came to the glen where he'd last said goodbye to Heather Flower. Across the meadow lay the opening to the trail Heather Flower used to go down to the river. He would wait here until he saw her.

He didn't wait long.

She walked toward the path carrying a birch bucket. She stopped at a bare-limbed maple tree, and he watched a few moments as she pounded a wooden spout into the tree and placed the bucket underneath. After a few long moments sticky sap started to run. He dropped the reins and walked up to her. "*Hoe gaat het?* How are you?"

She hopped back a step, but her lips betrayed a small smile. "I knew that was Miss Button nickering, Dirk. You do not surprise me if that is what you thought you would do."

"I couldn't stay away."

"I wouldn't want you to." She stepped closer to him.

"It's the season to draw the sap."

"*Nuk,* yes. I do this for Winnie. There is but a short time we can draw it. Dirk, there is but a short time for us."

He looked from the sweet syrup dripping now into the bucket to her eyes, so dark and troubled. "What do you mean? Are you all right?"

"My aunt will send me back to Montauk when my brother comes. It will be soon." She raised her chin as if to challenge his reaction. She would go, that he knew.

An eagle swooped above their heads and both drew in their breath to watch.

"The nest is not far from here," she said. "They return to the same one every year. They must have eggs by now to watch over."

"Once the eaglets leave the nest they never go back, *ja*?"

"No, my friend, they do go back that first year. But when they are strong, they leave and never return."

"Do you think that is what you must do? Return for a while until you're strong and then leave for your new nest?" He tried to swallow, but his throat felt like it was clutching his heart.

Her chin lowered to her chest, and he could see puddles under her closed eyes. He hadn't realized he'd not seen her cry before. How he wished he did not see it now. He grasped her shoulders and drew her into him. His chin touched her soft raven hair and he rested against her.

"I don't mean to make you weep. I don't know what to do, what is best?"

"There is no best. But it is what I must do." She pushed away and turned from him.

"*Ja.*" No wonder he'd avoided this love thing. It hurt.

With both hands she hoisted the bucket half full with sugary sap. "I want you to meet my aunt and the other people of our village, but I fear for your safety."

Dirk tethered Miss Button, rubbed her muzzle, and lifted his musket from the saddle. "I've taken care of myself for a long time, Heather Flower. I would be honored to meet your people." He took the bucket from her and they walked toward the palisade. If Captain Youngs or one of the Hortons showed up, he could be arrested. But the desire to be with her pulled him along.

"Your people do much trade with our brothers on the west side."

"We've traded for years with the Iroquois Nation," he said. "They trade further north, their corn for fur pelts. We trade guns for the fur."

"Our English neighbors do not like our people to have guns."

"How does that make them your friends then? To have arms means you can defend yourselves from your enemies, the Narragansett. How is that wrong?"

"They say you give our people guns, then fire water, and that is wrong. But they have militia, Dirk. Since the Montauk attack, they have offered to protect us. And they do."

He shook his head. "What have they done to bring back the women who were captured with you? How did they protect them?"

She stopped at the gate and looked up directly into his face. Hurt flooded her beautiful opal eyes, but the fire was there too. "Sometimes I feel as sad for their loss as I do for my Keme. I long for them to come home."

"I know. I share that desire with you."

He pushed the stick gate open and they brought the sap to the birch bark dwelling where it would be boiled down to sugary crystals. Several women worked over iron cauldrons given in trade by a Southold merchant. Covered sugar buckets lined the walls. At the end of the large room, little girls played with their dolls and twigs, pretending their dollies drew sap. The sugaring season was short, but after the cold winter the community came together in a festive spirit to get the chore done.

Winnie scraped a pot clean and turned for Heather Flower's bucket.

Dirk noticed her irritation at seeing him,

but she did not comment — only took the bucket from him with a nod of thank-you.

"I am glad, my niece, you are here for the sugaring. It gives me pleasure." She lifted the bucket, but Dirk stepped toward her and took over the process of pouring. He held back a grin when she sighed and murmured her gratitude.

"I could stay," Heather Flower offered. "If you need my help, I would like to stay."

For a long moment there was silence. Dirk's mind raced back to his earlier thought that it would be better for her to go home, away from Southold, away from Benjamin. He would miss her sorely, but if she had that time to become strong of mind about what she wanted, she might come back to him.

He said "no" at the precise time Winnie said "no." They looked at each other at the same time too, and he saw Winnie smile.

"Wyancombone will come soon. It is time for you to gather your things, say your good-byes. The sugaring is soon finished. You will go home then."

Heather Flower looked from Winnie to Dirk and back. "I will do your bidding, my aunt, because I know my mother grieves for me. It is time for me to accept the blood of my warrior."

Dirk set the empty bucket down. He sought Heather Flower's hand as he turned toward Winnie. "I would like to take your niece for a ride on my horse. May I take her away from her duties here? For just a short time?"

Winnie looked at her niece. "You would like to ride?"

"Yes, I would. I won't let us be long. Yes, Dirk?"

"*Ja*. We won't be gone long. I must say my goodbyes."

Heather Flower rode in front of Dirk, her braid flying back over his shoulder as Miss Button cantered in an easy lope. One hand clutched Button's mane, but the other rested on top of Dirk's. They'd already ridden through the woods and across the salt marsh and entered the endless forest between the Corchaug's principal place and the invisible line that marked the Dutch west side of the island.

His guidance of Miss Button through the thick trees was expert as he reined her down a narrow deer path. Silence, but for the fall of hooves, had enveloped them like a mist, and she did not want to break through it any more than he appeared to.

The day grew long and he brought his

horse first to a walk, and then to a stop. Miss Button shook her head and he gave her rein to nibble at grass before they began a slower ride back. Heather Flower leaned back against him and her head rested in the space between his shoulder and neck. Would he ask her to come with him to New Amsterdam, or return her to her aunt?

She pictured herself as his wife, living among the Dutch in their bustling establishment and busy trade center. Would they accept her there? But when she imagined the townspeople all staring at her, Benjamin's smiling face kept appearing and the love the people of Southold had shown to her and her aunt. Benjamin had told her the stories of Pocahontas and John Rolfe many times. Did he think they could marry and bring a stronger alliance between the English and the natives?

But then Keme's face drifted in among the others, just as she remembered him from the last moments of his life. His face filled with courage as the Narragansett held him, spears at his neck and sides, and she was forced to watch in horror as the ruthless warriors buried the spearheads into his side. Keme dying without a cry, a strong brave.

She'd wept, but she had not let those

despicable warriors see that. She'd been strong and true to her people and Keme. It was most likely why they agreed to free her in exchange for the wampum, but at the last minute Ninigret had gone back on his word and left her in the forest to die.

Was that why she was attracted to this man? Was it gratitude that he'd found her? Saved her? Most likely, and now it was time to go home.

"You are quiet, my friend, but I feel you are at peace with my leaving?"

He picked up the reins again and gave a little pressure to Miss Button's sides. She started back, plodding along this time, in no hurry at all.

"*Ja.* I don't like it, but I think this is good for you."

She could feel his breath close. "Do you find love for me, Dirk?" She felt him straighten and she twisted around to face him.

"I — I cannot talk of that. I know what we must do. If I let you go now, perhaps someday I will be able to tell you what I find in my heart for you. Here, I have a present for you." He pulled a small metal drill from his knapsack. "This is for you. For your wampum beads. It will be easier than using the flint to drill the holes."

She held it close and ran her fingers over the point. She looked up into his bay-blue eyes and wondered how he could give her something so wonderful while he talked of going away.

He bent forward and his lips lowered to hers. It was a funny custom of both the Dutch and the English, this kissing, but she found it warm and to her liking. It was a light, but lingering kiss and she could tell he was conflicted in giving it. That was okay. She was too.

20

March 17, 1654

The bay was as smooth as glass and reflected the cloudless blue sky. Heather Flower watched the canoe glide across, paddled by Wyancombone. He gave one last strong sweep of the paddle and landed on the beach with force. Benjamin stood beside her, and once her brother secured the boat, the three walked up to Winnie's wigwam. The Hortons and Fannings had gathered, along with Abigail's family and Patience. Her heart thumped in her chest and felt heavy. As hard as it was to leave these people, it was even harder to go home and face her sorrows.

With the sugaring done and her aunt's health returning, there was little reason to stay. Certainly Dirk had not given her a reason to remain — in truth he'd pushed her away. Now Benjamin could not bring himself to smile.

Wyancombone did not let that go. He folded his arms. "*Aquai,* friend. Why the dark look?"

"You know the answer to that. You're glad your sister is coming home, but you forget that we will miss her here."

"Some more than others?" He pushed lightly against his friend's arm with a fist.

Heather Flower could see the redness in Benjamin's neck as it crept upward. "Brother, you must leave our friend alone. This is not easy for any of us, except for you and our mother and father."

The three walked the rest of the path in silence. All eyes turned to them as they entered the fort. The soft-gray wolf pups chased around the trio, yipping and licking any fingers they could.

After a meal in the longhouse, they crowded Winnie's wigwam, and it reminded Heather Flower of the day they'd all shared when they buried her uncle. Benjamin had sat opposite her that day around the fire, and she remembered the sweetness of his glances her way. She did not know what to do with this Benjamin, so glum and so unhappy.

She watched her aunt with Mary, Patience, and Elizabeth. They were sisters in every sense, one minute teasing each

226

other, the next heads together sharing secrets or gossip. They pulled her into their circle. She could be a sister to them, she knew. They welcomed her with open arms already.

With Sarah long ago lost to the arms of Rachel, and Ruth waiting her turn to hold her, Mary sat in a chair, two of Smoke's offshoots curled at her feet. Winnie and Lizzie sat on each side of her. Patience lowered herself next to Heather Flower and Abigail.

Mary leaned down and fluffed the fur of one of the wolf pups. "My, don't you look just like our Smokey? Yes, you do." The pup squirmed with delight. She looked at Heather Flower. "Prithee, come visit us with your brother often. There is always a place for you here."

Heather Flower looked up at her as Lizzie and Patience leaned in to hear her reply.

Patience nudged her. "You will want to come back, yes?"

"I will. I will want to come back the moment I step out of my brother's canoe. But I don't know if I will return." She sensed rather than saw Benjamin's look.

Mary was persistent. "But you could come back for a day. Bring your mother with you. It is always so nice to see her. Is it not,

Winnie?"

Winnie looked from Mary to Heather Flower and back at Mary. "It is."

Heather Flower looked down at the fire, but the burning in her cheeks was not from the flame.

Winnie took up her cause. "It is too difficult for my niece to live between the two worlds of her family and her friends for now. Let her spend time in Montauk before we have her back."

Benjamin sat down next to her. "I will miss you, but I think that is good. Mayhap I could come see you there."

She looked sideways at him. His face was soft again, understanding. He reached for her hand and she let him take it in his. "I will miss you too, my friend."

Patience's giggle sounded like hundreds of little jingle shells. She hugged Heather Flower. "If anyone can get you back here, 'tis Ben, is it not?" Her blue eyes danced.

"Now, Patience." Lizzie shook her head, curls bouncing. "We all know how you like to see a good romance blossom, but give them time." She glanced at her sister with a grin.

Crinkles deepened around Mary's hazel eyes. "Time and warmth, Patience. Like our dough. She needs time and warmth."

Heather Flower raised her chin. "I am more like the eaglet fallen from her nest than dough. My strong brother comes to scoop me and carry me back, but I will survive."

"That's because you are a survivor, Heather Flower." Benjamin squeezed her hand. "It is all right. I can wait. You will be back, I know. But I will not be happy until you are." The last he said with a reassuring smile, which was his way. "Would you take a walk with me?"

She stood and tugged at his hand in answer and didn't even hear her friends make a peep as she and Benjamin started down a shaded trail.

As they rounded a bend, Benjamin stopped and pulled her close. His warm breath tickled her ear. "May I come visit you?"

She nestled her face into his shoulder. "Yes, my friend. I would be sad if you didn't come. And my father and mother would be upset if you didn't." It would be so easy to love him as a wife. The Hortons and her parents had been friends from the time she could remember. Benjamin had always been so kind and caring. Her loyalty was with him, but where was her heart?

"Well, they will be so relieved to have you

back home." He held her back and his baby-blue eyes sought hers. "Would you make me a promise?"

She'd thought he was about to kiss her. "What promise, Benjamin?"

"That you will wait for me? That you won't go home and find someone else?"

"Why do you ask for a promise? Do you think I am so simple that I would fall for the next man who would woo me? I have told you I am not ready to love, but don't you think you will be the first I tell when I am?" Her cheeks burned and she took a breath to steady her voice.

"Whoa. I didn't it mean it that way at all. I am just glad you want me to come visit. And you don't have to promise. You just gave me your word that at least you'll let me know who the lucky man is."

"That is right, Benjamin. We should go back now." She studied the path for a minute and then turned into him, her chin raised. "Could you kiss me first? I want to remember your kiss."

He bent and their lips met. His kiss was light at first, and gentle. As she returned his kiss, he drew her closer.

"I am learning your English ways, *nuk*?"

The time came for Heather Flower to carry

her small cloth bag filled with her few possessions down to the bay. After many goodbyes, and a long hug from her dear aunt, she climbed into the long canoe and waited for her brother to follow. She had not thought about how she might feel about sitting in a blackened birchbark again, after her last ride of terror. Even the crossing on the ferry over the East River did not cause her to panic like this did. She clung to the side, her large dark eyes pinned on Benjamin.

They pushed off and she watched as he stood waving. As he grew smaller in the distance, she at last let go of the side and raised her hand in a small farewell. He could not see it, she knew. But maybe that was best. She belonged with her people. Not the English or the Dutch. She turned in the canoe and spotted Fort Pond Bay, the entrance to Montauk, in the distance. But stepping back into the life she'd been dragged from seemed almost impossible.

Thankfully, her mother left her alone with her thoughts much of the time, and she watched the labors of her tribe from a distance.

The women were busy with gathering wood. They had a large store of seasoned

231

wood — buried in the sandy ground all winter — but this was the time to gather new wood. Many others worked in the fields, breaking up the ground and getting ready to plant their corn, beans, and squash.

By summer they would be wading in the shore, looking for the quahog, or clam shells, and the swirly whelk shells that the men would craft into wampum beads.

As the daughter of the sachem, Heather Flower did not have to labor in the fields or search for shells, but she was allowed to make beads and wampum. She enjoyed grinding and drilling the beads and stitching them onto her tunics and headdresses. She made wampum belts too, and hers were highly prized.

Today she worked on a star, cut from a soft piece of deerskin with her knife. She concentrated as she stabbed the bone needle into the hide, filling in the surface with tiny, dark purple beads. They glinted in the sunlight and she smiled at the pleasure her work gave her.

She had told her mother about the story Benjamin's mother liked to share. About how stars were little windows in heaven for the angels to peer down to earth and send their love and light. Aunt Winnie said it was just a story, and not from the white man's

Bible. But she and her mother liked it just the same.

She'd also talked about Dirk and Benjamin with her mother, and as she listened to her counsel, her throat ached as if she'd swallowed splinters, and she'd held back tears. Her mother's concerns were much more about their race being obliterated by intermarriage than about her heart and love. But if she married Dirk, or Benjamin, or any white man for that matter, wouldn't there always be pieces of her in her children and their children? Could a race ever really be lost as long as the Great Spirit was over all?

The laughter of young boys caught her attention and she looked up to see two young braves tussling with each other like young bear cubs. One looked so much like Keme when he was younger. She stared at him, and he glanced up and shot her a wide grin, then plowed into the stomach of his playmate and the two rolled in laughter to the ground. Recognition registered. It was Keme's brother. He had six, and this one was the youngest.

She looked at the star she'd made and gathered her tools and beads and stood to leave. She saw Keme's mother bent over a piece of hide that she scraped with a shell.

She walked over to the woman who mourned for him as much as she. She was plump with long braids to her waist, and she looked up with sad eyes as Heather Flower pressed the star into her hand. Turning it over and running her thick fingers over the shiny beads, she smiled, and it gave Heather Flower much pleasure to see her happy. Perhaps they both could heal, both be strong.

"I am glad you are home, my child," the older woman said. "You are what I have left of Keme."

"Yes. I know you are as sad as I am. You have been strong, and at times I feel I have been weak. I miss him very much."

"He hunts in the eternal forest and thinks of us as he runs. I will place this star on the pallet that holds his tomahawk and wampum belt."

"That would please me." She patted the woman's hand, then wandered down the path toward the bay. She came to the place she'd last seen Keme and turned to look at the exact spot where he was held before they killed him. She put her fists to her heart and beat rapidly several times and then held them up to the sky, her cheeks glistening with tears.

She continued to the water's edge and

listened to the gentle lap of the water. A little red crab ran sideways between the yellow and orange shells. She'd felt like running when she'd first come home, like the crab, but confusion held her here. It should be good to be home. She wanted it to be good.

She heard footfalls behind her and turned to watch her brother make his way down to the beach. They both sat in silence as the sun sank to the west, casting a silvery glow across the bay. She should be glad to be home, comforted by the familiar and her family. So why did it feel like her heart was somewhere across the bay?

21

March 30, 1654

Heather Flower sat on the beach, a bearskin blanket wrapped about her shoulders against the brisk March wind, and watched the men prepare their canoes. The northern right whales, done with spawning off the warm southern shores of the Atlantic coast, had begun their annual migration north.

The men of her village were expert fishermen and for generations had paddled out beyond the surf to spear large fish. But the largest was the right whale, given its name from the Basque people of the north because it fed from the ocean surface, swam slowly, and was easy to spear. When it died, the carcass floated.

Occasionally one would beach itself on the shore and die, and the tribe would have a ceremonial feast of the fin and tail, and trade the whalebone and oil to the English. But the whale hunters never waited for the whale to come to them. Their excitement was in the chase.

Wyancombone tossed his bow, arrows, and a harpoon tipped with bone and attached to sinewy ropes into the bottom of his canoe. He was as fine a fisherman as the rest, and he took pride in his knowledge and skill. When Heather Flower was younger, she had begged her father to let her go on these expeditions, but he said no and she became accustomed to watching them from the beach until they disappeared on the horizon.

She'd heard her brother's stories enough to know they would swarm their canoes around their prey and attack with their weapons until the great fish could struggle no more. The English of Southampton were impressed with the Montauketts' skill and brought in great fishing vessels with offers to the tribe's fishermen to work onboard as crew.

A few of the men had already accepted jobs in return for clothing and sailcloth, and even guns and rum. Benjamin would disapprove of that — the English had their laws regarding the supplying of guns and alcohol to the native people — but the fishing companies were exempt from such laws, so eager were they to hire the expertise of the Montauketts.

The companies sent out two thirty-foot vessels at a time, each reinforced with cedar ribbing and equipped with iron harpoons, four oarsmen, a steersman, and a harpooner. It was dangerous work, even with the protection of the big ships and the additional crew, but not as perilous as hunting in the small canoe. Still, her brother was against working for the white man, even distrusted their motives, and continued to hunt the old way with his own primitive tools. Her father disagreed, though. He said that to have trust was a thing of honor, and that Lion Gardiner was his friend. He said they must learn to work side by side. But he was the first to agree that the commodities the white man had to offer them were things they did not need.

Heather Flower stood up, put her hand above her eyes, and squinted east, into the sun. The canoes were specks where water met sky. The wind blew sand at her legs and she pulled the blanket tighter before she followed the path toward home. The incessant calling of gulls overhead drew her attention, and she watched a flock as they flew toward Shelter Island.

She came to a curve in the path and skirted a mound of sand leading to a secluded spot that was her favorite retreat. She could sit, out of wind and sun, and listen as others passed by within feet of her without them ever knowing. She pulled her leather pouch out of the neckline of her tunic and emptied out the bone needle, some sinew, and a few beads. She untied her wampum belt and began stitching a row of beads at the end.

As she stabbed the needle through the bead and into the deerskin, she wished her life could be sewn back together so easily. But Keme was not coming back — he could not be stitched back into the pattern of her life. She would sit here and sew until her brother came back.

After killing the whale, they would tow it to the shore, something that could take hours. Once the fins, tail, and mouth bones were removed, the blubber was cut out. It was a long process and one she never stayed to watch. But she always liked to be at the water's edge when Wyancombone's canoe struggled in, dragline taut.

At length she settled back into the sand and fell asleep. She dreamt of Keme and dancing, of flowers and feasting, and for a moment when she woke she thought she heard him calling. But it was her mother's voice that broke through her dream, and she jumped and gathered her needles and pouch before running to the path.

"Quashawam, where were you?" Her face was stricken, though her words were calm, stoic.

"I was beyond the path, Mother. I came as soon as I heard you. Are you all right? Is something wrong?"

Tears sprung to her mother's eyes. "Wyancombone did not return with the men. There are ten missing. They threw their spears into a big whale, but it fought and pulled two canoes over. The water is freezing. Only six men were helped into the other canoes and came home. We don't know what happened to your brother."

Heather Flower grabbed her mother's hand and pulled her toward the ocean shore. Her father was there, with the exhausted hunting party. He was preparing to leave with his own handpicked rescue party and Heather Flower ran into the surf.

She grabbed her father's hands. "Take me with you, please. I must help you find Wyancombone."

"No, my daughter. You must stay with your mother. She needs you and you would not be safe out there. I cannot lose my son and my daughter in one day."

She blinked the sting from her eyes and

fell to her knees. "Please. I must go."

Wyandanch looked from her to her mother. "You must understand. Someday you might need to lead my people. If I am gone, and your brother is gone, it will fall to you to take care of your mother and all of our people. By staying behind, you are strong. Do this for me and your mother."

She pulled back, her head held high. "Find him, Father. Bring him home." She waded back to her mother, the icy water biting her ankles. They embraced as they watched the men paddle out to sea. The crowd of villagers gathered round them and together they walked back to the village.

She asked Keme's mother to build up the fire and instructed an elder brave to put up a smoke signal after she sent their fastest runner to carry the news to Momoweta. She pulled her mother to her near the fire and listened as the medicine man began a chant. The wait began.

All night they clung to each other. At dawn's first light Benjamin arrived with Jack, a young Indian brave who lived on Shelter Island. He was called Jack by the Sylvesters, and Abooksigun by his people, and was a good friend of Wyancombone.

"How did you know?"

Benjamin swung down from Star, but his

241

eyes never left hers. "I saw the smoke signals. I knew something was up. I came through Shelter Island, and Jack said he would come with me. When we came ashore, we talked with some of the boys that were playing along the path. They told us about Wyancombone and your father."

"There is nothing we can do but wait."

"No, I think we can do something. I'm going to ride to Southampton to get a whaling ship dispatched to look for them."

"Benjamin, I feel as lost as my brother. We must bring him back."

"We'll take a full search party out." He stepped close and brought her into his arms. "We'll find him."

He nuzzled the top of her head and she looked up. His mouth lowered to hers and they shared a tender kiss. In that moment she knew if anyone could bring her brother back, it would be Benjamin. He was always there when she needed someone.

"*Nuk.* Thank you, my friend."

She watched him leave, urging Star to a full gallop, Abooksigun close behind him.

How long could Wyancombone survive in the water? Could someone have found him and picked him up? She had so many questions. What frightened her most, of course, was she knew the answers to her questions.

■ ■ ■ ■

Mr. Bennett granted the ship and crew required for a full search. Benjamin and Jack sailed with them, and as the wooden hulk, seeped in whale stench, pitched and slammed against the sea's surface with the impending storm, Benjamin gripped the rough rail. How could he have thought for a minute he might long for the sailor's life?

As the ship lurched one more time and the rain began to pelt, his stomach revolted and Jack grabbed him as he heaved over the side of the ship. More miserable one could not be. Jack pulled him down the hatch and they settled onto a trunk tied to the planks of the lower deck. Benjamin lowered his forehead to his knees and tried to get a grip on his stomach. When he felt in control, he sat up.

Jack handed him a rag and he wiped his face. "Some hero I am." They both chuckled.

"Your heart and mind are both trying — it is only your stomach that does not know how to follow."

"You are so right. Has anyone said if they think we are near where Wynacombone and the other men were lost? And has anyone seen Wyandanch?"

"Not yet. I don't think we are anywhere close."

He closed his eyes and a moan escaped. His stomach clenched and he pressed the rag to his lips, willing his insides to be still. He drew in a breath to clear his head.

The storm picked up and sent waves over the rail, washing everything in their path across the slanted deck. They both stayed below, with Jack coming close to being as sick as he was.

All he could think about was Wyancombone, Wyandanch, and himself all lost at sea, with no one there for Heather Flower. Why had he not stayed with her once he had the ship commissioned? And if Van Buren was as in love with her as he'd like to pretend, where was he? He needed to survive this, for Heather Flower. Please, God, help him survive.

Hours passed with Jack and Benjamin heaving, their clothes waterlogged, and each clung to anything that seemed to be bolted down. Late in the afternoon the wind abated, the sun sent streaks of light between the clouds and the ship bobbed like cork on a placid lake.

Benjamin raised his head and found Jack sitting up rubbing the back of his neck. "I think the worst is over."

"If we're lucky, everything is over." Jack clutched his stomach.

Benjamin stood up, his legs feeling like the straw Mary used to stuff Hannah's little poppets. "Let's go find out if anyone knows where we are." They climbed the ladder to the top deck. A few sails were torn, but the oarsmen were at work righting their course.

He listened as Captain Foster gave them a briefing on their location and the plans for the evening. The captain mentioned food and Benjamin's mouth soured. "I, for one, can forgo a meal, Captain." He turned to Jack, but as he did, a commotion on the starboard side brought all of them to the rail.

A man with a telescope pointed far out to the west. "I see something. It could be a piece of shipwreck, or even the whale, but we need to go and look."

All eyes were on the dark spot in the water. Benjamin caught the man's arm. "May I look?"

"Of course."

He took the scope and trained it on the dot. "I think I see something moving on it. Let's get on with it. Go, men."

The oarsmen struck their paddles to the water with great strength and the ship plowed through the water with speed. As they came up alongside, they discovered the battered canoe of Wyancombone, who lay in the bottom, a broken arm held close to his side, and one other hunter who had also survived. Benjamin and Jack helped lower men into the canoe, and Heather Flower's brother was quickly lifted into the ship, along with his companion.

"Easy. Be easy with him." Benjamin helped the men lay him down on the deck. Jack ran below to find dry blankets. Wyancombone was incoherent, but he looked like he would survive with some fresh water and his arm set.

The other man suffered from exposure, but otherwise seemed in one piece. He described the ordeal of wrestling with the whale with the harpoons in its side, but fighting them all the same. When the canoes began to roll, he thought they were all dead. But he'd managed to get back in and pulled Wyancombone in after him. He'd worked for more than an hour trying to save the other two men, but they drowned. He was certain the whale had survived, as a northern right whale would have floated if dead.

Benjamin looked up to the darkening sky with mountainous clouds threatening more rain and thunder. He shook his head as he thought of the last storm and how Wyancombone had survived it. But his thoughts trailed to Wyandanch, and he prayed father and son would both live to reunite with Heather Flower.

Somehow the ship limped into port, just ahead of the storm. As soon as everyone was debriefed and a wagon could be secured, Benjamin and Jack hitched up Star and brought the two men home. As they turned the wagon down the road into the village, a crowd gathered. He reined in Star in front of Wyandanch's wigwam and crawled off the wagonboard. When the Grand Sachem himself appeared, new strength flowed through Benjamin's veins.

"I thought we'd lost you, my friend." He clapped Wyandanch's back and brought him into a Horton bear hug.

"I am too stubborn for that. I see you have my son." His words came out in short, raspy syllables. "I have his life to owe to you."

Heather Flower rushed out of the wigwam with her mother and they ran to the wagon. There was fire in her opal eyes.

"He looks rough, Heather Flower, but with the medicine man's help, he will be all right."

She came to him and he took her in his

arms once more, rocking her. "There, it's all right. Everything is all right."

Jack returned to his work on Shelter Island, but Benjamin stayed for a few days at the invitation of Wyandanch and kept Wyancombone company while he mended, which didn't take long. Soon Benjamin and Heather Flower joined him for walks to the beach, his arm bound to his side. He loved to tell them the story of fighting the great whale, and his plans for someday finding him again and taking him in the hunt. He called him Scar Fish, and said his name was carved in his side.

Each night after their meal Heather Flower worked with her beads in a corner by the fire while he and Wyancombone traded stories of tracking and hunting. Finally the day came for Benjamin to return to Southold, and Wyandanch presented both him and Wyancombone with wampum belts made by Heather Flower. He explained to them they told the story of both his son's hunt and Benjamin's rescue.

Benjamin fingered the beautiful shell beads. Should he tell them how sick he'd been and what little use he was for the rescue? But Heather Flower looked so happy he couldn't say anything that would diminish her joy. "I watched you working with the beads. Thank you for this. It will be an honor to wear it."

"No, Benjamin, the gratitude is mine. And it is an honor to present you with the wampum. You have given us back my brother. My family has known much grief. His loss would be too much to bear."

He glanced around the wigwam. Wyancombone slept and her parents seemed to busy themselves with their backs turned. He didn't miss their intention of giving the two privacy. He stepped closer and pulled her near. "I didn't do much, really. But I'm thankful he's safe and home." His voice lowered, almost husky. "It's hard to stay away, Heather Flower. You know that I miss you, don't you?"

"Yes. I am needed here, and I know my mother believes this is where I should be. But my heart is in Southold."

Her last words were like poetry and his fingers caressed her cheek. "That's all I need to know for now." His lips sought hers in a brief kiss that promised not to be the last.

He squatted next to Wyancombone's pallet and found his slumber to be a ruse. After jesting with him about eavesdropping, they said their fond goodbyes. He said a more formal farewell to Wyandanch and Wuchi and promised to return as he pulled himself into the saddle and tipped his hat to Heather Flower. He guided Star on the path, but when he came to the point where he could cross to Shelter Island, he decided on a whim to ride around to the fork, and check on the property out at Wading River before riding all the way home. He could stop by Southampton along the way and give his thanks to Captain Foster and Mr. Bennett.

The ride home was long, but uneventful. It gave him much time to reflect on the last few days. He would not have thought it possible, but Heather Flower seemed closer than ever to him and her family as well. Mary had been right. It did indeed seem that this was where he was meant to be, and Heather Flower seemed to be coming to a place where she might be able to love again.

The Dutchman seemed to have disappeared or at least given up, and that was so much the better. He could go home now and start tending the land. He glanced around as he rode, noticing the young green shoots sprouting in every direction. He saw some wild iris in bloom and breathed deeply the fresh scent of the spring air. Mary always had a list of what needed to go into the garden at each turn of the planting year, so he imagined she'd already started one.

He hadn't thought about the apple blossoms and wondered if any had opened yet. He'd have to make a point of looking.

As he rode past the Corchaug fort, he noticed the women working the fields. That meant Mary would have him and Joseph out in the garden soon. She'd learned a lot from Winnie and had quickly passed it on to her boys. But it was true the Corchaug way of farming and the rich, fertile soil of the north fork grew the best corn — the best crops — on the whole island.

He was blessed to live here. This was where he belonged. And he couldn't wait for Heather Flower to join him.

22

April 4, 1654

Wyandanch watched his daughter wander through the village and sit on the bank of the bay day after day and could not bear it any longer. He instructed one of his braves to take Heather Flower and Wyancombone to visit Grissell Sylvester of Shelter Island. Pogaticut was her uncle and sachem of the island. He still lived there but had sold the land to Grissell's husband and three of his business partners in 1652. Nathaniel Sylvester had a large house built for his young bride before they arrived. She'd loved her home, but found it lonely until she met Heather Flower.

Heather Flower found the home lovely and the exporting business that Nathaniel ran fascinating. He'd been attracted to the island because of its large stands of white oak, and he produced barrels to use in Barbados for shipping sugar. It had made him a wealthy man and his home reflected his status.

Though his and Grissell's sympathies lay with the Quakers of New England, they attended church services at the meetinghouse in Southold. It was known that many Quakers found refuge in their home, but as long as the Sylvesters did not preach in their town, the Horton and Youngs families tolerated them. Heather Flower was a friend to all.

Wyancombone, annoyed he could not paddle the canoe himself, rode with his sister to the little island, sheltered on two sides by the north and south fork of Long Island, and to the east by Isle of Wight, Lion Gardiner's island home. Heather Flower helped the brave turn the canoe upside down on the bank, and the three walked up to the house.

The center door had two windows to the left of it and two to the right. A second floor had another set of four windows and a porch chamber used for sleeping on hot nights. It was a large house for the young couple and their first child was already on the way.

The large estate required much help, and some of Pogaticut's family lived in the house to care for it and would help with the babe's arrival in August. Black slaves brought from Barbados, and even Africa, worked on the estate and had quarters within the house as well. Heather Flower was not sure how she felt that they were made to move far from their land to work for the white men. But they seemed pleasant and happy and healthy.

While Heather Flower visited with Grissell, her brother helped with whatever chore Abooksigun — Jack to the Sylvesters — was involved with. Occasionally, they were permitted to go fishing and such they did on this day.

Grissell welcomed Heather Flower warmly, and they walked to the back garden to sit and take refreshment.

"It is good to be away from my home. I find it confining and filled with much sadness, yet my parents forbid me to return to Southold."

"That's terrible. Why do they not let you stay with your aunt? Especially after what happened to Keme?" She ran her hand lightly over her belly, which was barely there.

"They say it is best for me to come home to get on with my life, but I know it is because of a Dutchman who is in love with me. They fear I would run off with him."

"And would you?" She smiled at her friend.

"A part of me would. But it is Keme's memory that holds me back. And Benjamin too." She tossed her head. "I don't know what I want."

"Ah. You are doing the right thing then." Her blue eyes danced with merriment.

"What am I doing that is right? Everything seems wrong."

"Oh, no, Heather Flower, you are here with me. We are friends and friends help friends. You made a right choice. Now, I want you to tell me everything about this Dutchman that makes you want to be with him. Is he handsome?"

"Oh, yes. And Dirk has a kind voice that sounds like the ocean in a conch shell. And he is gentle, like he finds me delicate and breakable, and I am not but it is good. He looks into my eyes like I matter to him more than anything here on the earth."

"Is he smart?"

"He is. He can track like an animal, like my people. He found me in the middle of dense forest. He saved my life. He is an officer in the Dutch militia, and his men look up to him. Even the men who command him look up to him."

"And Benjamin? Isn't Benjamin as smart

and handsome?"

"Yes. And he cares for me so much. My heart is torn."

The young niece of Pogaticut came out to take their cups and plates, and Grissell thanked her and told her she and her guest would take a walk and explore.

They walked along a row of boxwoods Nathaniel had planted toward the creek. Grissell told her she had brought the cuttings for the plants from England. She breathed deeply before she posed a question. "Are you in love with either of them? Like you were with Keme?"

Heather Flower's eyes barely fluttered, barely gave away that they stung with salty tears, and in an instant they were dry again. "I do not know."

Her friend nodded. "It is too soon to know. You must not think of these things for a good long while. When you married Keme, you were fresh and so full of strength and confidence. You rejoiced in your youth and innocence and celebrated each other. When you lost Keme, you lost all of that. It will take time to rebuild, and you will not ever feel the same way toward another what you felt for your first love, but it does not mean you will not love."

Heather Flower looked at her friend. "You

speak like an old woman. How do you know these things?"

"I don't know. My mother always said I had ideas beyond my years. Perhaps I think like an old woman." She laughed and the breeze carried it away.

They found themselves where the creek emptied into the bay, facing the north fork. "You didn't know Keme. He wanted to be a warrior from the time he was little. We would run through the woods, and when we tired, we would lay down in the sand by the bay. He would tell me stories he saw in the clouds as they drifted by. There were always rabbits and elk and great hunters in the story. And he would say, 'Oh, look there! A great warrior and who's that? A girl? Ah, yes, I think he wants to marry her.' He would look over and smile at me and say, 'Look! Is that you I see in the cloud?' And I would giggle and get up and run and he would chase me all the way home."

"Was he mad he couldn't catch you?"

"Oh, no. He could have caught me if he wanted to. But when he grew up, his story came true. He was a great warrior and the Narragansett hated him for that. My father and Keme were the aim of their attack. I was only the means to make them suffer more."

"Heather Flower, you must not blame yourself. Stay with us for a while. We have plenty of room and I crave your company. You would be between the two worlds that trouble you so much right now. You would see Benjamin when we journey to church on Sundays — but you would not need to talk to him. Unless you wanted to. But it will give you the time you need."

She watched the choppy waves as the breeze picked up across the water and pictured herself once again forced to lie in the bottom of Ninigret's canoe. Helpless. She felt helpless now, and Grissell's invitation tempting. She wasn't sure if her parents would agree, but she would plead with them if need be.

"I do not want the power of what Ninigret did to me to keep its hold. I want to be free again. I will come to you after a moon. I must sit at my parents' feet and give them my respect. Then I must tell them it is time for me to stand again."

Grissell looked surprised at her decision, but it was the right one.

They walked back up to the house and Grissell took her up to her room and showed her pretty frocks that Nathaniel brought back from his travels for her. She insisted she had too many and that her husband would have more for her when he returned from his trip to France. She asked her to pick one. Her buckskin dresses and leggings were so much more comfortable than the stiff fabrics of the colorful dresses, but still it was fun to try them on, and she picked a lovely purple gown to take home.

"It bothers me I have nothing to give you, my friend."

"You have given me the gift of your visit. The gift of yourself. You do not know how I long for company."

"But I hear you have many visitors."

"Oh, yes, we do — but not women my age. Not women who talk with me about handsome, charming men and love lost and found." Her giggle was infectious and both laughed at what they knew they enjoyed talking about the most. "I love a good romance, even if I'm advising against it." They were lost in laughter again and it felt good.

Wyancombone and Abooksigun returned with a large catch of cod, and they cleaned the fish and fried it in a cast-iron pan over the fire. Grissell had a cook, but when Nathaniel was gone, she sometimes enjoyed preparing meals herself. She'd become quite proficient in the kitchen when she'd lived with her sister and brother-in-law, the Coddingtons.

The meal was delicious. "That was good fish, Grissell. Thank you. And thank you for the dress. We should go now, before the sun sets."

As they walked down the path to the canoe, the wind picked up in earnest, and fat, cold drops of rain pummeled them.

"You cannot go in this weather. Come, stay with me tonight. We shall sit by the fire and tell stories. It will be such fun and you will stay safe. Your parents would not want you to cross the water now."

They hurried through the storm back to the house and huddled by the fire to dry. Wyancombone stretched out on a pallet across the room, but Grissell loved telling scary stories, and Heather Flower stayed up listening until they were both too frightened to sleep. Her friend settled into telling her the story of her life and how she grew up in England and, at age fifteen, came across the pond to Rhode Island as the ward of her brother-in-law. She soon met Nathaniel and they wed.

With thoughts of flowers, sweet cakes, and promises of true love swirling, she curled onto a bolster and pulled the quilt Grissell had given her about her shoulders. As the embers glowed, she fell asleep. But her dreams were not of flower girls or feasts, but of war and terror.

In the morning, with the sun shining, Heather Flower and Wyancombone paddled home. She'd said her goodbyes to Grissell with sadness. Washing in the pretty floral basin that morning, she'd known she would not be back to stay. They were worlds apart, and even Grissell could not change her life. She must face her fears in her own world. Alone.

Dirk lifted the saddle over Miss Button's withers and settled it on her back. She looked around at him and nuzzled his elbow. "It's all right, girl. This will be an easy trip. Long, but easy. Just some mapmaker that needs escorting and showing around." He tied his musket and knapsack to the saddle and patted her flank.

The horse outfitted for the mapmaker, a tall, white gelding with a few years on him, stood patiently waiting. He'd picked Cotton for this trip because he knew Nicholas Visscher was not much of a horseman. He lifted the saddle to his broad back. "There, steady now, old boy."

He adjusted the cinch and picked up the knapsack and tied it to the back of the saddle. The army treated their mapmakers like royalty, so he figured he'd be doing most of the physical work on this trip. But he had to admit he admired Visscher. He came from a long line of Dutch mapmakers, and his work was worthy of masterpiece status.

Visscher walked out with the governor and tied two long cylinders to the pommel of his saddle.

Dirk stretched out his hand. "Hallo. I'm Lieutenant Dirk Van Buren, and I'll be your guide, Mr. Visscher."

"Hallo to you. It's Nicholas, and thank you very much. I appreciate you giving time to assist me."

Dirk nodded toward the governor. "I do as I'm requested, with pleasure."

After a farewell that bordered on ceremony, the two departed with a salute. Not much was said during the first four hours of the ride, and Dirk had plenty of time to think about what he'd like to accomplish on this journey. He didn't need maps to travel, but he respected the men who could put on paper what he could see and feel instinctively. And he looked forward to observing Nicholas at work.

The journey was almost identical to the rescue trip for Heather Flower, and he found his mind preoccupied with thoughts of her, so when his charge finally broke the silence, he was almost grateful.

"I've mapped to the Mohawk River, but they said that for me to proceed further east, I needed your services."

"*Ja,* it would be foolish to journey into this land without a guide. The Narragansett people are fighters. They do not care who they fight — Dutch, English, or other tribes. It is sport to them and they are mean. But I'm looking forward to our journey, so do not think of me as a service, but as a companion."

Night came and they built their camp next to a small creek. The heavy dark clouds that had hung about them gave way to a brief dusting of snow as Dirk searched for dry firewood. Nicholas surprised him by pitching in and making camp. He snared a rabbit before Dirk had the fire lit.

By firelight, Nicholas unrolled the stiff parchment scrolls. One was completely blank, but the other contained detailed mapping of Hudson's valley. The detail and richness of his drawings impressed Dirk. The river depicted the fur trade and the abundance of wildlife. Bear, elk, fowl, and fish were all drawn with a keen eye and artist's hand.

Dirk's curiosity was piqued. "Did you ever

think of making a living as an artist?"

"Not for a minute. But my sister is both an artist and a poet."

They discussed their families and leaving Holland as the mapmaker worked on sketching a tiny portion of the territory they'd covered that day onto the page, his notebook open before him. But the night was too dark and the firelight not sufficient and soon he put away his work.

They would travel for a few more days, with frequent stops for Nicholas to fill his notebooks, and then make camp for a few more days while he sketched. Stretched out near the fire on the hard, frozen ground, they joked about the feather beds they left behind at the fort.

Nicholas told him that when he finished the maps he'd been commissioned to draw he would return to Holland. He pulled out a small travel Bible and showed Dirk the illustrations of maps it contained, all drawn by his father.

"So you travel with your Bible."

"*Ja.* Don't you? I would think if ever a time you need it, it is out here in this wild land."

"Maybe. I feel closer to God here than anywhere else, though."

The night was dark with no moon and

nary a twinkle in the sky. In the next few days they would be very near Ninigret as the tribe prepared their fields for planting. How he would love the chance to right the wrongs done to Heather Flower. What did God think about that?

23

April 8, 1654

They had covered quite a bit of territory for as often as they'd stopped. A stand of river birch now hid their presence.

A thin gray layer of clouds obscured the stars, but they were thankful the journey so far had been dry. Still, Nicholas needed a clear sky. "I need better night navigation for accuracy. I can observe and count paces and apply certain mathematics, but without the stars, all of my calculations are incomplete."

"We can remain here as long as you need to get your bearings set. Do what you need to get your work done."

But as he spooned the *stampotten* into bowls for supper, his mind wandered to Ninigret. They had to be close to the tribe. He didn't need to stick around the camp all day — he wasn't here to protect the man he was guiding — he might be able to do a little scouting.

He took two sausages and put them on top of the bowls of mashed potatoes, carrots, onions and kale. They ate near the fire and Dirk listened as the mapmaker talked of learning his trade at his father's knee. He enjoyed the companionship and the myriad stories Nicholas could tell, but if he'd thought the trip would take his mind from Heather Flower, he was wrong. In any given moment, the memory of her walking away from him could materialize and cause a ragged pain to clutch his throat.

The following morning he was up before dawn, packing his knapsack for his scouting expedition. The cloud cover remained, even a little mist in the air, but Nicholas was content to sit under the shelter of thick branches to work. They ate *poffertjes* and dried blueberries to break their fast. "Do you have a weapon, Nicholas?"

"Nee."

He popped the last *poffertjes* in his mouth, stood up, and brushed crumbs from his leather doublet. He walked to his knapsack and removed a leather pouch with care. He withdrew a wheel-lock holster pistol and laid it down next to Nicholas. "Do you know how to use one of these?"

"If I'm scared enough, I suppose."

"Good enough." Dirk tied his knapsack

267

behind the saddle on Miss Button and led her out. He needed to stay close to the ground while tracking.

It didn't take long to find what he looked for. *Ja*. His instincts were correct. He swung himself up on Miss Button and urged her into a walk. They continued most of the day at a quiet pace, stopping only to eat a few biscuits and give Miss Button some water. When he could see an opening through the trees, he whispered, "Whoa, girl."

He slid down. "Stay here, missy." The backs of ten wigwams stood on the other side of the glen. Across from them he could make out additional huts and a longhouse on the far corner. Women and children sat under an open area with a thatched roof. The children played with little toy canoes and dolls. The women were mixing dried ground corn and water into a mash. A fire pit had two turkeys roasting on sticks. The smell was irresistible, but he reminded himself to keep all senses focused on his mission.

The men would be fishing or hunting, but by the slant of the sun he reckoned they would be back with their catch soon, before dark. He studied a large field to the south. Most likely they would come up the side of it if they were returning from the coast.

Cornstalks grew in the field, surrounded by sprouts of pole beans and squash plants. Several women, clad in plain deerskin tunics that hung loosely on their thin frames, worked the earth on their knees. He hadn't noticed them at first, so close to the ground they dug the dirt with their clam shells. He inched his way to a better vantage site. They had baskets of small fish they buried to fertilize the soil.

Were these women the Montauketts? The Narragansett were known to keep their captives together. It was unusual they had separated Heather Flower out, but then she was the daughter of a Grand Sachem. And the only one they offered for ransom. It would be a long time before these women were assimilated into the tribe.

He waited to see if they would notice him, but not one looked up from her work. Were they afraid? His keen gaze skirted the perimeter of the field. He saw no guards, no means to detain them. But where would they run? They were far from the territory they knew. If they tried to escape certainly they would die, for either their captors would come to look for them or they would not survive the elements.

He pulled out a few dried apple slices as he watched them. Guilt pricked his thoughts as he chewed his meager meal. He'd give them some if he had enough. If he could without alerting their captors. Their young faces held no joy, not even sadness, but grim exhaustion worn like a mask. It wasn't right that one man could give the order to take women from the people who loved them, never to return, their parents or husbands left to wonder if they were dead or alive.

As he'd anticipated, the returning braves filed in with their nettle-fiber nets dotted with sea bass and reed baskets of clams and oysters. They barely looked at the women who labored late into the afternoon. And the women did not look at them. He decided to wait and see how much longer they would work and in what manner they would be summoned. His most fruitful tracking involved waiting and watching.

The sun was nearly down, and two of the youngest women appeared on the verge of fainting, when three braves returned to herd them back to the common area of the village.

Dirk considered repositioning himself to observe how they were treated and where they were kept at night, but it was best to come back the next day. It wouldn't do to push his luck. He would have time enough as Nicholas sketched to learn more about the plight of the Montaukett women. Hunting grounds for the tribe were north of the camp and they wouldn't be moving anytime soon, so he was pretty certain the mapmaker would be safe. Besides, his orders said to guide him, and that he did. At least that was how he looked at it.

He rode half the night, and when he arrived back in camp the mapmaker sat much like he'd left him.

Nicholas looked up and smiled. "I thought you were lost."

"I was gone long enough, *ja*? Your maps? They are looking good?"

"*Ja.* I'm able to get much done here. It's difficult to sketch or write in the dark, but the stars are out and I've taken notes by firelight."

Dirk looked around the camp. "Have you eaten?"

"I was working and didn't think about it."

The mash from the night before still sat in the pot, a bit dried out, but warm over the fire. Dirk pulled a small slab of bacon from their provisions and fried it in a pan over the hot fire. A whiff of the meat as it crackled in the pan made his stomach growl and his mouth water. He broke up the crisp slices with a wooden spoon and stirred them into the mash, grease and all.

As he scraped the pot into two bowls, he considered telling Nicholas about his discovery of the Narragansett village and the Montaukett women, but he decided to wait until he had more time to observe them and form an opinion of what — if anything — could be done.

They sat next to the fire with their bowls and ate with only the rushing stream and noisy geese to break the silence. Eventually Nicholas looked at him. "Did you find what you were looking for?"

"Looking for?"

"*Ja*. Scouting. You were looking for something, weren't you?"

"Oh." His forehead wrinkled as he tried to measure what he would say. He liked this chap and didn't mind talking with him. Just how much he should say, he wasn't sure. "I'm trying to put behind, rather than trying to find, I suppose."

Nicholas looked at him like he was a bit daft. "What would you be putting behind?"

"A woman, of course. Isn't that always the case?" Dirk's wry grin spread.

His eyes lit up and he nodded. "Ah. And is she the pretty maid who packed the *poffertjes* for us before we left?"

"No, not the one." He raised his eyebrows, and a warm flush crept up his neck. "You would not know the lady. She is Heather Flower, the princess of Montauk."

It was the mapmaker's turn to raise his brow. "A princess?"

"*Ja*. Daughter of Wyandanch, Grand Sachem of Montauk. I was sent to find her when she was kidnapped and left for dead in these woods. When I did, I could not believe my eyes. She is beautiful, and regal, but much more than a princess. She is strong and tall like the reeds by the river, but her heart is tender and soft as the dandelion puff, though she tries not to show it. I fell in love with her, and I thought she might love me too."

Nicholas put his bowl down on a flat stone next to the fire. "How do you know she does not?"

"I could see how torn she was between her people, her friends, and me. It was not an easy choice for her, and indeed she could not make a choice. So I did. I let her go, and she walked away without looking back. I thought coming on this journey would take my mind away from her, but it doesn't. In fact, she is in my thoughts all the more."

"Well, then. Don't run from her. Go back. When we finish here, go find her."

Dirk stood and walked to the edge of the camp facing the deep woods. "No. I cannot do that. But there is something I can do for her. It will not win her heart, but it will bring her peace and joy. Just to see her smile will be sufficient. It is all my heart needs."

Nicholas fell quiet, and though that suited Dirk, their talk made him feel restored in some way. He wasn't sure exactly how, but it was good. *Ja?*

He was up early again the next morning. The abundance of little puff pancakes made Dirk shake his head as he put together their meal. He glanced at the mapmaker, studying the stars and taking notes. As he packed his dried apples, he looked back again at the many *poffertjes* and stuffed as many as he could in his knapsack. He slipped on some leather moccasins and saluted his goodbye. He was glad to set out from camp on Miss Button and knew exactly where he was going. He wanted to watch the Narragansett village from the time they started their day to the time they brought those women back for the night.

He left Miss Button a safe distance away. He walked in slow motion, his moccasins silent on the path. He inched his way toward the viewpoint he'd selected the day before. The wind picked up, whistling through limbs, and he was thankful it would keep all trace of his scent from the village below. He appreciated the cover noise too.

He squatted next to a large hickory and began his watch. It didn't take long before he saw the women leave the huts of their husbands and gather near the central fire. They cooked what looked like a samp, and the men and women did a dance of thanksgiving for the sun as it rose in the east. The captive women watched.

They served the village and only when the people finished eating were the women allowed to eat what was left. He strained to see how much that might be, but with just a bite or two, the women were done. After the area was cleaned, they were led out to the field. They fed their wolf dogs better than they were feeding those women.

He crept back to check on Miss Button. She could sleep standing anywhere. He gave her an appreciative pat and slid his knapsack off. He continued back to watch the fields where the women worked. He watched the men march down the path in the direction of their canoes with spears and nets in hand.

The women began again on a different section of the large field. How would they react if he walked into the field? Terrified, most likely. Still, he had to try. He had to make contact. These women were starving.

He couldn't just leave them. But he couldn't take them with him either. They'd be found and he and Nicholas strung up like pigs for a roasting before the end of the day.

He brought out a few *poffertjes* and started toward them one quiet step at a time. He guessed his hope was they'd see the food first. Lord help them to see the food he offered. As he closed in, a woman raised her eyes and froze. Her mouth was open but no sound came out.

"*Yeowdi.* Here." He stretched out his hand. "*Meech.* Eat it."

Her eyes were on the food, but she didn't move. Instead she called softly to the other women, something he did not understand. His hand shook a bit as he considered what could happen next.

The women crowded around him, and he said *"Meech"* again, holding his humble offering of food. They began to take the *poffertje* and eat, and tears gathered in the corners of the younger women's eyes. He wanted to tell them they needed to leave this place, but he didn't know how he could help them. Instead he put his finger to his lips and he left.

As he entered the cover of the woods he turned and watched them at work again, no trace of his contact with them left behind.

He tied his pack to the saddle and swung up on Miss Button with a heavy heart. He knew the whereabouts of the women. He knew how they were being treated. He just did not know how to fix it and he hated that helpless feeling. *Lord, if You want me to follow You, I'm ready. Show me the way,* he prayed.

24

April 10, 1654

Benjamin's boots crunched on the jingle shells as he reached Hallock's Landing, the name the founders had given the beach they'd landed on in 1638. He pulled his hat down over his eyes and his doublet a little closer as ice-cold raindrops pelted his face. The squall had not abated since the night before. Letting the hard earth soak up the rain was to their advantage before they began to plow, and his father had given him a rare day off. He was accustomed to working hard during planting season because once summer came his construction season went into full swing with no time to spare.

James showed up shortly, ready to row with him across the bay to Montauk. He preferred rowing and walking to taking Star on the ferry and across to Shelter Island, then another ferry over to the south fork. And it beat riding all the way around like he'd done last time he went to see Heather Flower.

He was bringing gifts of food from the bakeshop, but most likely they wouldn't survive the trip in this downpour. At least it wasn't windy and travel would be safe if not dry. His mind had been on Heather Flower ever since he'd left her. Mary knew that without asking and encouraged him to make the trip.

He placed the leather pouch in the bottom of the canoe and James handed him a paddle. They pushed off and worked their way swiftly across the water. When they reached the shore, they pulled the canoe up on the beach. Benjamin retrieved the bag and helped James turn the canoe over on the sand.

The two discussed everything from Johnny's latest adventure to how many sheep were in the town green as they trudged the wet sand path to Montauk. The downpour eased into a sprinkle, but Benjamin didn't notice. As they neared the shore, his thoughts were all on Heather Flower while he tried to keep up with the conversation with James.

The little boys playing at the edge of the village sprang from their hiding spots as they approached and pretended to take them prisoner, leading them to the center where the ladies sat scraping hides. Heather Flower sat off to the side stitching wampum a distance from them, and she jumped and ran to Benjamin with wide eyes.

"Everything is all right, we've come to visit." He shook his head and lowered his voice. "I couldn't stay away."

He held out the leather pouch and she took it and peeked inside. Her pouty smile showed her delight as she brought out the inner wrappings and carefully unfolded the crumbled but miraculously dry ginger cakes. "We must take these to Keme's mother. She has many children and it will make them much happy."

"There are crocks of honey too, for your mother. Take some to Keme's mother too."

He and James followed her to Keme's wigwam and were greeted by his mother with warm arms. Her face was wreathed in a smile as she accepted the gifts. She settled them near the fire pit, and they told her stories of Southold. Her sons gathered and listened too, and nibbled on the sweet treats.

Later James went to seek out Keme's father, and Benjamin and Heather Flower took the honey to her mother. She donned a warm blanket, and they went for a walk up to the bluff of sand on the very tip of the south fork. They sat and stared at the gray ocean; Benjamin occasionally picked up a clam shell and tossed it as far as he could, its splash lost to the crash of waves.

"I can't wait for you to come back to Southold. Everyone asks about you."

"I miss them, my friend."

"How are you now? Is it helping to be home?"

"I think it helps, but I have moments when the memories haunt me. My brother brought me across the water to visit Grissell on Shelter Island and that was good to be with her for a time."

His arm stopped midair, shell in hand. "You are friends with Grissell?"

"Yes, you know Pogaticut, my uncle, lives there. When Grissell came to the island we met. She is very friendly to me."

A cold, wet wind sprung up and stung their cheeks with sand, and they turned their backs to it and scooted closer. She pulled her soft doeskin tunic over her leggings. He settled the blanket around her and took her hand. "You know they are friendly with a lot of people, and not always those we would want to have living near us."

"What do you mean, Benjamin?"

"They are friendly to Quakers. Some even suspect the Sylvesters are Quakers themselves."

"And what is a Quaker? What is bad about them?"

"Oh, they are good enough people, but they persist in coming into our communities to preach their own beliefs, and they don't always agree with ours. There's plenty of space for them to go and establish their own communities with their own beliefs." He gently squeezed her hand. "Grissell and Nathaniel are good people. They attend our church in Southold and they don't stir up trouble. But we know they allow Quakers who are threatened with imprisonment up north to come and stay until they can figure out where they are going next. I don't think it is a good idea for you to be staying with her."

She drew back, her eyes huge, fiery black opals. "I do not see what is wrong for her to give shelter to people who are in need. And I do not see what is wrong for her to be my friend. I am surprised by you."

He smoothed her hair as wisps escaped her braids in the wind, and ran his fingers down to her chin. "I'm sorry. I don't mean it to sound like I'm forbidding you to see her."

"But it does sound like that. *Nenertah,* that is mine to decide. Does it surprise you if I say that I'd already decided not to go back to stay with her? It makes me sad, but when I stayed with her, I knew we walked different paths. Her world is not my world. She is my friend and always will be, but I will not stay in her world."

A sigh escaped him. "Well, that's good and I guess that takes care of that. I regret I made it a concern when it is not." He pulled her close, the blanket rough to his touch.

They sat for a long time, huddled together until the biting sand was too much. They stood without a word and silently walked back, against the wind, to Montauk. The savory scent of turkey greeted them as they entered the village. Women tended the fires, protecting the flames from the weather as the meal cooked. Small packets of corn were nestled in the coals and pots of rabbit and squirrel stew sat on the rocks near the many fire pits.

"You and James must eat with us and stay the night. It is dangerous for you to cross the bay in this storm."

He didn't need much urging. He felt a strain between them and welcomed the chance to make amends for his thoughtless comments. James was distressed to not make it home to Abigail and Misha, but agreed his wife would rather have him safe.

Wyandanch and Wuchi were happy to share their wigwam, but Heather Flower remained aloof and let her parents entertain their guests with conversation. Benjamin lay awake on his pallet, listening to the cadence of rain and whoosh of wind throughout the long night. With dawn the storm broke and he and James prepared to return home.

But the firestorm in her eyes did not diminish and he took her by the hand and led her to the place where she worked with her beads. They stood apart. "You have something on your mind and I think you should tell me before I leave, Heather Flower."

"My thoughts are mixed, my friend. I am troubled by the words you spoke yesterday. It is the white man's way to rule the woman. But it is not my way. I came to my home to heal, and I think to do that I must ask you to go. I need a time to think about us."

Her words cut like sharp-edged obsidian. His throat clenched as he answered. "Are you saying you don't want me, Heather Flower?" He didn't want to hear the answer.

"I will always be grateful that you saved my brother. But I do not think we should plan marriage. Now go. I do not like to cry when someone sees me." She turned away from him.

He wanted to take her in his arms. If he left now, would he ever see her again? Would she cut her world, her Montauk world, off from his? "I will do as you ask, but I pray it is not the last time we speak. That would tear me apart."

He said his goodbyes to her family, grateful no one spoke of the tension between him and Heather Flower. With James well on his way to the canoe, Benjamin's stride was swift as he left the village, the possibility that he would not see her again piercing his heart with every step.

It was his father's generation who held a strong belief that they must keep those who professed a different faith out of Southold. They had suffered much in their homeland and wanted the peace of worshiping in their own way, without interference. But were they not on the verge of treating others in the same manner that they had been? It was something he and Joseph and Johnny had discussed from time to time, and they agreed it might be time for change.

But was that the issue between him and Heather Flower? Or did she hide deeper fears? She didn't like it when he cautioned her about Grissell, and he wasn't certain if she'd been more upset because he'd said the Sylvesters were sympathetic to the

Quakers, or if it sounded like he was telling her what to do. Was that her fear? That if she married him, she would lose her voice? Her fierce independence?

25

April 15, 1654

Benjamin stood in the field. It was manuring season, not a pleasant task. But with the whole clan, it would go quickly. Even Mary was out today, Abigail left in charge of Hannah and little Sarah.

Winnie had come to help them, as she did most years, and she would take some of the bounty home with her, come harvest. She was not herself though, and Mary worried she was declining since Heather Flower left.

Patience and Lizzie worked in the bakeshop and planned a hearty dinner for the planters when they came in at noon.

He paused behind the manure sled and ran his fingers through his hair as he scanned the field. Carrots and onions would go in this field, and he figured it would take about ten cords of manure to do the planting properly.

His mother worked side by side with Jane.

They gathered stones into their aprons from the broken earth, then hauled them over to the edge and the already tall pile. Joseph had married well. Jane's father was well respected and Jane was not afraid of physical work. Not that any of the women around here had a choice.

Heather Flower was another story. She was raised as a princess. Not expected to lift a finger. That was one reason he fell in love with her. She didn't have to do a thing, and yet she was always the first one to lend a hand, to brighten someone's day if she could, like she did for Winnie.

He needed to stop thinking of her. He watched Joseph make his way through the rough dirt with shovels and hoes and walked up to meet him halfway. Barnabas had Starlight in a harness and the old horse plodded behind him. They waited for their father to catch up.

Caleb and Joshua grabbed shovels and the four started flinging the smelly compost over the ruts. They'd worked their way down one row behind Mary and Jane, and Barnabas led Starlight as she pulled the sled to the next row. Rachel and Ruth followed behind with hoes to spread the manure.

They were halfway through the field when a bolt of lightning zigzagged through the sky and hit a large maple tree with a loud clap. The bark from the trunk flew off in huge chunks and a thin line of smoke snaked from the center, scenting the air with a burning wood smell that was odd and not at all like the smoke that filled a room from the hearth.

The rocks tumbled from the women's aprons as they flung their arms over their heads with screams that rivaled the rumbles. With a hearty chortle, the Horton men grabbed the women and pushed them toward the house as the rain battered down and more lightning danced between thunderheads.

Barnabas raised his face to the rain as it began to pelt the earth and everything in between. "An early thunderstorm brings a fine growing season." And his rich baritone sang out a "Hallelujah!"

They charged through the back door to the bakeshop and stood dripping puddles like yesterday's wash. Rachel and Ruth began shivering as Lizzie and Patience stood, mouths agape before they ran to find rags and blankets.

Barnabas went straight for the kitchen rags and began mopping Mary's face, hair, and arms. She laughed and pushed back on the cloth, but let him tend to her.

After they had dried off, they warmed themselves in front of the fire and Lizzie gave them mugs of hot broth to sip. Mary set hers aside to help her sister and Patience bring the meal to the long tables. She carried steaming bowls of stewed rabbit seasoned with wild onion and dried sage, while Patience tucked early lettuce around slabs of cold venison. Lizzie pulled crusty loaves of bread from the oven and placed them on the sideboard, along with chunks of cheese and fresh churned butter.

Abigail and the younger Horton children, along with little Misha, joined the family near the fire. Barnabas picked up the old family Bible to read a Scripture and led a prayer of thanksgiving for the food prepared, the family and friends gathered, the good earth, and the mighty rain.

Benjamin picked up Hannah and swung her into her spot at the worn oak table, hauled over so long ago from England. She squirmed and he stepped back and folded his arms. Joseph led Jonathan to the place next to her and she grinned at the chance to sit near her big brother.

Joseph straightened and drummed his finger on the corner where a *B* was scratched, encircled with a heart.

Benjamin nudged him with his shoulder.

"Takes you back, doesn't it?"

His brother's face was serious, but his words gave way to myriad emotions. "We had a mother who loved us, didn't we? Sometimes when we're all gathered it can bother me that there are only three people here who even knew her. But then, I look around and think how wonderful this family is, how we've grown, and how much we've been given, and I know how blessed we are to have had it all. Mother, Mary, the whole Horton tribe." He rolled his eyes. "But I'm not the sentimental one, now am I?"

The Horton chortle erupted between the two brothers and everyone turned.

Joseph cleared the space between him and Mary in three long strides. "In the spring when we are planting, I always feel a gratefulness to you." His eyes sought hers and his arm slipped about her shoulders. "I look at the apple blossoms and think back to how you entrusted me with your little pippin tree at a time I was so angry with everyone, especially you. Planting that little twig and caring for it as I watched it grow somehow gave me a connection to you that I cannot explain. I only know that I've grown right along with the pippin in my love for you."

Mary's hazel eyes pooled until they looked blue. She smiled and kissed his cheek. "Thank you, Jay. It's so good to hear you say that."

The room was silent except for Hannah's chatter to Jonathan and the insistent patter of rain on the steep roof.

Benjamin heaved in a big breath. "Very well, then. I say we eat. Talk about planting, there's much to do, and as long as there is no more lightning, we'll be back out there after dinner rain or no."

They would work up a sweat before they caught their death of cold. Indeed, the rain would feel good by the time their work was done.

Though his muscles ached, the hard work took his mind from Heather Flower, and Benjamin worked late in the fields with his father and brothers to accomplish as much as they could before the Sabbath. The muddy smell of their labors clung to their clothes and skin, and they retired to their respective homes and rooms to shed sodden clothes, damp-mop their skin with rags, and put on dry shirts and breeches.

Mary stayed in to prepare food that would take them through the evening on the morrow, with Patience, Winnie, and Jane joining in to help her.

Benjamin and Barnabas trudged across the road to the church. Tonight would be a town meeting, with all men in attendance. They entered and sat in their box pew at the front of the hall. Reverend Youngs sat at the clerk's desk next to the pulpit, and Joseph sat on his left, ready to write the notes of the meeting.

John Budd and his two eldest sons sat in their pew across from the Hortons. Benjamin craned his neck and watched as the Wells brothers settled in their pew box.

When the townsmen were assembled, the reverend cleared his throat. The change in Reverend Youngs the last month saddened Benjamin. Johnny hadn't been heard of in over two months, and the possibility that he'd been murdered by one of the Connecticut tribes couldn't be ruled out.

Reverend Youngs stood and went to the podium. He put his hands on either side and leaned into it. "We've some information that leads us to believe my son is held prisoner in New Amsterdam. While I am grateful to know he most likely is alive, there is no way to know he is well. Or what they might do to him before they are done."

Silence fell among the men. Benjamin glanced at his father's grim face. He looked older than when they walked in. He was certain his first thought was thanks be to God it was not one of his own sons.

Barnabas stood up. His arms crossed as he looked down at Benjamin, then swung around to look at his good friend. "John, when something like this happens to any of our children, it's like it has happened to my own. I know you'd feel the same if it were Joseph or Benjamin. I say we send the horse troop out to get some information. You know how it is out in Hempstead. They don't think much of Stuyvesant. They tell us more than we need to hear, they're so anxious to complain."

"I warned Johnny there was only trouble to be had if he kept going out there." His tone was soft, but his voice shook.

Joseph stood now. "Have you told Margaret?" Jane and Margaret were close friends.

"Aye. I told her right before I came over. She's taking it hard. Her parents are just sick. I'd told Johnny he needed to settle down for Margaret's sake, if not for his mother's."

"If there's anything we can do, tell us. Don't be afraid to ask." Barnabas paced.

"Father, we cannot sit and wait for him to be released. I'll get the word out tonight that we leave for Hempstead in the morning." Benjamin looked at his brother. "You agree?"

"I'll be there."

After the meeting the two brothers left Barnabas deep in conversation with the reverend and crossed the road toward the Horton house. They paused outside to finalize their plans for the morning.

Joseph stood with his fists at his sides and looked down at his boots. "You know, we should just keep on pushing through to New Amsterdam. Run them out of there."

Benjamin scanned the dark sky. The air was thick like it would pour any moment. What about Dirk? And why should he care? He cared because Heather Flower would be devastated if something happened to him. She'd care about Johnny too, if she knew he was missing. "I don't know. I agree we will never be at peace with the Dutch. But I'm not sure now would be the time to attack. Not while they have Johnny. And we don't even know for sure they do. We're just going on a field expedition."

Joseph studied his brother's face and rolled his eyes. "You are sounding like Father. But I think there is more to it than what you are saying. You don't care what happens to the lieutenant, do you? I mean, you'd just as soon have him out of the picture, true?"

Benjamin just stood there.

"You can't let a woman get to you like that. Not when you are making decisions about the safety of everyone else. You are in the militia."

He started up the flagstone toward the door. "You don't have to tell me that. I'm quite aware. I just don't think we have to react with our guns just yet. That should never be our first course of action."

"Very well, we'll ride out in the morning for Hempstead. But if we find they've got Johnny, I say we go after him."

He watched his big brother walk up the road to the Budd house before he pushed open the door. The young ones would be asleep. Mary sat in the little mahogany rocker Elizabeth had brought over from England, and worked on a piece of embroidery. She looked up and smiled.

"That was a short meeting. Where is your father?"

"He's talking to Reverend Youngs. Word is Johnny might be held by the Dutch in New Amsterdam."

She stopped rocking and her eyes flew open. "Why would they do that?"

"He's been up in Connecticut with

Captain Scott trying to raise trouble with the Indians, keep them from getting between us and the Dutch." He picked up the iron rod and sparks flew up from the logs he poked at in the fireplace. Small flames began to lick around the logs casting a warm glow.

She gazed at the fire and shook her head. "What does that mean?"

He sat in the chair opposite her with his hands on his knees. "You know the Dutch have been giving the Indians firearms. Johnny just wants to be sure our interests are not compromised and the natives don't interfere."

"Ben, are we at war with the Dutch or not? I cannot keep up." A smile played on her lips, but her eyes gave her away. She was serious.

"You've a right to be confused, Mother. Word travels slowly, even to New Haven. Father has been elected to be deputy to the court, and I think he will be well suited to help them get things sorted out, eh? But I think the latest rumors are that we are at peace, though most of us do not accept that."

"I think your father would like to. And Reverend Youngs. 'Tis you young whippersnappers who cannot." Her soft laughter erupted like the tinkle of a bell.

"Joseph and I will ride out at dawn with the horse troop. We'll just be out gathering information about Johnny's whereabouts."

"But that is dangerous, is it not?"

He stood up and bent to kiss her cheek. "It's nothing to worry about, Mother. We'll just be nosing around, staying out of trouble."

"Why take the whole troop then?"

He walked toward the stairs. "We don't want to wind up like Johnny, I guess. We'll be safe."

He entered his room and the wood floor creaked. He paused at the foot of his siblings' bed. They slept soundly, and he moved to his bed and sank to his knees. He wished Heather Flower was not so far away. If he could but talk to her and tell her what was planned. But then, would she care what he had to say? He doubted it. She was already upset with him. This would just add to it and seal his fate with her. Joseph's comment shattered his reverie. He should not be thinking of her. His brother was right. It would interfere with what they needed to do. He prayed for safe travels and God's presence for the morrow. They would need it. Lord be with them.

26

April 17, 1654

Winnie welcomed the ride with Abigail and James. Little Misha cuddled with her in the back of the wagon as it made its way over the bumps and ruts. She used to ride with Mary over this same trail after Jeremy brought Starlight over from England. How she'd loved the feeling of freedom sailing across the countryside, holding tight as Mary expertly guided the horse.

Heather Flower had come to visit only once since she'd returned home, so Winnie did her best to make the trip to Mary's Wednesday ladies meeting whenever she could. Often she walked, but today James had some supplies he wanted to deliver and they offered to bring her back with them.

James turned on the bench. "Do you know that the Southold troops rode west yesterday morning?"

Winnie looked up from Misha. "No, why?

Where are they going?"

Abigail spoke up. "They are riding to Hempstead to find out about the disappearance of Johnny Youngs."

"I knew he was gone a long time, but how do they know he disappeared?"

The wagon hit a rock and Abigail grabbed the backboard. James stretched out his arm to secure her. When it stopped rocking, he glanced back to see if Winnie and Misha were all right. "They've gotten news that he might be a prisoner in New Amsterdam. The boys are just out scoutin'."

They rumbled into town, splattering mud with the wheels. It'd been a wet April so far, with heavy clouds still cloistering the sky. As they pulled in front of the Horton house, a few fat drops fell.

James hopped down and raised his arms for Abigail. She landed softly and turned for Misha as he helped Winnie out. "All right, ladies. Have a good time with Aunt Mary." He kissed the baby's hair, then climbed back up. "I'll be back to get you before supper."

Mary heard the wagon and pulled open the door. Her apron was dusted with flour and the scent of dough greeted her guests. "Come in, come in. 'Tis starting to rain again. Don't get wet."

She smiled at Misha, and the little girl held out her arms and fell into Mary's. "Ah, sweet girl. Come to Auntie."

Abbey helped Winnie off with her cloak and hung their outer garments by the fire to dry as they all moved back to the big kitchen.

Lizzie placed dough mounds on the peel to transfer into the hot oven, and Patience, with Hannah by her feet, bounced Sarah on her lap.

"Good morrow, Abigail. Winnie, so good to see you." Lizzie wiped her hands on her apron and gave each of the ladies a hug.

Patience stood and kissed Winnie's cheek, then turned so the older woman could kiss baby Sarah's cheek too. Hannah waited and was showered with hugs and kisses.

"*Aquai,* friends. I am always glad to be here." Winnie's smile was hesitant. "Is it true the Dutch have Johnny?"

Mary's eyes glistened and she blinked. There was quiet for a moment and she set Misha down next to Patience. She picked up her apron and dabbed at the corner of her eye. "Well, yes. It might be. Jay and Ben left yesterday to find out. They took the whole horse troop, so I think they expect trouble. Of course, they won't tell me that.

They make light of it. I've a pile of breeches here for mending, if you all don't mind helping me with them. I thought we could work on them in between putting the bread in the oven. Lizzie and I worked half the night and all morning getting the dough ready."

Winnie picked up the first pair and sat next to Patience. "I need something to sew. It is calm to my soul."

"Good. I'll fetch the Bible and we'll start with our prayer and a Scripture." When she returned with the Bible, she sat opposite Lizzie. She opened to Proverbs 29:25. "Barnabas read this to me last night when I told him how afraid I was for our sons to be going into Dutch territory. He reminded me they'd been there before and God always went with them. Here's what it says: 'Fear of others will prove to be a snare, but whoever trusts in the Lord is kept safe.' "

She looked up. The angst that had veiled their faces faded and she was encouraged to lead them in prayers.

At her "amen" Winnie raised her eyes. "I feel stronger, Mary, thank you. And I know I must tell Momoweta to send a smoke signal to Wyandanch. We will get the word to our people to keep them safe. We are sisters, I will send out the word they go in peace."

"Thank you. You've always been the wise, strong one of our group, Winnie, and I want you to know how glad we are to have you back." She wasn't convinced the men went in peace, but certainly the object of their discontent was the Dutch. "Ben didn't say it, but Jay told me before they left that he's concerned about Heather Flower's reaction to this."

"Why?"

"I suppose because she knows how he feels about the young lieutenant, Dirk. Ben is one of the sweetest men I know. He always has been. But with Dirk I'm sure it's the competition over Heather Flower. He'd never admit it, though. I wish I could help him. But you know how love is."

Lizzie's laughter erupted. "Little sister, you are the last person I would expect to hear that from. Prithee, tell me all about love."

Mary could feel the warmth of blush flood her cheeks. "Only that it took me a long time to find it, did it not?"

They all laughed and stitched for a while in silence. Mary kept her eyes on her work. Were they all lost in their own reverie about love, or were they all thinking about the years she craved Barney's love and he could not give it? Goodness, it felt like a long time ago now, but an eternity while she went through it.

Lizzie made amends. "I will say, Benjamin would be a wonderful husband. Any girl would be blessed to have him. I don't know what Anna Budd was thinking when she married that Tucker boy."

Patience grinned. "Benjamin is a shy one. Nothing wrong with that, but it leaves the girls not sure if he has an interest, so they go with the ones that show them they do." She bounced Sarah. "Don't we, Sarah? 'Tis what we do, isn't it, little one?"

Mary gave her a dour look, very reminiscent of Lizzie's when she lectured. "Do not teach my poppet about love, Patience. And Ben is not shy. Not in the least. He's a gentleman and the girls should appreciate that."

"Oh, they do, Mary. But they also want to be wed, so they marry the first boy that asks. 'Tis just the way it is. Nothing bad about Benjamin at all."

Lizzie set the breeches down in her lap. "Then how is it that you haven't married, Patience? Many a man has asked you. We all know that."

Mary looked at her, waiting for her

friend's answer, but she knew what she would say. Patience returned her look.

"When I was a child, I dreamed of marrying Barnabas. But of course he was married to Ann and then to Mary. You know Barnabas — there's really no other man like him. When Mary and I became friends, I made a vow to myself I would not marry unless the man who asked me could measure up to Barnabas. And I have not given up my vow." She breathed out like she had been holding it.

Mary's eyes crinkled as she smiled at her friend. She twisted a stray curl with her finger. "I know you have always felt that way, and you are right — Barney is an honorable man who has known much pain, but he learned to trust God with it. Thank you, my friend. Those are kind words and I pray you find the man who is right for you and will love you with all of his heart. You deserve that."

Mary caught the look Lizzie and Winnie exchanged. She raised her brow. "Well, you've known for a long time how Patience and I feel. 'Tis nothing new to you, now is it?"

The smell of baked bread permeated the room, and Lizzie jumped up. "I almost forgot." She threw open the oven door and

Mary got up to help her.

The bread was golden — another minute, it might have burned — but they brought out loaves baked to perfection. They used kitchen rags to move them to the table. Abigail got up and stirred the stew that simmered in the pot and took bowls from the shelf above the sideboard. "James will be here soon to pick us up, Aunt Mary."

"Stay for supper. We've plenty, and with Jay and Ben gone, Barney would enjoy James's company."

Before long Barney came in from the field with Caleb and all eyes were on him. "Heigh-ho. What's this, pray thee? Do I have mud on my face?" He rubbed his forearm across his brow.

Mary tiptoed and kissed his cheek, but stayed clear of his dirty clothes. "Nay. We just appreciate you, Barney. We love you."

"Very well, then." He wiggled his eyebrows and chortled and everyone joined the laugh.

James arrived, and after prayers and Scripture they ate fresh bread with the pottage left from dinner.

Zeke had ridden out with the boys, and now Lizzie walked home with Patience. It was chilly, but they had their cloaks. Winnie and Abigail climbed into the wagon, and Mary handed Misha to them. James shook hands with Barney, who clapped him on the back.

Mary stood back and watched them leave. Winnie would spread the word to her people and that would be a good thing for Ben and Jay. But what about Heather Flower? Where would her emotions take her? To Ben? Or would she be worried about Dirk? Was Dirk one of those men Patience was talking about? The kind who won the girl because they were not shy about saying what was on their mind? She'd never thought of Benjamin as shy. Why, he was just polite, was he not?

27

April 20, 1654

Sarah lay in her basket, close enough to the fire to keep warm, but far from stray sparks. Abbey would be here soon to take her upstairs for a nap.

Mary stood on a box and stretched to bring down the carved wooden candy molds. Most of her molds were from France, presents from Jeremy. But her two favorite were carved out of walnut wood by Jay. She gathered up the sugar loaf and shears and spread everything out on the old oak table. Today she and Lizzie would make sugar candy.

She set out several dozen eggs and a red-ware bowl as Hannah climbed up on the bench to be her helper. She brought out a small wooden pestle and mortar and began to grind the almonds that the boys had hulled for her the evening before.

Lizzie arrived in a flurry of kisses for her

nieces, and soon they were up to their elbows in whipped egg whites. She saved the yolks to mix into a pudding for supper. Hannah got to stir as Mary snipped the sugar with her silver sugar shears and Lizzie poured it into the egg whites. They worked the ground almonds in with their hands, and Hannah had to be reminded to save licking her fingers until after they patted the candy into the molds.

Abbey came in with Misha, and after sampling the confections, she picked up a sleepy Sarah and took the little ones upstairs. Hannah held onto her skirt and looked back at the candy making with big tears as she followed Abbey upstairs. "Come, little one. There will be plenty of sugar for you after a nap."

Mary blew a kiss to her little girl and then brought out the cross-buns Barney had baked. His beautiful manchet loaves and ginger cakes were hard to match. He was the baker, but she was the sugar-baker and spring was a busy candy-making time. Lizzie arranged the candies on wooden trays.

The chilly spring morning turned into a warm afternoon, and with dinner behind them and a good portion of the sales done, the two women mopped their damp brows.

Lizzie smoothed her salt and pepper

tendrils that curled about her face. "Do you have any news from the boys?"

Mary took a couple of the sugar crumbs and dropped them into steaming mugs of water with sprigs of mint. She handed one to Lizzie and they wandered to the front parlor. Her eyes took on a watery blue tint. "We haven't heard from them or anyone in the horse troop. But we didn't really expect to. I pray for them every day."

"How was Benjamin doing before he left? Does he miss Heather Flower?"

"Oh, yes. But we all do. I think this is good for her, to be at home with her people. She needs the time to find what's in her heart and maybe Ben does too. When he came back from Montauk the last time, he was very quiet about her and seemed to want the separation."

Lizzie sat opposite Mary. "What if her heart is for Dirk?"

"I fear her family would disown her. Certainly Ben and Jay would be unhappy. And Johnny too. I don't know what they would do. But I think she must follow her heart, do you not agree?"

Lizzie nodded. "Of course she must."

"I mean, look at Patience. We all have wanted for years for her to find someone to share her life with. But she shares her life with us, and God fills every need she has. She teaches young girls and sometimes the boys. She has found purpose and fulfillment in that, and is in her own way following her heart."

"That may be true, but just the same, do you remember how much you wanted a baby? It seemed you wanted to follow your heart but God had something different in mind. At least for a time."

Tears pricked at Mary's eyes as she thought back over the years. It wasn't just a baby she longed for, it was Barney's love. And she thought she could get both all on her own. "The lesson there was we need to seek God in all that we desire. Barney and I have been blessed, but not because of anything we did."

"Do you think Heather Flower might never marry then?"

Mary sipped her minty water and looked at Lizzie over the rim of her mug. "I think God will fill her needs. And if a husband is that, He will do it in His own time, do you not agree?"

Her sister's silvery laugh filled the room. "Yes, I believe that, but 'tis such fun to try to figure it out too. And you know you long for Benjamin to marry."

Mary bubbled with laughter too. "True.

But for a man, a good wife keeps him out of trouble. And continues the generations, and the family name. I know Ben loved Anna very much, and I know he has had a special place in his heart for Heather Flower since they were young. I just don't know —"

The small bell at the back kitchen door rang as someone entered the bakeshop, and Mary and Lizzie hurried to greet their customer.

"Oh, Patience, I'm glad you're here." Mary gave her a warm hug and stepped back to allow Lizzie a hug too. "We are sipping a mint tea. Would you like some?"

"I would love some."

Mary handed her a mug with the cooled beverage, and she sipped as they moved to the long oak table.

"I heard the weaver is making his way through Southold next week and thought you might like to know. We might want to all get together and sort our thread and plan what we'd like made up."

Lizzie's violet-blue eyes lit up. "Yes. And do you think he shall have some news? He's been all over by the time he makes it here. I so love it when he tells us what's been going on over in Southhampton."

Mary put up her hand to stifle the gossip

she knew would follow. "I thought you were going to talk to him about getting your own loom? Are you still entertaining the idea of a hat shop?"

"Oh yes, I am. Do you think Heather Flower would like to help me? She does such beautiful beading."

Mary thought a bit. "Perhaps. I would love for her to become more involved with our town. That might be the way to encourage her."

Patience raised her eyebrows. "Encourage her to what?"

Mary wagged her finger at her friend with a grin and a tsk. "Oh, 'tis not what you think." But then again, why not?

Mary sat down to pen her candy recipe into her book.

MARCHPANE CANDY

Two pounds almonds
Two pounds snipped sugar
Two dozen whipped egg whites
Rosewater

But her thoughts drifted to Heather Flower and she didn't finish. Her obsession with finding a place for Heather Flower in their community went beyond her desire for

Winnie's niece to fit in. She didn't want Ben to be hurt, so perhaps if she could give them opportunity to see each other, the feelings they'd always had for each other could grow.

Not all the townspeople would agree with her. Certainly Patience and Lizzie would. But many of her neighbors felt that intermarrying was not right. Indeed, they would just as soon the natives pack up and move westward, deeper into the forest. But she didn't feel that God had called them here to drive out the people He'd already planted. And surely they were all the same in God's eyes. Heather Flower's parents felt much the same way as some of the townspeople, though for perhaps different reasons. They worried about diluting their heritage, losing their identity.

Both Sarah and Hannah napped, so she wandered to the apple orchard, now dotted with pink and white blossoms, and settled beneath her cornerstone tree.

If marriage for Ben and Heather Flower was meant to be, they would find the way. She reminded herself "in God's time." *Not my time nor my will, dear Lord, but Yours. Amen.*

The new grass rustled and she looked up to see Barney standing next to her. He lowered himself to the ground. "Abbey said

I'd find you out here. Unloading your troubles to God?" His smile spread and she smiled in return.

"This little tree has always reminded me to be strong. God's given me some good answers and some blessings while sitting right here." The afternoon sunshine felt good on her face and she turned her eyes heavenward. Should she share what was on her mind? Or would he think she was meddling?

"There are rumors going around."

"Oh?"

"Aye. I've heard you favor a wedding for Benjamin and Heather Flower."

She giggled and leaned into his shoulder as he wrapped an arm about her. "There's been no secret in that."

"True. But if I know Benjamin, there will be no courting unless he's certain her feelings for that Dutchman have cooled. He was burned by Anna's fickle feelings. It's made him cautious, which is not a bad thing. Mayhap his mission to western Long Island will be the test. He was worried Heather Flower's concerns would be with Van Buren. We shall see."

"I don't want misunderstandings to keep two people who love each other apart. But then again, I don't want Ben hurt."

"Whether it's misunderstanding or circumstance, it's nothing you can change." He leaned into her and kissed her forehead.

Abbey came out with Sarah on her hip and Hannah running beside her. Mary opened her arms as her little girl tumbled into them. "Ah, and here's two of my biggest little blessings. Did you have a good sleep?"

"Yes, Mama." She blinked her eyes up and down and giggled.

Barney chuckled. "She reminds me of the young girl that I used to give ginger cakes to back in Mowsley. She looks just like you, my sweet."

Mary hugged her close as Abbey lowered Sarah to Barney's arms. It didn't take long for their littlest to start squirming. "Here, Hannah, Mama must get up." She stood and took Sarah into her arms as Abbey chased Hannah around the orchard. "I'll take her in. She's a hungry little girl, but so good." She walked toward the back kitchen door. Barney was right. There wasn't anything she could do. But she could pray.

28

April 22, 1654

Heather Flower lay on her mat near the fire waiting for daybreak. She listened to the rhythmic breathing of her parents and brother and wondered how they could sleep. They'd had smoke signals and runners with much news. The Southold horse troop had gone west and trouble was in the air. The reverend's son might be held captive by the Dutch. It was Momoweta's wish that the English party be treated with respect, and in the event of a skirmish with the Dutch, the tribes were to support the Hortons and their troop.

Had Momoweta forgotten the land belonged to no one? They were all caretakers of Mother Earth. How could they forbid one people over another their right to walk the land?

Tears trickled down her temple to the mat below. She never wept in front of her family

317

and especially not in front of the paleface who showed their emotions so freely. But in the dark, with the earth and those who walked it asleep, she allowed herself to let them flow.

How could her heart be so torn? She feared for Dirk. But she feared for Joseph and Benjamin, and the other men riding with them too. They had gone into enemy territory with their fire sticks. Did they not know how dangerous that would be, for surely Dirk's people would not tolerate them if they did have Johnny. He would not hurt anyone, she knew that. But his countrymen could.

The thought of Dirk brought a wave of emotion and she clenched her eyes shut and tried to squeeze back the tears. Her throat burned like a hot rock lodged in it, and her stomach was sick, though she'd refused to eat food since she heard the news.

Her mother talked of nothing but the young warriors who attempted to woo her and bring her wampum gifts. They came day after day and would sit for hours in the center of their fort, playing their flutes and hoping she would accept their gifts. But she always spurned them, and her mother left no doubt that she was unhappy with her. But what could she do? Every time she imagined a wedding here on these sacred grounds, she wanted to flee. She wanted to climb in her brother's canoe and paddle to Southold.

But to whom would she run? Winnie. It would have to be Winnie because she did not know which of these two blond-haired, blue-eyed men she could give her heart to. But now both were in jeopardy and it frightened her in a way she could not imagine.

She'd approached her father after the smoke signals were received and reminded him Dirk had found her and brought her back. He acknowledged that, but he told her their allegiance to the English was much stronger. It had been her father's friend, Lion Gardiner, who had paid the ransom. The Southold horse troop had been willing to travel to Connecticut to get her, but when Ninigret went back on his word, the Dutchman Van Buren had volunteered to find her. Yes, he was grateful to the man, but no, his allegiance was to the English.

Heather Flower could not lie still any longer. She rose quietly and softly padded out of their wigwam. She walked until she was at the shore, with only the Peconic Bay between her and Southold. The night was warm for April and the clouds had parted, leaving stars that danced like tiny rush lights in the moonless sky.

She could not stay here while her mind filled with worry over Benjamin and Dirk. She needed to be close when news came so she could learn their fate. When the sun brought the day, she would tell her mother she must go. Wyancombone would take her across. She looked at his canoe, tied to the reeds. How easy it would be to leave in it now, without the words she would have with her mother. Her brother would be angry she took his canoe, but he had friends who would gladly come across the bay to help him retrieve it.

She released the tether and slid her leg over the side. With both hands she balanced the canoe and swung herself in. She picked up the paddle from the blackened bottom and quietly dipped it into the water. She pulled at the water and began to glide. Pull, glide. Pull, glide. She skimmed across the surface like a water bug. She went around Shelter Island — she could not face Grissell. Her friend would beg her stay, and this she could not do.

The canoe finally beached on the agate-strewn beach of Hallock's landing. She took the tether and pulled it as far as she could out of the chilly water, then wound the leather strap around a large piece of log. She started up the road toward the town green. It would be a long walk to the Corchaug fort, but she was determined.

The sky to the east was a faint gray and she wanted to be through the town before it was light enough to be seen. She picked up her pace. As she neared the Horton house, she saw Barnabas with a hoe over his shoulder heading to his fields. She ducked behind a large chestnut tree and waited for him to be gone. It was good most of the men had left with Joseph and Benjamin. Fewer out and about, like Barnabas.

She avoided more homes by taking the trails through Indian Neck. She picked up her pace after Dickerson Creek. She came to the palisade around the fort and rushed through to Winnie's wigwam. This was more of a home to her now than where she grew up. She whispered at the door, "Winnie."

She feared her aunt would be upset with her, but when she came to the door, Winnie's tears were accompanied with a smile and a hug that swept Heather Flower into the room. The wolf dogs did circles around the two, welcoming her back as well.

"What are you doing here, my child?"

"I — I was with my father when the smoke signals were seen. I heard of the troubles with the Dutch. I didn't know what to do. Have you heard anything more?" She struggled to look calm, serene as befit her station, but her inner voice was crying out.

"No. I think there are troubles, but I don't know anything more. Come sit." She pulled her down by the fire. "Is it Dirk you worry about?"

"You know me well, my aunt, yes. But I worry for all of the men too. For Benjamin and Joseph, and the troops that go with them."

Winnie nodded. "We all worry. But you know, if anything happens to the Southold men, Dirk would be arrested the minute he came near you. You must give up on him. You must not think of him." She stood. "Let me get you food. You must eat something."

Heather Flower got up. "No, I'm not hungry. I cannot think of food. I'm going down to the river."

"I'll go with you."

"No, please, Aunt. I must go by myself. I need to think. I need to mourn the loss of another love."

Winnie put her arms around her. "You cannot mourn a love you never had."

She pushed away for fear Winnie would see the tears. She hurried out the door and through the gate, down the path. As she neared the clearing where she last saw Dirk, she hoped he would be there waiting. Had he ever returned to this spot? Had he ever waited for her and she hadn't come? He might have and given up.

She saw the young Corchaug runner who had delivered Dirk's message the day she and Winnie walked back from Mary's house, and a thought struck her. She must warn Dirk of the troops. It was the only way she could be sure he'd be safe. "*Muckachuck,* come here."

He grinned and walked over.

"Do you remember the man who gave you a message to give to me?"

"Yes, he was nice."

"Would you take a message to him for me? To meet once again at the tulip tree? I will give you a wampum bead."

"I can do that. I would do that for you without wampum." He smiled at her.

"I know, but I can't ask you to do that without payment." She removed a deep purple shell bead from her belt and pressed it into his hand. "Go now and tell him I will wait on the morrow by the tulip tree when the sun sets."

He took off with the speed of a wildcat.

Would Dirk meet her? She must warn him — or was she hoping for more?

Why hadn't she been strong and let him love her? The thought struck her as funny now and she turned down the path to the river. Yes, all this time she thought by keeping a distance from Benjamin and Dirk she'd been the strong one. But perhaps to love was to be strong. She'd worried that living in the white man's world she'd lose a part of herself. With love comes sacrifice. But how much could she sacrifice and still be true to herself?

A young brown eaglet sat on a branch above the water and watched her. She'd seen its parents here many times, and they probably weren't far. The eagle was protection, seeing all that happened from above and spreading truth and healing with his wings. Wasn't that like the white man's God? Did God use nature in that way? Was God watching over her like Winnie said? She hoped so.

But she would not tell Winnie of her plan to warn Dirk. Her aunt would be upset and fear for Benjamin's and Joseph's safety. Tensions were high, but Dirk would not hurt them. She was not quite certain that the English troops would go easy on Dirk, especially if he had anything to do with holding Johnny prisoner. Yes, she was doing the right thing. *Nuk?*

29

April 23, 1654

The sun dropped low in the west and Heather Flower slipped out the door. She could not lie to her aunt, so she left without a word. It was terrible to do that, she knew. She thought about how glad Winnie was when she'd opened her door and found her standing there. But this could not be helped.

She would go back to Fort Amsterdam with Dirk if he would still have her and marry him. She would not have to face her father and mother's consternation or the Hortons. That would make her sad, of course, but it could not be both ways. She was certain of that.

The forest was thick, but she enjoyed her freedom as she swiftly covered the ground. She made it to the meadow where the tall tulip tree stood on the edge of the opposite forest just as the sun was igniting the treetops with rays of brilliant orange. She studied the base of the tree line as she closed the distance, straining to see if Dirk had arrived first.

She approached the tulip tree and circled it. A whippoorwill called, and for a moment she thought it was Dirk, but when she called back, no one answered. She settled next to the tree. The young boy had said he found Dirk and gave him the message, but there was no message back. Likely because it would be too dangerous to tell anyone his plan, even the messenger boy.

But as the sun sank lower, hunger pangs attacked her for the first time since she'd left home. She still had on the same clothes she'd laid down in the day she found out about Benjamin and Joseph entering Dutch territory. She stood and foraged for berries, and when she'd had her fill, she lay down next to the tree in the sodden grass. Even her shivers could not keep her awake. She was exhausted from the past two days, and her last thought as she drifted off was of Dirk's blue eyes, the color of the bay on a summer day.

She woke stiff, cold, and wet as the spring rain gently pattered on the tree leaves and over her body. She pushed herself up and looked around, her arms clutched at her sides. Slowly she remembered why she was there. She'd asked Dirk to meet her at the tulip tree. He hadn't come. She'd waited all night and Dirk had not come. Her breath was shaky as she drew it in, and her eyes stung, but she willed herself not to cry. No, it was her fault. She must face the cruel reality.

She'd put a wall between her heart and the man Dirk. She could not have expected him to wait when she gave him no hope.

She began walking back. But she was not the free, happy person who had almost run to get here. Her feet dragged, and she could not bring herself to think of what her aunt would say. She did not want to face the shame, to face the words Winnie would have for her.

As she came to the Corchaug fort, she kept walking without a plan. Her body was racked with pain and her mouth was as dry as her clothes and hair were wet. She cut through Calves Neck and stood before the Horton house. She swayed as she tried to think of what she might do. Then everything went dark.

When she awoke, she lay in a bed and someone looked down at her. Slowly Mary's soft face came into focus, her hazel eyes first, and then the reassuring smile on her lips. The quilts tucked around Heather Flower were warm, and a fire crackled in the fireplace.

"You gave us a fright. But you shall be all right now. Abbey is going to bring you a nice broth. And James has gone to fetch Winnie."

"Oh, no. I wish he wouldn't." She raised her head quickly as she said it, then just as quickly her head dropped back to the bolster, black spots blotting her vision.

"Careful now. Stay down and rest until Abbey brings the broth. You've been through quite a shock, to be sure." Mary ran her hand over her hair to smooth it, then rested it on her forehead. "You don't have fever, but you are at the least exhausted. That is not good."

The fire popped and sputtered and Mary stood up to add another log and nudged it into place with her boot.

"Mary, I don't want to go back to my aunt's."

"Why not, dear? She loves you. What has happened?" Her brow raised and she swiped at the curly lock that always was a problem as she settled on the edge of the bed.

"I — I left home without telling my parents. She let me stay, but then I left her too. I'm afraid I've been terrible. I think

Winnie will make me go back to Montauk now and I do not want to do that. Please, Mary, don't let her send me home." She tried to sit up again, but Mary put her hands gently on her shoulders and made her lay back down.

"Hush. You are not in any condition to travel anyway, even if 'tis only across the bay. You shall stay here, of course. Now rest." Mary patted her shoulder and stood.

She huddled under the cover and closed her eyes. It did feel good to lie in the bed. She wasn't used to such softness. And she was tired. She drifted off once more, though this time she did not fight it.

How long she slept she did not know, but it was dark again when she woke and Mary told her Winnie had come and gone. Abigail had gone home too, but Mary brought her the warm broth she'd promised and Barnabas came in to sit and read his Bible to her. Before he and Mary went to their chamber upstairs, he said a prayer for her and the men on the west end of the island. It gave her a peace she hadn't known for a long time.

With the Horton children in bed, and now Mary and Barnabas, Heather Flower lay awake for a long time, reflecting on the last few days. She'd been foolish to think she and Dirk might marry. He had certainly run at the first chance. She thought she knew him, but perhaps she did not.

She should not think of him anymore. She would let go of her dreams. Let go of Dirk. And if Benjamin came back, she would tell him she was glad and never leave his side. At least he had always been there for her.

Her thoughts drifted to Barnabas's prayer. He'd prayed for them all, not just his sons, and not just the English troop. He'd prayed for the Dutch troops too. If he could do that, then she could forgive Dirk for not coming to her when she needed him. But it didn't have to mean they would be friends. That was over.

Benjamin led Star into the barn and brushed the Great Black. He gave her some hay, patted her flank, then crept into the still, dark house. A week and a day had passed since he and Joseph had left with the horse troop. He was tired, but he went to the fireplace in the back kitchen and stirred the embers. As they sparked, he put three small logs in a triangle fashion on top and stuffed a bit of dried moss to get it going good.

He settled in his mother's chair and picked up the Bible.

Barnabas appeared, tucking his long white linen shirt beneath a leather belt. He ran his fingers through his dark hair, streaked with silver strands. "I thought I heard you. Did you ride all night?"

"Yes, and half of yesterday. We went out to Flushing."

His father picked up the bucket of water brought in the night before and poured it into the iron pot hanging from the trammel. He swung it over the flames and sat opposite his son. "Let's start our day in the Word. Then you tell me everything while I get the fire in the oven started. I want to know it all."

Benjamin handed him the Bible and they studied a passage, ending with prayer. He watched his father as he prepared for the baking day. It had been the routine for many years now. Barnabas would come down early for his time with God and then get the bakeshop ready for the day while Mary tended to the younger children. Once Abigail arrived, Mary would spend the day baking, and Barnabas could take care of the farming chores early in the day and the affairs of the town in the afternoon.

It was an arrangement that worked well. In England, Barnabas had been the baker in the hamlet at a time few households had their own oven. Here in Southold, the homes the founders built all had an oven of some sort. But the townspeople still loved the Hortons' treats, and the Horton hearth was the largest in the village. Mary still couldn't bake pippin pies fast enough for the town, and Barney baked the family recipe for crisp little ginger cakes almost every evening.

"I thought you'd gone further when you didn't return. What did you find out?"

Benjamin stood and walked to the north-facing window. It was still dark but for a tinge of orange-pink sky to the east. He folded his arms and leaned against the casement. "They have Johnny. They are keeping him on a ship in the harbor, the *King Solomon*. The charge is that he was privateering."

Barnabas held his armful of logs midair. "Privateering? How can they claim that? Wasn't Johnny up in Connecticut?"

"He spent most of last year doing that, trying to rally some volunteers to attack New Amsterdam. But apparently, of late he sailed straight into the harbor at New Amsterdam, I suppose under the guise of trading. Who knows what he was planning. He has quite a few friends in Flushing and Hempstead. Mayhap they thought they could overthrow Stuyvesant by themselves."

Barnabas stuffed the logs into the oven and added moss. He picked up the flint box from the shelf above the hearth and struck a spark. He left the door open as the wood started to burn and watched it, bellows in hand, ready to get air to the fledgling fire. "The reverend's son has always been a bit rash, has he not?"

"Father, he believes passionately that we will not have peace as long as the Dutch are on the west side. I agree and I rather admire him for taking a stand. People in this town criticize him, but I believe one day they will thank him for his efforts."

Barnabas chortled. "Very well, but the news we have is that Cromwell has declared peace with Holland. A messenger from Cromwell's army notified New Haven that he is now the First Lord Protectorate of the Commonwealth, and has instructed New Haven to set our policies in alignment with that treaty. We've had a boundary now on Long Island with which we need to abide. Johnny should have known if he entered their harbor, they'd take him prisoner. Mayhap he wanted that, though who could begin to imagine why."

He closed the oven door. "But no matter how he got himself in the predicament, we must find a way to get him home."

Benjamin fell silent. He wasn't sure if he should share the plan he and Joseph had talked about just yet. He wasn't even sure if he agreed with Joseph, or at least his heart didn't. He had not successfully put a wall between it and Heather Flower yet. But right now he should be thinking of Johnny.

"Father, perhaps our troop should ride into New Amsterdam on the attack. Perhaps that is what Johnny was thinking — that if he couldn't convince anyone to attack with him, he'd risk himself to bring on the troops. He's got many friends out there that would ride beside us to overthrow the government and free him, all in one swoop."

Barnabas sat there, his mouth open, moss-green eyes penetrating. "Surely he would not do that?"

"Joseph and I think we should go back, this time prepared to fight and free Johnny."

"If you take our militia and our horses again and engage in battle out west, the Narragansett will no doubt attack the east end. We have known for a long time they wait for the opportunity. We are under orders from New Haven to train every week, and indeed it has been difficult without Captain Youngs here to supervise that. But we cannot send what we do have off on a war with the Dutch."

"It's the Dutch who make the Indians to the north dangerous, trading them guns for pelts."

"That may be, but no — you will not be riding out there again. Wells and I have been elected as deputies to the court and will be going to New Haven within a fortnight. We'll petition the court to negotiate his release. I'll talk to John today. Mayhap we can leave sooner."

Benjamin rubbed his neck. Thank goodness. He didn't like the plan anyway. But he'd rather it be Father who told Joseph. He scooped some oats from the old oak cask and dumped them into the pot, the water now a rolling boil.

The chatter of his younger siblings drifted down from the upper chambers and he heard Mary come down the stairs with them. He startled when he overheard her greet Heather Flower at the bottom.

His father gave him a curious look. "Oh. I forgot to tell you we have Heather Flower with us."

30

April 25, 1654

Benjamin rushed out to the front hall. She looked frail like a bird. Her dark eyes lacked their fire and had the softness of a frightened doe. She gave him her small smile, almost as if she felt shy with him. But she possessed the kind of beauty that could weather rain, hardship, or whatever life tossed her way and it would not be lost.

Mary stepped forward and threw her arms around him. "Ben, you are back. How I've prayed for you and Joseph. You are both safe?"

"Yes, Mother. Everyone is. We're all back. Heather Flower, I am both pleased and surprised to see you here."

Mary turned and put her arm around her. "She became ill, Ben. She'll stay with us until she gets well."

Heather Flower's voice was soft and tentative. "Thank you, my friend. I am grateful to see you. Grateful you have returned."

"What about Winnie? Does she not want you there?"

Mary spoke for her. "She does. Very much. And I think soon she will go there." She looked at Heather Flower. "You get stronger every day. And Winnie has told me that she will let you stay. You don't have to go back to Montauk. Not until you are ready."

Benjamin hoped she would never be ready to go. Mayhap this was his chance to convince her to stay.

After everyone had some porridge, his father kissed Mary goodbye and walked across the road to meet with Reverend Youngs. Before he left he said he expected they would call an emergency town meeting in the afternoon and he hoped Benjamin could get some work done in the fields before that.

Benjamin was reluctant to leave Heather Flower, but labor in the fields was a family obligation. His three younger brothers followed him out and they gathered tools, the wheelbarrow, and the stone boat — a large flat sled without runners. He let Joshua help Jonathan hitch up Star and they led her out to the field.

He loved this time of year when winter's quiet gave way to bird songs and insects chirping. Mary kept honeybees out back by the orchard, and they just now were waking and drowsily buzzing about. He could remember how happy she'd been when Uncle Jeremy had been able to bring over a shipload of hives from England. Not a favorite cargo of his, however.

Caleb and Joshua both favored their father and looked like Joseph at a younger age, except Joshua had Mary's lighter, hazel eyes. But Jonathan looked much like Mary's papa, and bore his name. All three boys were at an age where they could be helpful in the fields. They were pretty good with a sling and a bag of stones too, and could bring home quail and occasionally a pheasant.

Today they would be doing a man's work, pulling the larger stones from the field that the women had not been able to remove.

The first stones they dug around, and while Joshua and Caleb both pried with shovels, Benjamin rolled them onto the sled. When they had the sled full, they worked on a couple of larger stones that they would not be able to move as easily. They dug a deep hole next to each and then pushed the rocks into it. They shoveled enough dirt to give them something to plant over it and called it done. They worked throughout the morning with little talk until they headed back to the house for dinner.

Joshua looked up at his brother as they walked. "Ben, do you like Heather Flower?"

He laughed, his dimples showing. "Why, yes, I'd say I do. You do too, do you not?"

"Oh, yes. I just thought maybe you'd marry her and then she could always stay here. I don't think she wants to go home."

"Well, little brother, I wish it were that simple. But life is not like that, I'm afraid." Oh, how he wished it were.

Caleb smiled a knowing look. At fourteen he'd begun to have some thoughts of his own about the girls in their small hamlet. "You've had a sweet spot for her for a while now, haven't you?"

He thumped Caleb's shoulder. "You've found me out, but you mustn't tell her."

Caleb laughed and ran ahead, calling back. "Oh she knows. I know she knows." Joshua and Jonathan took off after him and the three chased each other in circles while Benjamin went inside.

Barnabas came home for a dinner of ham, beans, and a hearty brown bread. He said little except Benjamin needed to come back with him for the meeting. Joseph would meet them there too.

Benjamin wolfed his food quickly, watching Heather Flower pick at hers. Finally he asked her if she would like to take a walk in the orchard. They got up, leaving the rest of the family with eyebrows raised, and walked outside.

The day was a cool spring day, but the sunshine warmed his face. Hopefully it felt good to her. "I wanted to tell you about my trip to Flushing."

"Your mother did, Benjamin. What Barnabas told her."

"Yes, well, I want you to know that I didn't receive any word about Lieutenant Van Buren. He didn't show in Flushing and there were no attempts of contact with the Dutch militia. And Father will handle matters from here on. He intends to leave for New Haven as soon as possible. We'll be discussing that at our meeting."

"You do not need to explain, my friend. I know you dislike Dirk, but I don't believe you would harm him."

"It's not a matter of disliking him. It's more disliking the Dutch interfering with our lives. They are not peaceful neighbors, though they sometimes pretend to be. They'd rather take us over. But the issue now is Johnny."

"I think you dislike him."

She wore her pouty smile and he wasn't

sure if she teased or if it truly made her unhappy that he didn't like Van Buren. "All right. You said it and I suppose it's true. I don't like him. He makes my teeth grind and I want to punch him. There. Is that what you want to hear?"

"Yes, because it is true."

The apple blossoms were in full bloom and she plucked one from a branch and brought it to her nose. A bee followed close and Benjamin swatted it away. She moved toward him and he could not help but take her in his arms. He wanted to protect her. He held her tight and she rested against him. He'd never stopped loving Anna, even after she'd married the Tucker boy. It would always be the same for Heather Flower, he feared. She loved someone else. But did that mean they shouldn't be together?

"Benjamin?"

"Yes?"

"I should go back to my aunt. We should have a courtship. An English courtship."

"We both have broken hearts, Heather Flower. We need to be honest with each other. I love you, but not in the same way as I loved Anna. Is that all right with you?"

"*Nuk,* my friend. Yes. Winnie tells me today is God's gift. We do not know if we have a tomorrow. Dirk is gone from me and

I cannot stop loving him, but I must not think of him."

He lowered his cheek to hers and whispered in her ear. "Yes, then. We'll court. And then will you marry me?" Why was he pushing? She'd just told him what he wanted to know.

"I think so, my friend. If your family will have me."

They walked toward the house and already doubt beat at Benjamin's resolve. If this was right, why did it feel so bad? This would be so much like his father's marriage to Mary. A marriage of convenience. For the first time he could understand what it had been like for his father when his mother had died. But there was a difference. He was pretty certain Mary had loved his father when they wed. Heather Flower came to this union from the same place he did. In love with someone else.

They walked into the kitchen and no one looked at them, save for Hannah. But the raised eyebrows had been replaced by merry little smiles, and it was a forgone conclusion that his family would welcome her with open arms.

Abbey arrived for the afternoon, and took Hannah, Sarah, and Misha to the upper chamber for a nap. Mary and Heather Flower worked in the bakeshop and the first afternoon hours were busy with patrons. They said hello to Mrs. Corey and Mrs. Wells and sent them home with loaves of thirded bread, Mary's specialty, next to her pies.

Mrs. Case and Mrs. Budd always stopped in to sample, whether they bought or not, and shared a little gossip. Today they exclaimed about the apple blossoms in full bloom.

Mary nodded. "We'll have quite a crop to be sure. I'll be drying the pips all winter."

Patience and Lizzie finally came by to pick up sacks of ginger cakes. Lizzie's home, built by Zeke, Barney, Jay, and Ben, had its own large kitchen complete with baking oven. She had the joy of filling her own home with the delightful smells of baking. Times had changed since those early days in Mowsley, and as harsh as things could be, they had settled into a nice life in Southold.

Lizzie nibbled on a crust of bread. "The weaver will be coming through tomorrow, Mary. Did you remember?"

"Oh yes. I did some spinning last night. I've plenty to give him. Patience, let me put your bread order together."

343

"Give me a few biscuits, too, for the little poppets who are good."

Mary smiled. "According to you they are all good. I'll give you a baker's dozen."

As much as she enjoyed the company, she was a bit relieved when they were gone and she had a few minutes to talk with Heather Flower alone. "You look so much better today, really this is the first day I could say that. I've been so worried."

"I do feel better, Aunt Mary, and I know it is time to go back to my aunt's home." She stood by a bucket of water, washing out the bowls and platters from the earlier meal. She ladled a bit more water from the hot cauldron.

Mary wrinkled her brow. "Is that because Ben is home?"

"Yes."

How did she mean that? "Because he makes you uncomfortable?"

"No, my friend. He makes me feel good. Happy. Happier than I've been for a time. I told him he could court me, but I must go to my aunt's for it to be right."

She rushed to hug her. "Oh, Heather Flower, I'm so happy. 'Tis good for both of you. Ben has loved you for a long time."

"I know. I want it to be good for him."

Mary drew back and fell silent. She busied

herself with wrapping the remaining loaves in cloth and brushing the crumbs off the table. Muffkin rubbed her side against her leg and she stooped to pet her. She sensed something in Heather Flower's answer. Was Heather Flower just giving up? Was her heart truly with Ben, or had it shattered when Keme died? Or worse, was she in love with that Dutch lieutenant?

31

April 28, 1654

Mary was encouraged to see Ben spend his spare time, short as it was, at Winnie's after Heather Flower returned. She'd had her doubts in the beginning, but the more they saw each other, the more she became convinced they shared an enduring love. Ben had been crushed when Anna married. Now it was his turn to be happy.

The courtship was more a formality, like the banns. As soon as those could be posted, they could marry. They both knew each other well enough.

She'd helped plan several weddings, and with Lizzie's and Patience's help, this one would be lovely. In Boston a wedding was hardly an affair at all, but Southold tended to keep the celebration a slight bit reminiscent of old England. The men seemed to tolerate it, even enjoy it. And for Mary with her Anglican upbringing, it just seemed natural.

The women were gathering today. Abbey was already here to watch the girls, the men and boys were out working in the fields — except for Barney and Mr. Wells, who'd gone to New Haven — and Winnie was on her way with the bride-to-be.

Mary finished with her baking for the morning, set out platters of little cakes and tarts for the ladies. Lizzie and Patience arrived and they pulled out some of Mary's best laces, bolts of blue brocade, and soft silk from her trunk. "I'm not sure what Heather Flower will want to wear, but if she would like a nice gown, I've got the fabric."

Lizzie didn't waste a second. "I'll make her dress. I'd love to."

"I'll help you, Lizzie. And Mary, I'll help you set up for the dinner. We can decorate with wild iris and it will be so beautiful."

"Thank you, Patience, and thank you, Lizzie. We'll need to see how much she and Winnie will let us do. But she did tell Ben she'd like a Christian wedding."

Rachel and Ruthie joined them and soon everyone arrived. Winnie's face glowed as they talked about the plans. Mary and Barney would prepare the feast and include both English and local dishes. Baked fish and roast turkey would be on the menu, but venison would be the focal point of the meal. Barney would bake the cake, and of course the table would be laden with English savories and sweets.

Heather Flower was quiet through most of the chatter, but when they looked at the fabric and lace, her face brightened. She ran her hand over the smooth, shiny blue and cream satin and listened as Lizzie told her how she could embroider the blue brocade for the fitted bodice, and create a full skirt with the blue satin. Billowy sleeves of cream-colored satin would be tied above and below the elbow with blue ribbon.

Mary hugged her. "It will be a dress truly for a princess, Heather Flower."

The ladies decided they would not wait for the banns to be posted to begin the dress, and they all helped cut the fabric, holding it up to Heather Flower and measuring. They moved her arms straight out to her sides, turned her this way and that, smoothing, snipping until finally they had all of the pieces cut for Lizzie to take home to stitch.

They began to fold the pieces and Mary told the story of the cake Barney baked for their own wedding day again, and they all listened like it was the first time.

Lizzie giggled. "Tell them how you cried

and he had to promise to bake you one every year."

"Oh, they've heard that too, I'm afraid. But he does, no matter what." That still meant as much to her as it did on the day they married.

"Winnie, you've sent a message to her parents, haven't you? Have you heard from them?" Patience loved the details of a wedding and was always good at keeping track of what had been done and what still needed to be accomplished.

"We sent a messenger, and yes, they will come when we set the day. Benjamin will journey to Montauk. He tells me that he must ask permission of Wyandanch."

Mary straightened from her folding and put her hands on her hips. "What if we say the twenty-seventh of May? That way Benjamin can tell Heather Flower's parents when it will be and it gives us one month to prepare. 'Tis a Saturday, a good day for a wedding feast."

"That is good." Patience was the first to agree.

Everyone looked at the others and nodded their heads in agreement, then broke out in chatter much like clucking hens. Heather Flower found a chair in the corner and settled into it. Mary meant to say something to her, but Barney entered. His presence still filled up a room and the ladies still noticed him. All eyes turned.

"Barney, you are back. What did they say at the court?"

He looked from her to the group of women. "The men will meet tonight and William and I will give our report. The men will then tell their wives. It's best I keep it that way." He bowed to the ladies. "Prithee, understand."

Patience nodded. "Of course."

"Very well."

Patience stood up. "We were all getting ready to leave." She nudged Lizzie.

"Oh, yes, Barnabas. We are just gathering up what we need for Heather Flower's wedding dress."

He turned to Heather Flower. "Good morrow. Have you a date for this wedding?"

She stood. "Benjamin and I would like to marry soon."

"We've decided just now on the twenty-seventh of May. Do you think that would be suitable, Barney?"

"Aye, my sweet, more than suitable." He bowed to Heather Flower and kissed her hand. "Welcome to our family."

Lizzie gave Heather Flower a hug, and hugs began all around as the ladies left.

Abbey handed Sarah to Mary as she gathered up Misha to go home.

With the baby on her hip and Hannah at her skirt, she stirred the pottage on the fire. "You must be hungry. I've never known a Horton man to not be." She smiled up at her husband.

"That would be true. Give me Sarah and you dish us all up."

She handed over the baby and he grabbed Hannah's hand. "What say you we go find Benjamin and the boys? Are they in the barn?"

"Yes, Papa." They started out the door.

"Barney, wait." She stopped stirring and tapped the wooden spoon on the side of the pot. "I know you said you shouldn't say anything until after the meeting, but I just have to know. What did you find out about Johnny? Will they help get him back?"

He cocked a bushy eyebrow. "I suppose it doesn't matter if I tell you before or after the meeting. It will be the same either way. Aye. Stuyvesant set bail and we'll pay it. New Haven also requested the reverend write a letter asking for his release, which I expect him to do of course. I'll take the letter and the bail with me this Monday. Joseph will go with me."

She wiped her forehead with the back of

her hand and a smile flit across her face. "Good. I will be so happy when Johnny is back safe and Ben and Jay can stop having wild thoughts about rescuing him." She turned back to her pottage.

He sat at the head of the old oak table and looked around at his family. With another meeting at the church planned for after supper, Barnabas sent Caleb to fetch Joseph and Jane to join them. Now they all clasped hands for the blessing of the food.

Joseph sat to his right with Jane beside him. Benjamin sat to his left and then Caleb and Joshua. Next to Jane sat Hannah with Jonathan on her other side. Mary sat at the end of the table with little Sarah on her lap. She looked tired but so content holding their babe, and smiling — no, glowing — at their large family.

Tonight he was thankful for his family as he led them in grace, and humbly spoke of his love toward them as well as for the Lord. "Amen."

They all looked up and waited for him to spoon the pottage into a bowl, add a hunk of bread and pass it. The first bowl was passed to Mary and each bowl after was passed until everyone had their supper. When Barnabas served himself, they began to eat. Old memories were treasured, but making new ones was important to him and Mary.

Barnabas mopped up the gravy with the last piece of bread. "That was good, Mary. Thank you." He stood and looked to his two eldest sons. "We need to get over to the meeting." He glanced around the table, nodding to Jane. "Prithee, excuse us."

Jane gave a pat to her husband's hand as he stood, and Barnabas walked to the end of the table to kiss Mary's cheek and the top of Sarah's head before leaving with his sons.

The men who were gathered inside all turned as the Horton men came in. Barnabas walked up the center aisle to the clerk's table, where William Wells and Reverend Youngs sat. He and Wells would not begin to serve officially until May 1, but the reverend requested they sit up front for this meeting because of the gravity of the situation with his son.

Joseph and Benjamin sat in the Horton pew up front. The room was silent save for the door and the shuffling as the rest of the townsmen entered and took their seat.

At length, Reverend Youngs called the meeting to order. The reverend led the men in prayer and then Barnabas stood to read the report from New Haven, including a bail to be paid for Johnny and a letter request from the reverend stating he desired the court to take action. The men voted to accept both items, and John Youngs said he would write the letter that night.

"Thank you for your prompt action in the matter," the reverend began. "I cannot tell you how concerned his mother and I have been. I still worry for his safety after the release and would like to request an escort on his behalf."

William Wells tapped the table. "I ask for a show of hands of who is in favor of sending the horse troop to meet Johnny and bring him home."

Every man raised his hand.

Barnabas raked his hair back with his fingers before he stood. He turned to Reverend Youngs. "Joseph and I will sail before dawn on Monday and deliver the bail and letter directly to the court."

"Thank you, Barnabas. It is settled then, and we are close to having Johnny home. I thank you all. I know he has been something of a rascal, but you all understand a father's love. If anything happened to him, I would blame myself."

"Hear, hear, John — we all understand.

Prithee, no explanations required."

"I appreciate that." He folded his hands on the table before him. "Is there anything else we should discuss while we are here?" Reverend Youngs sounded tired.

Timothy Brush stood up. "What about the wedding, Horton?" He nodded at Benjamin.

"Thank you for asking. I'm proud to say my son will be marrying the daughter of Grand Sachem Wyandanch." Murmurs trickled through the group. The custom of whites taking a native woman as a wife was not always well received by either the English or the Indians. But did not God create mankind equal?

Barnabas knit his brow and looked around the room. The issue went far beyond the intricacies of living with the native people. He and Mary both thought the Quakers, and others who did not share the same religious beliefs, were precious in God's sight too. He prayed for them continually, and his fervent desire was for those people who followed a different theology to find another place to live and worship, as he had done when he left England.

He cleared his throat. "Mary informs me they have selected the twenty-seventh of May for the date, and you know how the ladies are. They are already busy with the preparations. I am certain that includes a feast at our home. The wedding will be here in the church, but I, as magistrate, will officiate. Benjamin, is there anything you want to add to that?"

Benjamin stood, running his hand through his hair much like his father. He grinned, dimples creasing deeply into his cheeks. He glanced toward John Budd and nodded. "Just that I am looking forward to my marriage to Heather Flower and I appreciate all of your support."

The men rallied and applauded, but were they really supportive? His second eldest was getting married and he was creating a bit of a stir. Certes. Nothing wrong with that. He kind of enjoyed starting stirs. Ann would have been proud of their son and would have loved Heather Flower. She'd liked a bit of controversy as well.

32

April 29, 1654

Benjamin sheared the last of the sheep with Joseph and Zeke, and the three trudged down the commons to make sure they hadn't missed any. They'd be able to export half of the wool and still keep Mary, Lizzie, and Patience busy with spinning.

Lizzie was looking to make her own hats, like Mrs. Haskins in London, except she wanted to control the process in every step. She would be spinning her own wool, dying it with the precious blue that the indigo-peddler sold and with the vivid reds and yellows from shrubs and trees that grew right there in Southold. She'd had a loom shipped down from Boston. Soon she would be carding, and then weaving the wool for hats.

He was pleased Heather Flower consented to do the beadwork for Lizzie. He'd worried about blending their cultures when they wed, but she took everything in stride, like she'd been born to it. Mayhap her upbringing as a princess helped, though his mother said she doubted that.

The men gathered in the barn after they'd put the fleece in barrels to soak and washed the sweat and dirt of the day off with a bucket of water and rags.

The women had supper ready — they'd prepared a big dinner at noon for all the men involved in the shearing, and now it reappeared with a few refreshments added. Heather Flower and Winnie were visiting, and Benjamin sat with Heather Flower on his left and Hannah on his right. She wanted to sit next to Heather Flower and so they traded places. He could see who the favorite was around here.

Benjamin took the opportunity to invite the ladies for a ride in the wagon after they ate. All but Heather Flower declined, much to his delight.

Mary packed them a little sack of ginger cakes, and they wandered down to the barn. Inside the barn, Starlight softly neighed. Heather Flower stroked her muzzle as Benjamin hooked Star into the harness, and then he helped her to climb up to the wagonboard. They rode alongside the green commons, now filled with shivering sheep.

"Would you like a ginger cake?" He reached in the sack and offered one to her.

Heather Flower smiled and took the offering. *"Koekje."*

"What?"

"It is called a *koekje.*"

"Who calls it a cookie?" He grinned, for he knew, but he wanted her to say it.

She stared straight ahead. "I am sorry, Benjamin. It was Dirk. I forgot. I should not have been thoughtless."

He reined Star in and turned her face toward his, cupping her chin in his hands. "No, it's all right. I think it's good you talk about him. I want you to be sure that we are doing the right thing. If you can talk about him without sadness, then I think that is a good thing. Yes?"

"You are right."

"I wanted to tell you I'm glad you'll be working with Lizzie. You enjoy beadwork and I think you'll like Lizzie."

"I do, Benjamin. I like your aunt."

"I meant working with her. I guess I worry that you will somehow miss being at home."

"Winnie says God will provide, no matter where we are. No matter our path."

He clicked the reins and they rode across the fork to the North Sea. "She is right. I think the Hortons know that better than anyone."

They stopped at the bluff and walked down more than a hundred steps to the water's edge. "Joseph and I helped my father lay those stones. The first time we came down here we climbed through all sorts of snagging bushes. I didn't think I'd make it back to the top."

"It's beautiful here."

"I think so. But in a few minutes the sun will hit the water and you won't believe how beautiful that is." He looked down at her and pulled her near. He lifted her chin with one finger. The sun's light flickered in her opal eyes, and Benjamin thought how easily he could gaze into them from now until forever. Her pouty lips were soft as he bent to kiss them and he pulled her close.

They climbed the steps back to the top of the bluff, and Heather Flower stopped to catch her breath and take a final glimpse of the moon over the water. Benjamin stepped in close and she allowed him to pull her to him. She wished tonight would not end and yet her aunt waited to return to the fort. She was glad Aunt Winnie was feeling better and enjoying the company of her friends.

Benjamin lowered his lips to her ear. "What are you thinking about?"

She caught her breath with a little laugh. "My aunt. I should take her home. It's getting late." She looked up to his baby-blue eyes and immediately felt regret for speaking the truth. "Benjamin, I was thinking of you, my friend, and this beautiful night, but then I remembered we left everyone back at your house. They must wonder where we are."

He laughed softly. "You don't have to feel bad. I understand. And you're right. We need to get Winnie home. I'm driving you, of course." He kissed her cheek and took her hand. "Come on, I'll get you both home."

As he helped her up into the wagon, he said, "I like it when you think of your aunt. I think we should all have respect for our parents and elders. It's been a part of your and my upbringing and for that I'm thankful. See, our worlds are not so different."

She smiled. "Do you worry our worlds are different?"

"No, not much. I think our parents worry about that much more than we do."

They rode down Hortons Lane in silence. Heather Flower could hear the crickets singing their songs and a lonely hoot owl winging its way through the dark, even with the creak of the wagon wheels and the clop of

Star's hooves on the dirt road.

The white man had made many changes to their island. Some she did not understand, but most were good, she thought. It was strange they penned up animals, but then each family had their own. They even branded them with a special mark in their ear, in case one should escape. To ride horses and hitch them to carts and plows instead of using their own swift feet and canoes to do the work had been surprising at first, but a wonderful idea. Even with the new and different noises added to their landscape, she appreciated what the white man had brought to her people. And they gave back generously.

They pulled up in front of the Horton house, and before he could even help her down, Mary had walked out with Winnie.

Benjamin closed the gap between them in three quick strides. "Heather Flower was worried about you, Winnie. It's late. Are you all right?"

Winnie held onto Mary's arm, but brightened at Benjamin's question. "Yes, my friend. I'm very good. We heard you coming down the lane and thought it might be nice to meet you out here. It's such a nice night."

Heather Flower could tell she was tired.

"Benjamin will help you up, Aunt. We'll get you home. Would you like to sit up here on the wagonboard with us, or would you like to be down in the back?"

Benjamin took her arm. "Why don't you sit up with us? We'll keep you warm. It is a nice night, but the air is a bit cool."

"That would be good."

Mary stepped close and gave her a gentle hug. "I'm so glad you came back for a visit. You are looking good, Winnie."

"You are too, Mary. And those little girls are growing so fast. I don't want to miss a minute of it."

"I shall bring them out to visit you more, Winnie. I promise."

They waved their goodbyes again as Benjamin clicked the reins and they started the long ride home with Winnie snuggled between them.

Heather Flower thought her aunt was falling asleep, she was so quiet. But then she stirred and couldn't quit talking.

"Let me tell you of how I met your mother, Benjamin."

She told the whole story about how the shallop came into the bay and what it meant to her people. She told Benjamin she would never forget the palefaces as they played with the jingle shells and watched Momoweta approach in his ceremonial war paint and feathers.

Heather Flower listened, her amusement tinged with sadness. Her aunt told the story as if she'd never told it before and recounted how she was shy about approaching Mary at first, but Mary had been just as anxious to meet her as she was, and all awkwardness had dissipated quickly.

When they both discovered they had cooking and gardening skills they could teach other, the friendship was cemented forever. She laughed as she told them Mary loved to say who knew that milk from an English cow and Indian corn would taste so good together. And Winnie was as pleased to receive honey from the English bees as Mary was to receive syrup from the native maple trees.

Benjamin listened politely, thanked Winnie for her stories, and said good night. He kissed Heather Flower's hand and she walked her aunt to their wigwam. She helped her ready for bed, combing her aunt's long gray hair. "I enjoyed your stories too, Aunt Winnie."

Her aunt patted her hand. "I'm glad you did. Mary has been my friend for so many years."

"I know. It's comforting too, to know how

well our people can dwell together. I think at times Benjamin worries about this, and it was good for him to listen to your stories." She braided her aunt's hair. "Would you like to comb mine, Aunt Winnie?"

"Yes, my niece. I love to comb your hair."

She turned and sat so her aunt would not have to get up, and enjoyed the rhythm of the strokes on her hair. "Would you like to come and live with Benjamin and me after we're married?"

Winnie hesitated for just a moment, then continued to comb. "Why, no, child. I could not leave my hut. Winheytem lived here with me. I feel his closeness. You and Benjamin are so young and have so much ahead of you. You don't need me in the way."

"You would never be in the way, Aunt Winnie. I can't bear the thought of you alone. Have you ever thought of living with Abigail and James? You could help her with Misha."

"No, I love seeing Misha and Abigail. But I want to stay here. Don't worry for me, Heather Flower. I am where I'm happiest." The wolf dogs settled at her feet. "I've got my pups. They remind me of Smoke and your uncle."

She let her aunt finish her hair in silence, then she wrapped her arms about her in a hug. "I love you, Aunt Winnie. I had such a good day with you today." She took the comb and helped Winnie to her pallet.

As she put the ivory comb on her shelf, she thought of Dirk handing it to her the first time. It was more than just providing her with a necessity. She'd thought it had been a gift from his heart, but she'd been wrong about that. If only it didn't make her feel so very sad. She crawled onto her pallet and pulled the bearskin blanket over her.

How could she have been so wrong about him? And why did she keep thinking about him?

After Aunt Winnie's breathing evened out, she got up and wrapped the blanket around her shoulders. She crept out of the hut and hurried out through the palisade gate, down the path to the river. She wasn't sure why it was such a comfort. Perhaps it was because this was where he always came to find her. Was it terrible to come here? Did it mean she hoped he would be here waiting? She listened to the ever-flowing water and the bullfrog's occasional croak.

She shivered under her blanket and looked up just in time to catch a shower of stars blazing across the night sky. It was an astral display that her people believed was a sign of travel mercies. But who was traveling?

Dirk? She prayed to God that he would have the travel mercies promised in the shower of stars, if he be the traveler. She would never know, though, because traveling or not, he'd left her.

Sweet Benjamin was ever at her side, always there to pick her up when she fell — or when the world crashed in on her. She shook her head. She needed to go home, go to bed. She had people who loved her, and for that she could be thankful. She got up and padded toward the fort. She hesitated to listen one more time to the rushing water, then hurried to the gate and the wigwam.

As she curled beneath her blanket, gray light seeped in through the smoke vent and surprised her as the sun began to edge toward morning. She hadn't realized she'd been out most of the night. Her eyes seemed to close only for a moment, when suddenly she was conscious of meat sizzling in a pan, and Aunt Winnie preparing a very English breakfast of ham and chunks of bread and cheese sent home by Mary. The pups perched expectantly near the fire, intent on catching a scrap here and there.

She smiled to herself as she tried to close her eyes tighter and savor sleep and the smells all at once. Aunt Winnie would be all right. She loved her little home. Her little dogs. Her friends. And she would always be close by.

Finally, when pleasing turned to tantalizing, and she could not resist any longer, she rose and ate and told her aunt stories of growing up on the south fork of the island, of running free with Wyancombone, and learning to sew the wampum with her mother.

When they were done, Winnie asked if she'd like to go with her to hunt eggs, and Heather Flower said she could not think of anything she'd like more.

Aunt Winnie handed her a basket and they headed for the grasslands to the north. They hunted for mourning dove nests in trees and shrubs, finding a clutch of two eggs in each nest they discovered. They gently removed one egg and left one in place. When Heather Flower's basket was full, they headed for the reeds to look for goose eggs.

"Be careful with the nests. It may look safe to take the eggs, but if the hen is close, she'll bite you."

Heather Flower looked around and timidly followed Winnie. "I will let you take the eggs, Aunt. My basket is full anyway."

But as the morning wore on, she braved the threat of ambush and gathered some of

368

the large, warm eggs to put in Winnie's basket. The two headed for home, arms loaded.

"I thought we would bring some to Mary. It was so good of her to give us the ham. What do you think? We could see Benjamin too, if he is home."

Heather Flower's little smile turned the corners of her mouth. "Are you not trying a bit too hard to find ways to have Benjamin and me together, Aunt?"

Winnie smiled too, with a twinkle in her eyes. "Me?"

"Yes, you."

"My child, I believe Benjamin is a good marriage for you."

"Yes, I know, Aunt Winnie. You do not need to worry. That is what we think too." She would put the night behind her and move into the day. Move into the life ahead of her, and surround herself with the people who loved her.

33

April 30, 1654

Heather Flower arrived early to church with Winnie and watched Barnabas tack the banns to the front door of the meetinghouse. The day was blustery and the parchment fluttered as he tacked it to the wood. It was the wedding announcement for her and Benjamin and it would remain for three Sundays. She could not read, but the feeling in her stomach as she looked at the document was peculiar and she looked away. This was a custom not of her people, but she understood she was officially engaged in the eyes of the people of Southold.

Gauzy puffs of white clouds blew across the blue sky, sending shadows momentarily across the yard and giving her shivers despite her deerskin tunic.

Mary, dressed for church in her black silk with a white collar and cuffs, crossed the main road with Sarah in her arms and Hannah holding onto her skirt. They joined Heather Flower and Winnie and walked inside with them. Benjamin already sat with his younger brothers and he looked up with a deep smile as they entered. She followed Winnie into her pew and they sat in quiet, waiting for the service to begin.

At nine o'clock the bell began to clang, calling all to worship. Grissell came in with Nathaniel and waved at her with a grin as they took their seats opposite of her. She was dressed in a pretty yellow brocade, cut wide in the front to hide her growing belly, and looked elegant sitting next to her handsome husband. Heather Flower had never sent a message to tell her of her decision not to visit again and she regretted that. She did not mean to hurt her friend's feelings. Thankfully, Grissell seemed surprised to see her, but pleasantly so.

With the song leader to direct them, they began their worship singing "Shout to Jehovah All the Earth" from the *Whole Booke of Psalmes.* They sang for the first hour and then settled in to listen to the sermon.

Reverend Youngs stood and faced the congregation with his Bible. He opened it and set it on the pulpit. "This morning we will study prayer from Matthew 6, verse 9. In this passage, Jesus gives us the Lord's Prayer and tells us to pray 'after this manner.' "

Heather Flower listened intently to the preacher's admonitions. She liked that there was a book God gave to His people filled with everything they needed to know. If Benjamin would teach her, the Bible was the book she would like to learn to read.

The preaching lasted for almost two hours, broken up from time to time with another singing from the psalm book. She shifted on the bench to wake her feet and ease her back. Others were shifting about too, and she thought Mr. Wells might be asleep, except she couldn't really see his face. But still she heard most of the sermon and understood most of what the reverend was saying. And she was hungry for more, though perhaps in smaller doses.

At last it was the end of the first service of the day. Most of the congregation would stay and share a dinner on the church grounds and then reconvene at two o'clock for the second service. Winnie usually went home because she had so far to travel, but Heather Flower had asked her if they could stay, since it was the first Sunday with the banns posted.

Mary brought some samp like Winnie had taught her to make, and some cheese, bread, and two of her famous pippin pies. Lizzie brought a pot of beans and brown bread. Patience unpacked some cold meats and early berries, and they all assured Winnie there was plenty of food for them to stay and join them. Heather Flower thanked them, but then noticed Grissell and Nathaniel preparing to leave and she excused herself to say goodbye.

"Grissell, I am so sorry I did not tell you I changed my mind about returning to your home. I know you thought I might come back and stay awhile. It is hard to explain."

Her friend began to tell her no explanations were needed, but Patience interrupted. "Good morrow, Grissell. I was wondering if you and Nathaniel might join us for dinner here at church. I see you here at morning services, but we never have the chance to visit. I know it is a bit of a journey to travel over from the island each week, but I hope you might stay today." Her look was warm.

Grissell looked from Patience to Heather Flower. "I'm not sure . . ." Her voice trailed as she glanced at the post on the door.

Heather Flower waved her hand. "Much has happened since we last visited, my friend. I would love to have you stay so we could visit."

Patience giggled. "Yes, please do."

Grissell turned to her husband. "Nathaniel? May we stay?"

His look was one of adoration. "Yes, dear, if that is what you want. How do you feel?"

She ran her hand over her loose-fitting dress. "I'm fine. It might be nice to rest before going home."

"Very well, then. We'll stay. There's a thing or two I'd like to discuss with the reverend about his sermon this morning anyway, so if you ladies would excuse me, I might seek him out." He bowed and they watched him walk to the front of the vestibule.

Patience smiled and sighed. "Grissell, your husband is very dashing. Where did you meet him?"

"My brother-in-law introduced us while we were still in England."

"Your brother-in-law is from Rhode Island, *nuk*?" Heather Flower tried to recall the story Grissell had told her.

"Yes, in fact, after our marriage we sailed to Barbados and then up the coast to Rhode Island to gather my belongings from my sister's house. We were shipwrecked and lost everything." She shook her head. "We had such a difficult start on Shelter Island, but it is very comfortable now."

"Oh my. I had no idea you had been through a shipwreck. How awful. 'Tis my worst fear." Patience took her arm. "Come sit with us. You should get off of your feet." She took Heather Flower's hand and pulled both toward her spot on the ground, which was spread with a large quilt and Mary, Lizzie, and Winnie sat close by.

They settled and Patience brought out food and napkins. "Heather Flower, you know Grissell, then?"

Both women nodded and Heather Flower answered. "Since they moved onto Shelter Island two years ago. My mother and I made a trip to welcome them." She looked at Grissell. "When I left you last time, I knew I could not come back. I needed to face my problems alone. Then I heard that Johnny had been taken prisoner and Benjamin and Joseph would be going to west Long Island. I could not stay at Montauk, but came to my aunt's."

"I had no idea, Heather Flower. But I certainly understand. You know me, I just get lonely."

Patience put a plate filled with slices of ham and some red strawberries in front of Grissell and started dishing up some for Heather Flower. But she looked sideways at Grissell as she worked. "I thought you had frequent guests. From Rhode Island or Massachusetts?"

Grissell looked up quickly from her plate and glanced at Heather Flower. "Well, yes, we do. But mostly I like gossiping with women closer to my age like you and Heather Flower." All three giggled.

"I'm a bit older than you two, but I like being included." Patience smiled. "And I like gossip." They laughed again. But she became serious. She leaned over to Grissell and put her hand on hers. Her voice was low. "Your visitors would be safe with me. Truly. And I know Heather Flower feels the same way."

Heather Flower nodded, her dark eyes rounded. She had no idea that Patience would be a sympathizer to the Quakers. She knew how the Youngs family felt, but not so much Mary and Barnabas. Benjamin did not favor entertaining Quakers, that much she knew. But it was hard for her to understand and she could see Grissell wanted to be cautious.

"We give comfort to those who need somewhere to stay. Ours is a private home, away from many of the troubles that plague towns. Even Southold."

Hannah ran by, chasing one of the little boys her age, and they watched them for a moment. Heather Flower was sure they would fall and was relieved when Lizzie called out to the little ones to walk and they both slowed down. Mary brought a basket of bread and her bowl of samp over to spoon onto their plates.

The ladies thanked her, and they watched Mary rejoin Lizzie and Winnie. Patience turned back to Grissell. "I think the work you do is very important. 'Tis not right for any people to be persecuted. Not ever. I can remember what happened to my aunt and uncle who were not able to leave England with us. It was horrible and should not be repeated. Thank the Lord there are people like you and your husband who can give a weary Friend a hand."

Heather Flower was surprised when Grissell went on to share some of the atrocities that were happening in Massachusetts, but before she finished, Mary, Lizzie, and Winnie came over to sit with them and chat. As they settled on the quilt, Heather Flower looked about for Benjamin. She spotted him talking with Nathaniel, Reverend Youngs, and Barnabas and wondered when the men ate during these dinners.

"Did you read the banns, Patience? 'Tis official now. Benjamin and Heather Flower are to be married." Mary's excitement sparkled in her eyes.

"I did. I love weddings," Patience said.

Grissell smiled. "I love weddings too. Heather Flower, you have not yet told me that you are to marry Benjamin. I am so happy for you."

A small smile played on her lips. "I know. It happened suddenly." She looked at Mary and didn't want to go into all of the doubts she had poured out on Grissell the last time they'd talked.

Her friend understood and turned back to Patience. "You have a Dame School, do you not?"

Patience smoothed a corner of the quilt turned up by a breeze. "Yes, I do. Not much of an income, but I get by." She grinned.

"You should make hats with me," Lizzie said. "Heather Flower is. She is going to do beadwork for me." She smiled at Heather Flower.

Patience's brow wrinkled. "What would I do?"

"Why, you would help me. Cut, press, stitch. All of those things. It would go twice as fast and it would be twice as jolly. Grissell, would you like us to make you a hat?"

"I would love a new hat. May I be your first customer?"

"Why, of course."

Lizzie straightened her bonnet over her curls. "I have not thought of Mrs. Haskins for such a long time, Mary, but opening my own shop brings back so many memories."

"Memories I for one would rather forget, dear sister."

Grissell leaned in with a smile. "Oh?"

Patience frowned. "Mary doesn't like to talk about him."

Lizzie fluttered her thick lashes over her violet eyes. "Prithee, I did not mean to . . . So many wonderful times trying on hats in Mrs. Haskins's shop — that's what I was remembering."

"Of course. 'Tis me, Lizzie, not you. We loved going with Papa, riding to London, trying on the pretty hats — didn't we? Robert ruined it."

Heather Flower looked closely at Mary. "Who was Robert? What did he do?"

Color sprang to Mary's cheeks. She shifted and smoothed her skirt over her legs.

Patience glanced at Lizzie, then said, "She never speaks of him."

Lizzie slipped her arm around her sister. "May I explain it to Heather Flower and Grissell?" Mary nodded. "He was Mrs. Haskins's son and Papa wanted her to marry him. It was the one disagreement they ever had and it tore her heart to disobey Papa."

Mary leaned her head on Lizzie's shoulder. "There was a boy, Nathan. We grew up together and I loved him. We planned to be married. On our wedding day he abandoned me — left me at the altar. I was so ashamed. I never saw him again, but I heard he'd become an important lawyer. Papa was desperate to marry me off to Robert in London. It seemed the perfect remedy to him and he thought Robert was a good match for me. But I could not bear the thought. I never went back to London with Papa again." Tears squeezed from beneath her lashes.

Heather Flower took her hand. "I know your pain."

Lizzie hit her hand to her forehead, anxious to change the subject. "Mary, I just realized I need you to keep books like you did for Father. We need to make lists of supplies. There's so much to do."

Mary shook her head. "Have you lost your mind? I didn't have a family when I kept books for Papa. Where would I find the time? I have a bakeshop to keep too. And children. Yours are grown. There you have it. Ask Ruthie or Rachel. They both have a head for numbers. They'll keep your books."

They launched into a discussion of what a

perfect hat for Grissell would be — a pretty gray wool with a wide brim, bedecked with beads and feathers — and went on to decide that Patience's house would be a grand place to establish the shop since it was large and in a perfect location on the main road. She had so many rooms, she could still teach in the morning and help Lizzie in the afternoon.

"Zeke would like that. He's already complaining to Benjamin that he needs to build another room just for my loom."

"Mine is too big for me. And even with my school, there is much room for your hat shop, Lizzie."

"How did you come by such a large house?" Heather Flower had never heard Patience's story.

"Barnabas helped my father build it when we first came here."

"Ours was the first built," Mary added. "And then Patience's father was the first one he helped after that."

"My parents both died the following year when the fever swept through." Tears threatened and Mary leaned over to give her a hug. "At least they had a year to enjoy Southold and our new house."

Winnie spoke up for the first time. "The Terrys were kind to my people, Patience.

And they would be so happy to see how well you do with the children. And would your mother not love a hat shop?"

Mary smiled and patted Patience's hand. "Indeed she would."

The conversation came back to the shop and finally the wind died down and the afternoon took on a lazy quality they so seldom could enjoy.

Heather Flower noticed the children had gathered around the reverend and he was telling them a Bible story. Even the men stepped back and listened. When the story was over, someone rang the first bell and the ladies began cleaning up the dinner. By the last bell, all were sitting in their pews again, already reminded of how hard the benches were and trying to find a position that they could remain comfortable in for the next two hours.

When Reverend Youngs was done preaching that day, Heather Flower found she did not want to leave. She bid Grissell and Nathaniel goodbye with an invitation to the wedding and a promise that she would come out to the manor as often as she could. And in return Grissell promised to come over and buy hats. Often.

At last she and Benjamin were alone for a few minutes. He told her he'd give Winnie and her a ride home in the wagon, and they went out to the barn to hitch Star up. She watched him as he brushed his horse, then put on the harness. He did it with such care and she loved that about him. He was ready to lead the horse out, but she came to him and slipped her arms around his waist. He pulled her close. "Thank you, Benjamin."

"For what?"

"For being the kind person you are and for taking care of me."

"I don't do that to be kind. I do it because I love you."

She heard his words. She just wanted to believe them.

34

May 2, 1654

Barnabas walked into the large general assembly room with Joseph. The New Haven court was about to convene. His first day as deputy to the court would be difficult, given the nature of the situation. The men of the court did not have the same personal involvement, and his concern was the issue would be buried under other matters of the court.

They took their place on the bench designated for Southold, and Barnabas thumbed through the papers he'd carried with him. The pouch on his belt held the bond money. He was prepared but surprised when the judge called on him immediately after opening with prayer and Scripture.

"If it please the court, sir, I have a letter from Reverend John Youngs requesting the court's assistance in acquiring the release of his son, Captain John Youngs Jr., from New

Amsterdam. I have also brought the required bond."

The judge cleared his throat and his eyes held a peculiar gleam as if he enjoyed this. He leaned forward over the table. "Deputy Horton, I will accept the bond and the letter from the reverend, but I must inform you of the escape of the captain. Governor Stuyvesant has sent us a complaint that not only did their prisoner escape from the *King Solomon,* but they have thirteen horses unaccounted for, and he's suspected of being responsible."

"Your honor, that is absurd, if I may. If those Dutchmen cannot hold him on a ship, that is their trouble. But to accuse him of stealing thirteen horses? That is rather a jolly laugh, is it not?"

The judge pounded his gavel. "Hear, hear, Mr. Horton. That is out of place in this court. The court finds that the good men of Southold should return Captain Youngs to custody in New Amsterdam immediately. The bond is held until such time as the Dutch court is able to turn over the prisoner. The horses are to be located and returned immediately as well. And upon his release from New Amsterdam I hereby reprimand him to the court of New Haven." He pounded his gavel and it was clear he was finished with the issue.

Barnabas walked out of the church edifice with his son.

Joseph pounded his father's back once they were outside. "Cheers for Johnny!"

Barnabas shook his head. "Nay, it is not cheers for Johnny. He is in deep trouble."

"But Father, he wouldn't have stolen the horses. Surely it's the Indians. Or they don't know how to build a proper fence and the horses have escaped as well as Johnny." He chuckled. "Johnny can't be blamed for any of this."

"Oh you think he cannot? You have another think coming. For escaping he can expect to be fined about a hundred pounds. But if he's found guilty of horse theft that is another matter."

"If he didn't do it, how would they find him guilty?"

It was Barnabas's turn to chuckle. "I see you have been gone too long from merry old England. When did anyone ever have to do it to be condemned by the court for something? This is terrible news for John. He will be devastated."

They walked toward the port. The day was beautiful — green, fresh, and a bright blue sky — but it could have been gray, dreary, and dark for all they noticed.

"I know, Father. I think Benjamin and I had best go look for Johnny as soon as we get back."

He thought for a moment. "Your mother will not be happy if Benjamin leaves, especially if he's headed west. I don't think we can send him."

"Oh, but you can spare me?" He joshed, of course.

"Aye. For now we can. But before you go anywhere we must study the possibilities of where he might have gone. And when you do go, you'll take the horse troop, of course."

They walked the dock to the plank and joined the captain on the upper deck. He invited them to his quarters and they spent the rest of the morning discussing weather and tide. By high noon they left New Haven.

Heather Flower watched as the Corchaug people worked in the field, planting the corn so important to their survival. Those unable to work in the fields sat under open-air thatched roofs grinding dried corn.

Heather Flower made beads, but she also loved wandering the forest gathering yellow birch for brooms. The younger girls helped her make them, but she enjoyed searching for the twigs and smallest branches by herself. It gave her time to think of Benjamin and their wedding.

She was happy about the plans, and she did love Benjamin. Everyone did. Winnie, Mary, Lizzie, and Patience had most of the plans complete and a good start on the dress.

As she turned a corner, Winnie called from behind and she paused. Her aunt labored toward her, out of breath. "Where are you going?"

She took a breath. How should she answer? For surely she was on her way to the tulip tree. "I'm looking for the yellow birch."

"So far out here? You can find it much closer to home." Winnie scanned the greenery on the oak and chestnut trees. "There really isn't the right kind of tree this far into the forest."

"I'm not sure why I came this way. Let's head back, we can watch for the limbs on the way." She took her aunt's arm and for a while they were silent. "You are happy for me?"

"I love Benjamin as if he were my son. He's been in love with you for a long time."

"And what of Anna? Did he not love her?" She stooped to pick up a thin twig from the forest floor.

"That does not matter. She is married now." She offered to take the stack of twigs so Heather Flower could continue to pick up more.

"I think it does if he still loves her."

"Do you still love Keme?"

Heather Flower stopped walking to protest. "It is not the same."

"How not?"

"Keme died. He did not leave my heart. But he will not ever be here for me to touch. To hold. To lean on."

"I'm sorry. I know that. It is the same with my Winheytem. But we have mourned. It is behind us. But I think there is another in your heart. Another who is not Benjamin." Her aunt studied her.

"You mean Dirk. No, I have put him from my heart."

Winnie took her hand. "Heather Flower, marry Benjamin. You will be happy. He will treat you well."

They walked in silence until they were almost to the gate. "I want to do the right thing."

"Then pray, my child. Pray to God to guide you. Sometimes the best thing is right before us. We do not need to make it so hard."

"May we go to Mary's house, my aunt?"

Winnie looked to the ladies grinding corn. "Yes, we could. We could help Mary with the bakeshop. Tuesdays are busy for her and Barnabas is gone."

They continued on the path toward Southold. Heather Flower's demeanor was lighter and she'd have run except for her aunt. In some ways Winnie seemed to be improving, but her energy was not returning. She slowed her pace so her aunt could keep up.

Benjamin swung the axe, splitting the wood with a precise whack. He paused to mop his brow and noticed the two women walking up the lane. "I'm surprised to see you. Is everything all right?"

Heather Flower stood tall, smiling. "Yes. We thought it good to visit."

He nodded his head. "Ah. I'm not so sure if this is the right time. Father and Joseph came back today."

Winnie glanced up at the house. "Did they find out about Johnny?"

"Yes, I was just about to go in. They were waiting for Reverend Youngs and he just got here. Let's go in and see what's happened." He stood back as the ladies entered. How would Heather Flower take this? He didn't know much yet, but what he did know was not good with the Dutch.

They walked into the hall and Heather Flower sat on the floor as was her custom, but Benjamin found a chair for Winnie and one for himself from the kitchen. Sarah slept in Mary's arms across the large room. Everyone was grim save Hannah who sat on the floor and teased Muffkin with a length of blue yarn. Even little Jonathan looked glum as he sat watching his sister.

Barnabas paced until everyone settled. Then he turned and folded his arms. "John, Johnny has escaped."

He leapt to his feet. "What? What do you mean? Where is he? In New Haven?"

Barnabas put his hand on the reverend's shoulder. "They don't know where he is. The court took the bail and your letter. But they want Johnny returned to the New Amsterdam jurisdiction. When we find him. I think they are assuming he will come back here."

"That's what he should do." John shook his head slowly. "I don't understand. We were so close to getting him released."

Heather Flower sat like a statue. It was always dangerous when the men crossed the boundary line. She knew what would come next. Benjamin and Joseph would go back to find Johnny. And what if they came across Dirk? Who would hurt whom?

Joseph took a deep breath. "There's more, Reverend."

"More?"

He stood up. "There are horses missing. Quite a few. For some wild reason they think he had something to do with it."

Heather Flower could not help speaking. "Whose horses?"

"We don't know." Barnabas looked at John instead of Heather Flower. "And there could be a number of different reasons the horses disappeared."

"But what would he do with more than one? How many are missing?"

It was obvious John was having a difficult time imagining how this could have happened — Heather Flower was too.

Joseph went and stood by his father. "They said thirteen. I think that right there should show anybody with a mind that it's not him."

Benjamin had been sitting, listening. He gave Heather Flower a heartbreaking look before he got up. "Joseph and I need to ride in again and get him. We pretty much know where he would be hiding, but he needs an escort out. We need the horse troop."

His father raised his hands palms down.

"Hold it, I already told Joseph that you were not going. He can take the troop."

Mary's eyes were pools of gray as she listened. "Why do either of you have to go? That horse troop trains every Wednesday and they should be able to go — without Jay or Ben."

Benjamin shook his head. "Johnny is the one who was training them, Mother, and they need a leader. Joseph and I always fill in for Johnny. We can't just send them off."

"I'll go, Benjamin. You stay and get ready for your wedding."

He glanced at Joseph, then looked at his father. "You would send Joseph by himself?"

"He would not be by himself. He'll have the troop."

Benjamin looked at Heather Flower. She hoped her eyes said stay. He glanced down at his mother and her look definitely said do — not — go.

"All right. I imagine my duties as groom cannot be neglected." At last he looked at Reverend Youngs. "Joseph will bring him back safe."

Glad the issue was resolved without involving Benjamin, she was anxious to leave. He walked her to the door with Winnie trailing behind, giving them a moment alone. He bowed to her and took her hand, bringing it to his lips. She liked the warmth of his breath on her hand. The kissing habit from the Old World was quite nice.

Benjamin offered to take them home, but Winnie insisted the walk would do her good.

"Everything will be all right, my child. Joseph will bring back Johnny and we will all celebrate when he is home for your wedding."

If she told her aunt that she feared it would not be so simple, would her aunt understand? Or was she so counting on this marriage she would refuse to look at all of the implications of Joseph and that horse troop riding back into Dutch territory? And she could not help it — she worried as much for Dirk's safety as Joseph's and Johnny's. Why didn't Johnny just give himself up? New Haven would pay the bond and he would come home. Men made things so difficult.

And Benjamin, dear Benjamin. He wanted to go with Joseph, probably more than anything, except he couldn't hurt Mary. He would never deliberately do something she did not approve of. And Mary wanted this marriage as much as Winnie.

35

May 6, 1654

Benjamin brought the wagon out to pick up Heather Flower the following Saturday morning, and he helped her load it with her sacks of beads. She also brought her bead-making tools and sacks of shells. On the ride into town she did most of the talking and he listened intently. She liked the idea of helping Lizzie and Patience open a hat shop.

They pulled up in front of Patience's house, where Lizzie and Patience stood out front discussing a new sign. The ladies helped carry the sacks into the house, and Benjamin asked what they planned on naming the shop.

Lizzie looked at Patience with her brow raised. "I don't know. Something that uses both of our names?" She looked at Heather Flower. "And yours too, Heather Flower. You are in this with us."

Patience immediately protested. "No,

Lizzie. It has to be all yours."

"But we are using your house. And Heather Flower is doing all of the bead-work."

Heather Flower shook her head. "No, my friend. This is your dream and it should bear your name."

They wandered back outside as Benjamin chuckled. He pulled a ledger book from under the bench of the wagon and handed it to Lizzie. "This is from Mother. She said you must begin to use it right away and enter everything. She says Uncle Jeremy brings her a stack of these every year, and if you'd like him to bring you some too, she is certain he would be happy to."

Lizzie ran her fingers over the leather-covered ledger. "This is just like the ones Mary kept for Father. Tell her thank you, Ben."

"I will do that." He said his goodbyes and planted a quick kiss on Heather Flower's cheek before he climbed up into the wagon. "When you decide about the name, let me know and I will make you a fine sign." He clucked at Star and headed home.

"What do you think, Heather Flower?"

"I think Patience is right. I think you must call it Lizzie's Hatterie."

Patience's face lit up. " 'Tis perfect. It

shall be called Lizzie's Hatterie then."

Lizzie's laugh cascaded like tumbling thimbles. "I like it. But it shall always be our store, agreed?" She looked at both ladies until they nodded.

They went inside to figure out which of the front rooms would be the display room and which would be the workroom. Heather Flower sat down at a table with her shells and began to work on creating beads. She chose the inner white part of the shell for pure white beads, and made beads of three different intensities of purple — one almost black, one violet, and one almost blue. The yellow and orange jingle shells made tiny beads for bursts of color.

Lizzie supplied her with some small glass vials that Doc Smith had given her, and she stored each color of bead in a different vial. She worked through the morning while she listened to the two friends go over the floor plan and storage ideas.

Eventually they settled next to her with mugs of mint tea, and Patience wrote out a list while Lizzie told her everything she'd need. Bolts of wool, silk, brocade, felt, and threads and ribbons of all kinds. Straw was easy to come by, of course, and feathers — they had plenty of those. But she would need needles, pins, thimbles . . . the list went on and on. "And I have a whole box of dried roses in different hues, but we'll need to make more. They've already started blooming. Oh and dyes. I'll need to collect dyes. Indigo and cranberry red are my favorites."

Heather Flower and Patience smiled at Lizzie's enthusiasm. Patience fixed a small dinner in the kitchen and told Lizzie that the mother of one of her students mentioned she would like a hat.

The three returned to their project refreshed. "I have two orders already. Now let's sit down and this afternoon we will design my first two hats."

Patience provided the parchment, and for the next two hours she and Heather Flower sat and watched Lizzie dip her quill and sketch. "Now for Grissell, I think something adventurous with feathers and a beaded band. And for the lady down the lane — something a bit more diminutive, with flowers and ribbon? Do you agree?" She talked as she illustrated her ideas, her pen flying.

Heather Flower commented how beautiful her drawings were and Patience explained Lizzie was inventive and skilled, and very good with her ideas — as she was with most everything she ever set out to do.

"Your beadwork is the same." Lizzie

stopped drawing for a moment. "Your beads and how you stitch them together are works of art."

"I will make a wampum headband for Grissell's hat. It will be beautiful with many shades of purple from the quahog shell, and the whitest part of the whelk shell."

"What's a quahog shell?"

"A clam. I could teach you. It is not difficult." She made the offer to both of her friends.

Patience answered first. "Benjamin is coming back to build some counters and cabinets for us. Then you could show us how you make the beads?"

"*Nuk.* Of course."

Before Benjamin came, they moved what furniture they could out of the way and swept and scrubbed Patience's already spotless floors. When he arrived and set to work, they settled at a table in the next room, and Heather Flower got her tools out and the sacks of shells.

She spread her whelk and clamshells, a stone made of pointy flint, her metal drill, sandstone, sinew, milkweed bast, strips of soft deerskin, and bone needles all out on the table. She asked Patience for a bucket to fetch water as Benjamin walked in.

Heather Flower's heart twittered as he

stepped close to her.

"Did I hear you need some water? I can get that for you." He touched the tip of her chin with a finger.

"I will go with you, my friend." She wanted to share her knowledge of the beads with her friends, but Benjamin was making her forget everything she knew. Lizzie nudged Patience with obvious amusement and the two shared a giggle.

"I would like that very much. But I fear these ladies would be much more interested in teasing us than accomplishing anything else the rest of the day. Where's the bucket, Patience?"

His remark sent them into hysterics and Patience held her sides as she went to fetch it.

While they waited for the water, Heather Flower, with her cheeks a rosy bronze, explained to Lizzie and Patience the history and significance of wampum. The job of making purple and white beads was a highly coveted position for her people, she told them. The women found the shells in the mud or just below the water's surface off the shore and gathered them for the men who were assigned to make the beads. Because she was Wyandanch's daughter, she was permitted to perform that duty as well, as it was work befitting a child of the sachem.

The deep purple from the quahog clamshell was much harder to find, and considered more valuable than the white, which was made from the snowy inner swirl of the whelk shell. Many generations ago the beads were made for adornment. Headbands and headdresses, dresses and leggings, belts and moccasins, and jewelry were all bedazzled with the shell beads.

She picked up a shell and showed Lizzie and Patience where she would cut to make cylinders and disks. Strung on sinew or milkweed bast, they were then smoothed with sand and water. Each polished cylinder was cut and the finished beads were sewn onto soft deerskin, either directly on the clothing or on long strips to make belts, badges, and jewelry, and became wampum. So prized were they that often they were used as barter.

The stories that were told when they were presented at ceremonies became the story of the wampum being given. Soon the wampum was used as a way to record events, including war declarations and peace negotiations. Or ransom like the wampum belt paid for Heather Flower's release. The meaning of a particular piece of wampum was in the story that was told at the time it was given. That story would be handed down to future generations.

Lizzie's pretty eyes grew wide. "My goodness, I never knew there was such significance. I always thought it was just your way of money. Like our pennies and shillings."

Heather Flower gave her an understanding nod and a little smile. "In my father's generation they had no use for money. It is a white man's need. But our wampum has become the currency of the white man here. He gives us many things we can use in exchange, then he pays the northern tribes for pelts with it. He assigns a value like his coinage and tells us the purple are twice the value of the white beads. But our wampum is much more important than coins of silver or gold."

Patience laughed. "I think so, Heather Flower. Our silver and gold means nothing here in the colonies when it comes to survival."

Benjamin came back with the bucket of water, and while she taught Lizzie and Patience how she formed the beads, she could see him through the doorway as he worked. Every once in a while their eyes would meet and they would smile. He was proud of her, she could tell.

But when she came to the part of drilling the hole, she looked at the metal drill Dirk had given her, and suddenly she did not want to talk about it. She picked up the flint and hoped Patience and Lizzie would not ask about the other drill. She would tell them about the old ways, and long for them herself. Back when there were not so many choices to be made.

By the end of the very long day, the ladies had a counter and cupboards. Lizzie had brought a large looking-glass from England and it now sat on their front counter for ladies to view their intended purchase. Benjamin promised them a sign by the morrow. Now all they needed were the hats.

Lizzie told them while they waited for supplies they could make patterns, and Patience brought out more parchment. From the drawings she'd made of Grissell's hat, they began to sketch pieces, and after cutting out a few and holding them together around Heather Flower's head, they figured the size they wanted for the pattern. It was all great fun and Heather Flower's worries of living in a white man's world seemed silly at this moment. People were just people, *nuk*?

36

May 10, 1654

On Friday Heather Flower and Winnie traveled back to Mary's at her request. The day was beautiful with cottony wisps of clouds in the very blue sky and alive with the music of bird chirps and buzzing insects. They enjoyed their walk through the woods of Indian Neck, and when it broke open to the meadow that edged the town center, Heather Flower picked a nosegay mix of blue iris and crisp white daisies for Mary.

Joseph had ridden out with the horse troop, Barnabas and Benjamin were working in the fields, planting wheat. Lizzie and Patience came to work on the wedding gown. With Joseph gone, Jane joined them.

Mary welcomed them and fetched her pretty red slipware jug decorated with a yellow vine to fill with water and the flowers. She set it on the table in the hall, next to the Bible.

The ladies all sat in a circle, each with a piece of the dress, placing careful stitches as they chatted. Lizzie looked at the sleeve Mary worked on, and she winked her approval. Winnie worked on the bodice embroidery, and as she finished she handed it to Heather Flower. She stitched beadwork among Winnie's flowers, stems, and leaves.

She listened to the gossip, but her thoughts drifted to Benjamin and she wondered if he'd be coming in for supper before she and Winnie left. Lizzie wanted them to stop at the cobbler so he could make a foot form for her wedding shoes. She'd prefer to wear her moccasins, but she was allowing them to plan it, so she was agreeable to what they suggested.

She caught what Patience said at the very end. " 'Tis been a long time since he's been here."

"It has, but he warned Barney he would stay longer in Mowsley this year. Grandmother Horton is not doing well and he wants to be home if something happens."

Heather Flower leaned into Winnie with her voice low. "Who?"

Patience giggled with a tinge of pink flooding her porcelain skin. "Jeremy. I was just wondering what happened to Jeremy."

Lizzie put her fabric in her lap. "Jeremy is

Barnabas's brother. Have you met him, Heather Flower?"

"No. I've heard of him. We have not met. He has the ship that brought you here, Mary?"

"Yes, *The Swallow.* He's had some adventures on that ship. And some near disasters. I shall be glad when he is through sailing."

Lizzie stabbed her needle into the sleeve. "I do not see that happening anytime soon. The last time he was here, I tried to tease him about settling down and getting married. He wasn't having any of it. Not at all." She sniffed.

Winnie spread the piece she worked on flat. "Why do you think he is that way?"

Patience raised her arms, undid her straight blond hair, and rewound it into a neat bun. She pushed the small ivory comb back into her hair. "He loves his ship. He loves sailing. He always teases me that 'tis hard for any woman to rival that."

"Do you wish that were not so, Patience?"

The ladies drew silent with Heather Flower's question, waiting for the answer.

"No. Not really. Men who love the ocean do not easily give that up. I'm happy he loves what he is doing."

"You are right, Patience. That is where his

heart is. It has been that way since he was ten or twelve." Mary placed her work on the table. "I think we shall have a little refreshment, then we should pin this on Heather Flower and see how it's coming along." Her eyes lit up as she looked at their work.

She brought out a platter of little fruit tarts she'd made for the occasion and set them on a table. With the younger girls taking naps, Abigail, along with Jane, helped her bring out small glasses of cider pressed from pippins out of their orchard.

Lizzie watched as Mary and Abigail served each of the ladies. "You amaze me, Mary. You'd never know by watching you that you were so inept at anything housewifely when you married Barney. I used to think you would never earn those tongs." Her laughter tinkled.

Heather Flower leaned ever so slightly toward Winnie.

Winnie quickly explained. "It's an old English custom. The new bride gets the kitchen tongs — it means she is head of her kitchen. But Barnabas was a baker and much better in the kitchen than Mary." Her tone teased.

Mary caught her breath. "Why, that was true, but I learned. Once he let me in the kitchen." She winked and laughed with the rest of them.

Lizzie broke in. "Yes, you did. But what about Heather Flower, Mary? Will you be presenting her with the tongs?"

Mary looked at her soon-to-be daughter-in-law. "Would you like to do our custom, Heather Flower? It's a very important one to us, but I know you will take good care of Ben no matter if you take the tongs or not."

"I want to do the customs of my husband. I will take the tongs."

Jane pulled at a thread and tied it in a knot. "You have a good heart, Heather Flower."

A smile encircled the group as they finished their refreshment and bent back to their task. She was the daughter of the Grand Sachem, the English called her a princess. It was true she was not required to do much of the labor of her people. But she had been taught and she often helped in planting, harvesting, and preparing food. She would do what Benjamin needed to care for their family.

A stomping of boots heralded the arrival of the Horton men and boys. Heather Flower smiled at Benjamin, and Caleb jabbed at his brother with his elbow.

Benjamin smiled his dimpled smile at his

brother. "Hey."

"Oh, so sorry. I stumbled."

The ladies laughed at the two and Barnabas shook his head. "Good afternoon, ladies. We cleaned up in the barn. We'll just be going through to the kitchen."

Mary stood with her finished piece in hand. "We are almost done with this for the day. There are some sweets in the kitchen if you men would like some. We'll have just a light supper."

Winnie got up and set the bodice piece she worked with on her chair. "We must go, Mary, and we'll stop by and get Heather Flower's feet measured."

"I'll hitch the wagon and take you there," Benjamin offered. "Then I'll take you home, if that is all right with you."

Heather Flower's cheeks warmed, and she looked at her aunt.

Winnie nodded her approval. "We would both like that very much."

Caleb stepped in front of Benjamin and pleaded with Heather Flower. "Can I come?"

But before she could answer, his brother did. "No, but you can help me hitch up Star. Come on." Caleb took off at a run for the barn.

As they walked down the flagstone to wait

for Benjamin to bring the horse and wagon, Heather Flower overheard Mary ask Barnabas about Jeremy. She turned to Winnie. "Barnabas had two brothers, *nuk*?"

"Yes. His brother Thomas lived up north in Massachusetts. He died of the fever the year Caleb was born."

"Did he have a wife?"

Winnie nodded. "Her name was Mary Jane and they had a little girl, Mary Belle. They stayed up there and she remarried. I imagine by now Mary Belle is married too. Mary said they received the letter of his passing, and one later about her marriage, but that was the last they heard."

The wagon pulled up and Benjamin jumped down. He helped Winnie up to the bench first, then Heather Flower.

A short ride down the main road, around the curve to the left, and they arrived at the cobbler, just one lot up from Dickerson, the tanner. Winnie suggested Benjamin wander down to Dickerson's Creek while the willow mold was fashioned around Heather Flower's bare foot.

Later, they bumped down the road toward the Corchaug fort. After a stew of squirrel and wild onions, Benjamin asked if Heather Flower would accompany him on a walk.

"Shall we walk down to the river?"

Heather Flower looked at the head of the path. She could picture Dirk standing there, watching her walk away. Had he felt the same sorrow as she that day? Or had he been ready to move on without her? It seemed so, since he had not come to meet her at the tulip tree. Not even left a message.

"Yes, Benjamin. It is my favorite place here at Winnie's. There is a pair of eagles that nest there. It is a sacred place."

Benjamin held her hand and looked up at the treetops as they sauntered down the path. "All of God's creation is sacred, Heather Flower. The eagle is mighty and beautiful, but God knows how many feathers are on every bird and knows the number of hairs on our head. Isn't that amazing?"

"It is so hard to imagine."

"That is the beauty, Heather Flower. We don't have to. It says in the Bible we just need to have faith. When you look at what He has created, it is easy to have faith in what we do not see."

"My aunt has been telling me much about your God. I feel He is the same as our Great Spirit, but we did not know He had a Son until the white men came to tell us. Do you think that is true?" She sat now on the grassy slope to the river, her hands folded on her deerskin skirt covering her knees, searching the sky for the eagles.

He lowered himself to the ground a couple of feet from her and looked at her with his baby-blue eyes. "Yes, He sent his Son to us so that we might believe in Him and have everlasting life with God." He scooted close to her and put his hands over hers. "God knows our hearts, but He wants us to say we believe, not for Him but for ourselves. It's how we are saved."

"My aunt has told me that."

"Have you told God you believe in Jesus, that you accept His Son as your Savior then?"

Her heart was full. Tears she wished no one to see trickled down her cheeks. "I have felt emptiness for so long, and I have found it isn't something you or Dirk or even the memory of Keme can fill."

"It's Jesus who fills that, Heather Flower. The rest of us are just the ones He puts into your life to point you on your way. But it's Jesus who gives us all that we need."

"I want that. I want what you and Winnie and Mary have."

"You can have it. Just say it to God."

He pulled her to her knees and they knelt in prayer. Certainly she'd not ever been this close to the Great Spirit in the sky than she

412

was now, and she called Him by name and asked Him to fill the emptiness in her heart as she gave her life to God.

"The angels are singing hallelujah, Heather Flower."

Benjamin pulled her close to him and held her tenderly. She rested her cheek against his shoulder. He was a good man and sent to her by God. She loved him like a brother. She prayed now that the love they shared could someday grow into the deep, abiding love of husband and wife. Surely that was what God intended.

But what did God intend for Dirk? He rarely talked about God. She'd heard Benjamin say that the Dutch were here just to trade and make money. And that they did with the northern tribes. But she could feel a yearning in Dirk. He sought God in his own way, she was certain.

37

May 10, 1654

Heather Flower stayed up almost all night talking with her aunt. She told Winnie how she had given her life to God and how Benjamin told her the angels were singing hallelujah. Winnie was cold sitting by the fire, even though it was late spring, and she'd gotten her aunt a heavy linsey-woolsey blanket to wrap about her shoulders.

Winnie's two wolf dogs curled at her feet, one with its paws and nose resting on her ankles, the other's body snuggled as close to her side as he could manage.

"I have such a happy heart for you, my niece. I have prayed for you for many years. God is faithful." She shivered as she said it.

"Are you feeling all right, Aunt?"

"With that news I feel very blessed. Now tell me about you and Benjamin. And are you happy with your wedding dress? Are you certain you want to wear an English dress for your wedding?"

Heather Flower smiled. "So many questions. But they are music to my ears. I am so glad to see you with interest in life again." She hugged her.

"My child. Always know how much I love you. I have many children, but I have always considered you as one of them. And you have come to take care of me."

Heather Flower wasn't certain why, but she found what her aunt was telling her unsettling, so she just answered her questions. "I love the English dress. It will be a beautiful wedding. And Benjamin is happy. I am too."

With that Winnie closed her eyes, a smile on her face despite her shivers.

Heather Flower got up and brought her sleeping pallet to her. "Here, stay by the fire and be warm." She helped her onto it and then she lay next to her, warming her. She lay awake until the sun's first rays shot into the morning, watching her aunt until her heavy eyes closed and she slept hard.

Heather Flower woke to Winnie's raspy breath. She put her hand on her forehead — it burned with fever. She got up and ran out of the hut straight to the medicine man's wigwam. He followed her to Winnie's hut, and then she was off to find the mes-

senger boy. She sent him to run into
Southold and tell Mary her aunt was sick.
She promised the runner wampum if he
could return quickly. Mary would fetch Abigail and Doctor Smith.

She returned to the wigwam. Winnie lay
still with her eyes closed. Her breathing
remained ragged. The medicine man
chanted and had charms and potions. She
got down on her knees like Benjamin taught
her and began to pray. Her aunt was too
young to die and had much to live for. She
wanted her there at the wedding. She prayed
that she would get well.

She stayed on her knees until they ached,
then she got up and paced, but she did not
quit praying. At long last the runner came
back and told her that Mary would be coming. She would tell the people who needed
to know and then she would be coming in
the wagon. She thanked the young boy very
much, gave him the wampum, and then
prayed some more. She prayed without
ceasing until finally she heard the wagon.

She ran outside and Benjamin was already
helping Mary and Abigail down. He turned
to her and wrapped his arms around her.
"How is she?"

"She is dying, I'm afraid."

"The doctor is on his way. I thought he'd

get here first. I've been praying for her and you."

"Oh, Benjamin, I have prayed too."

Mary came over and gave her a hug and Abigail ran inside.

"We must go with Abigail." Heather Flower took Mary's hand to bring her in.

The inside of the hut was smoky and dark. The sad wolf dogs kept vigilance at Winnie's feet. Mary rubbed their ears before she embraced her sick friend.

Abigail sat on the floor and cradled her mother's head in her lap, running her fingers across her cheek. The medicine man continued his chants.

A "heigh-ho" at the door brought Barnabas into the hut. Mary looked at Barnabas with a questioning look. "Jane is with Sarah and Hannah. I came as soon as I could. Doctor Smith was coming, but then good Mrs. Haines began to give birth. He will come when he can."

Heather Flower looked at Benjamin. She was frightened, but she needed to keep herself under control. Especially for Abigail. She watched as he walked over and knelt next to Winnie.

Benjamin felt her forehead and looked at the fire, then her blankets. He looked up at the medicine man and Barnabas. "Father, I need to try to save her. All of this will not." Without another word he scooped her up, blanket and all, and rushed out of the hut, down to the bay.

Though it was already May, the water was cold. He stomped out into the waves until he could lower her into the icy water and immersed her. He brought her up and she gasped. He brought her down one more time, and when she came up, she opened her eyes and put a weak arm around his neck, hugging with what little strength she had.

He held her to him and walked back up on the shore. His parents, Heather Flower, Abigail, and the medicine man all waited there with horrified looks on their faces that quickly turned to joy when they saw Winnie awake.

They followed him into the hut and he directed them to leave the bearskin cover open on the doorway. He had Heather Flower move her pallet away from the fire and he laid Winnie down. She clung to his hand.

When she spoke, her voice sounded very old and tired. "Benjamin, I remember so clearly the day a little boy showed up at my door so frightened his brother would die and the woman who was to be his mother might never come back." She took a shallow breath. "You were at death's door. You burned with fever and could barely breathe. Your father was panicked. He could not bear to lose you. We sent the medicine man and he put the same icy cloths on your body Mary had prepared to use. The ones your father feared would be the death of you."

"Joseph has told me that story many times, and I was remembering it too. We didn't have snow today, but the water was cold and your fever is gone. You will get well, my friend."

Her smile lit her face and she squeezed his hand. "You did well. But I fear I am being called home. Do not cry for me. I'm going to a good place, my heavenly home."

Abigail sobbed and Heather Flower held her. "Hush, cousin, your mother still needs you."

Winnie released Benjamin and reached for Abigail and Heather Flower. They both sat beside her. "You must gather all of my children. I need them here with me as I go."

Abigail held her tears. "Is there something I can get you, Mother? Some water? Something to eat?"

"You may get me dry clothes, my child, and we will have everyone leave while I change into my finest dress." She laughed and everyone laughed with her.

Benjamin nodded to his father and they all left Abigail to do her mother's bidding.

Outside Barnabas stopped him. "You were brave to do that. Thank you."

"What the medicine man was doing wasn't saving her. I couldn't help think of how that snow saved my life." He turned to Heather Flower. "I'm sorry she thinks she is still dying. My fear is she may be right."

Heather Flower looked at him with sad eyes. "The dying usually know."

Barnabas took her hand. "The Lord knows every hour of our life. If it is her time to meet her Lord, she will be there. We will miss her, but we must not be sad for her. We can rejoice." He hugged Mary, and she finally spoke.

"I am losing my first friend on Long Island and it will never be the same." Mary's tears came fast. "I promise you, Barney, I shall be happy for her. But right now I am sad for me."

Heather Flower was glad to see the days linger for Winnie. Her family gathered around her. All six children, her friends from Southold, and Wuchi and Wyandanch came to sit with her and talk. Sometimes she would smile and look up as if she saw someone waiting for her. But then she would focus back on the present and seemed happy to be with her family and friends.

She took little drink and even less food. Heather Flower sang to her and often Abigail came to sit and sing too. Mary came out when she could and always brought her crisp little ginger cakes or pippin tarts to tempt her to eat something. On her last day, Patience had come out with Mary and it seemed to Heather Flower that with all of her friends gathered, Winnie was ready to say goodbye.

Heather Flower was not ready, though. She wanted her aunt at her wedding. She prayed daily that it would happen, and she even daydreamed about ways she and Benjamin could marry sooner. But that was not to be. That morning Winnie told her that God always answers prayer, but not always in the way we want.

When Winnie settled into Abigail's arms late that afternoon, she looked at Heather Flower and smiled. "I see you will be happy with your new husband, my child. That is all I need to see." She closed her eyes and looked like she slept. It was that peaceful when Winnie met her Maker.

38

May 18, 1654

Rain soaked the earth the day Winnie was buried, and Mary said the angels agreed with her that this was a sad day indeed. But Heather Flower comforted her by telling her, yes, the angels cried for them on earth, but they were singing hallelujahs up above.

The funeral procession braved the storm up to the bluff. Winnie already was in her grave, next to her beloved Winheytem, both facing west toward the setting sun. Before she was covered, Heather Flower draped the solid deep purple wampum across her aunt's body and said goodbye. Benjamin walked back with her to the wigwam, and Mary, Patience, Jane, and Lizzie busied themselves setting out pots and platters of food.

It was not a cold day, but the mourners crowded in, hugging their wet arms to their bodies, and Benjamin revived the fire in the pit with a new log. It wasn't that long ago they were all here for Winheytem's funeral; the only people missing were Johnny and Joseph. Barnabas once again offered seats of honor to Momoweta, Wuchi, and Wyandanch, and as before they talked of their daughter coming home, but this time to prepare for the wedding.

How could she think about a happy time when she was missing Aunt so very much?

Benjamin sat next to her. "It's hard, isn't it? Mayhap you should stay here until the wedding."

She looked around the hut and the wolf dogs came to her and sought her attention, nuzzling her with six black noses. She gathered them close. It struck her that she was always mourning, and her aunt would not like that. "Benjamin, you are right. I need to be here, not to mourn my aunt — she would not want that — but to celebrate her life. And to think on our wedding. That is what she would want for me."

He smiled deeply. "Well, I know I like that idea."

A pearl of a tear formed in the corner of Wuchi's eye as she told her parents her decision, but Wyandanch accepted what she said to them and allowed her to remain. Wyancombone would come often in the next

423

several days, and he would bring their parents on the day of the wedding.

To the rhythm of the rainfall, they sat around the fire and Wyandanch presented Abigail with a wampum belt Winnie had stitched herself and told a cherished story about her mother to be passed down to Misha and future generations.

Heather Flower walked out to the wagon with Benjamin as the Hortons said their goodbyes. The persistent rain was now but a drizzle. He told her he would come back out on the morrow.

"I will wait for you, my friend," she said.

Little Sarah slept in Mary's arms, and Mary gave Heather Flower an awkward hug and patted her hand. "I will have Ben bring you in for dress fittings, and you are welcome to come in to see us as often as you can."

Patience leaned in to hug her too. "You can stay with me, if you like. I would love that."

"We will be waiting for the supplies for the Hatterie, Heather Flower, so we can turn our thoughts completely to your wedding." A teary-eyed Lizzie hugged her tight.

Before Benjamin left, she hugged him and he pulled her into a long kiss. Finally she pulled back "They were precious days with my aunt that you gave to me and Abigail, my friend, and I thank you for that."

She stood in the rain waving until the last wagon disappeared out of the palisade. She walked inside and settled next to the fire in between her mother and Abigail, with James holding a sleeping Misha, and her father and Wyancombone opposite from them. All of Winnie's children remained, and they continued to talk of Winnie's life far into the night until they fell into slumber.

Heather Flower said her prayers before she drifted off to sleep. She thanked God for her aunt, for the wisdom and example she left as her legacy.

39

May 19, 1654

Benjamin's plans of going to see Heather Flower that morning changed when Joseph and the horse troop rode into town. He and his father walked outside when they heard the commotion over at the meetinghouse. The men were all dismounting and Joseph already stood at the porch of the north entrance, talking to Reverend Youngs. They turned as he and Barnabas approached.

Joseph was the first to speak. "Father, Benjamin — good to see you."

Horton bear hugs and hearty claps on the back were exchanged.

Benjamin glanced over at the men. Everyone, including Joseph, looked exhausted. "Where's Johnny?"

"No one's seen him. We talked to everyone who would have known. We checked every nook and cranny he could be hiding in."

Reverend Youngs looked out over the

small cemetery to the west of the meetinghouse. A few scattered stones dotted the field of wild grass. Fragrant bayberry and rosebushes, planted by the ladies, surrounded the lot. He rubbed his eyes. "What about the horses? Did anyone say if they found the horses that were missing?"

"No one knew a thing."

Barnabas folded his arms. "Do you think they were with-holding something?"

"I think they were telling the truth."

Benjamin put his hand on Joseph's shoulder and gestured toward the militia troop. "I'm going to help the boys put the horses away."

Barnabas nodded. "Do that — and thank you. Joseph, let's go inside with John. There's much more we'd like to know."

Benjamin led Joseph's horse to the barn kept for the militia. He hefted the saddle off the mare's back and straddled it over a stall wall. He brushed at the horse's coat as the animal cooled down. "There you go, girl. That's good." He talked to her in soothing tones and she flicked her ears toward his voice as he brushed the grime of travel from her coat.

Lieutenant Biggs worked in the next stall over.

"Did you have the same feeling as Joseph

about what everybody was saying?"

Biggs paused and rested his arms along the stall wall. "What do you mean?"

He tapped the brush against the side of the stall and dust billowed from it. "He thought they were telling the truth. They weren't hiding anything."

"Well, yes. I didn't see any reason not to believe them. We were talking to Isaac and a few of the others — they would be honest with us about Johnny."

"Yeah, I suppose so. It's just hard for me to believe that Johnny and all those horses just disappeared."

"If the Dutch don't have him, the Indians probably got him and stole some horses to boot. And Joseph said your mother wants this wedding to happen and it will. So you mights as well get on with it."

Benjamin chortled. "*Mights* as well, Biggs? Well, I don't think I have a choice there, and I'm glad I don't. It's time to settle down and get married, don't you think? I know the whole town thinks so." The Horton chuckle erupted again and he turned back to the horse.

"Aw, I suppose."

Benjamin got a bucket from the front of the barn. "I'll be hauling some water for the horses if anyone asks."

"Right."

He trudged down to Town Creek with his mind on the wedding. They hadn't even talked about where they'd live afterward. Most likely he'd ask his father if they could take over the small hall in the front until they built their own place.

Halfway down the road, just beyond a grove of walnuts, he watched a familiar figure coming toward him. "Uncle Jeremy!" He started out in a trot. "When did you get here?"

His uncle chuckled as he clapped him on the back and then wrapped him in a bear hug. "We docked less than an hour ago. Look at you, Benjamin. Let me see that muscle."

Benjamin smiled at the familiar request. "You say that every time you see me."

"That's because every time I see you, there is less baby fat and more of this." He squeezed the bicep Benjamin displayed.

"I haven't had baby fat since I was five, if you'll remember." They both turned to walk back to the village green. "I'll send Biggs to get water. I'm sure he needs something else to do."

"Who's Biggs?"

"His family came out from Flushing. He's a lieutenant in our militia. A dedicated fellow." He glanced behind them. "Don't you need help with your trunk, Uncle Jeremy?"

"Nay, my crew will haul it up in a bit. So bring me up to date while we walk. What's been happening?"

"You wouldn't believe it. Reverend Youngs's son — Johnny — got captured in the North Sea by the Dutch. They had him prisoner on the *King Solomon,* but he escaped."

"That's our Johnny. Good for him."

"Not really. Father took bond money up to New Haven and they were going to pay bail, except now they won't until Johnny surrenders back in New Amsterdam and then he's to go before the court in New Haven."

Jeremy shook his head. "Gracious. So he's doing that, right?"

"No, they can't find him and something very strange is going on, because a herd of horses disappeared at the same time as Johnny and they say he did it."

"What does your father have to say about all of this?"

"He sent Joseph and the horse troop to look for him and they just got back today. No one's seen him."

"Or the horses?"

"No."

They came up to the Indian cornfields and turned left toward the meetinghouse. Before they got far, they were spotted by Joshua and Jonathan and their friends, and the two were surrounded.

Jonathan grabbed Jeremy's hand. "Uncle Jeremy, Mama was just telling Papa that we needed to see you."

"Heigh-ho there! You both are getting so tall. How is that?"

Joshua walked straighter. "I'm almost as tall as Caleb. Mama says next year I will be."

"How is your mama? And Hannah?"

Benjamin answered as Joshua and Jonathan took off running to announce their uncle's arrival. "She is fine, Hannah too. And Sarah is all over the place."

"Crawling? Has it been that long? All those boys and now two girls. Your mother must be thrilled."

"I guess. She and Aunt Lizzie like to make them dolls."

"Like her poppet? The one she brought from England?"

"Yes, like that one."

They did not get much farther when Joshua and Jonathan came, pulling their mother between them.

Mary looked like she might faint, but

broke away from her sons and ran to greet her brother-in-law. He gave her a quick embrace, then held her at arm's length. "I am so glad to see you well, Mary."

"Oh, Jeremy, I was so worried about you. You have been constantly in my prayers. What took you so long?"

She looked up at him and he described for her and Benjamin the months of sitting by Grandmother Horton's side while she lingered before she went home to the Lord. Then there were affairs of the vast estate, which included the mill. He needed to hire caretakers and someone to run the mill, since he wouldn't be around.

Her eyes watered as she said how sorry she was to hear that news and told him of Winnie's death and how much she missed her dear friend. He hugged her again, telling her how sorry he was too.

Benjamin gazed ahead as they walked up to the meetinghouse. Joshua pulled the door open for them, and they were met by Barnabas, Joseph, and the reverend before they could all get through.

Barnabas and Jeremy clasped each other in a hug, pounding each other's backs. Joseph joined in, and Mary's eyes teared as she and Benjamin watched them rejoice in the homecoming.

"You've come on a good day," she said. "I've a joint of roast venison on the spit right now."

"You are always ready to feed an army."

She shook her head and a curly lock fell on her forehead. She brushed it back.

Jeremy turned to Reverend Youngs and extended his hand. "Benjamin was telling me about Johnny. I'm so sorry. You've no further word?"

The reverend looked tired. "Nay, Joseph's just returned. There's nothing. Not a trace."

"I've my own sad news, I'm afraid." He placed his hands on his brother's shoulders and his eyes sagged. "Our mother passed, Barn. She slipped from this world early in the morning, in her sleep. She's with God and our father."

"Why is it still so hard to hear those words, when I know she's in a better place?"

Reverend Youngs wrapped his arms about both men. "I'm so sorry. Shall we pray?"

He led the small gathering in a prayer. "If anyone feels the need to talk, my door is always open." He shook hands and gave Mary a hug, then trudged to the meetinghouse.

Barnabas was the first to speak. "As sad as I am for Mother, I feel at a loss of words for John. He doesn't know if his son is alive or dead. Come, Jeremy, I need to sit a spell, I fear."

Joseph went to fetch Jane, and Mary sent Joshua to find Caleb. She invited John to bring his wife, Mary, over for dinner. As they walked across the road to the house, Charles and Anna Tucker rode by in his wagon. He pulled over to inquire of Johnny, and before Benjamin could circumvent his mother, she'd invited them to dinner as well.

Looking around the two long tables in the big kitchen, almost the whole town seemed to have come for dinner. Abigail brought Hannah and Sarah downstairs as Mary made her way around to Benjamin with Muffkin at her heels.

She leaned close. "Ben, I know this might feel a little awkward — I don't know what I was thinking. But probably 'tis best for you to get used to being around Anna."

"I see. I thought you must have a plan." He could never be too upset with her, so he gave her a hug and let her go to her chair, opposite his father.

They all joined hands and Barnabas led them in a prayer for Joseph and Jeremy, for the safety of Johnny and a prayer for Grandmother Horton's passing.

Everyone began to find places to sit. Reverend Youngs and his wife sat to the right of Barnabas. Jeremy found a chair next to Patience. Lizzie and Zeke sat to Mary's right. The overflow took their plates out to the front parlor. Joseph and Benjamin offered their seats to Charles and Anna and wandered out front. Everyone was somber with the discussion centering on finding Johnny and getting him home.

Benjamin's discomfort with Anna's presence wasn't lessened by sitting in the parlor, and when there was a knock at the door, he jumped to answer it. There stood Heather Flower. Never was he happier to see her. He took her hand and pulled her in. In a moment he had her in the big kitchen and piled heaps of succulent venison and mounds of mashed pumpkin and baked onions on a plate for her.

He held the plate as he encircled her waist with his free arm. "Uncle Jeremy, this seems like a good time to tell you Heather Flower and I are getting married, and to invite all of you to our wedding on the twenty-seventh of this month." He looked at each of the guests seated at the table, then nodded toward his father. "Father will do the officiating at the meetinghouse, and there will be, of course, a big feast here afterward."

Jeremy stood up. "Hear, hear, Benjamin.

Congratulations to you and your bride."

Barnabas stood and went to Mary's side. With a hand on her shoulder, he bowed to Heather Flower. "We welcome you to our family. And Jeremy, if you might do us the honor of officiating, I know Benjamin would agree we would be honored."

"Yes, Uncle Jeremy. As a ship's captain, it is only fitting and would be much appreciated."

"I am the one honored by your request. And though we may treat marriage as a civil ceremony, I'd like to ask the reverend to close the service that day with a prayer on the union. Reverend?"

"It would be my pleasure. I only pray that Johnny is back to celebrate with us."

Joseph stood up. "If I have anything to say about it, he will be, sir."

Heather Flower's dark opal eyes grew large and round, her hand trembled on Benjamin's arm. "It is best to wait for him, Joseph. Do not go into that territory again."

Benjamin's brow wrinkled. "Why? It's not your people we suspect. If it's not the Dutch, it's the tribes to the north that are causing trouble."

Her smile warmed his heart. "You are right. I should not worry."

40

May 24, 1654

Johnny Youngs was not forgotten in the ensuing days, but the townspeople accepted he might not be coming back. Heather Flower's joy at her upcoming marriage increased as Benjamin made a point to spend more of his spare time with her, as limited as it was. He had purchased a wedding present for her in Connecticut, and it had taken him two days to bring it back. His excitement was contagious.

She sewed beads onto an elaborate headpiece that would bring unity between her heritage and her new life, and she thought much about Winnie as she worked. She went into town frequently for fittings with Lizzie and Patience. Her dress was beautiful, and she found herself twirling in it and feeling much like the princess the white men said she was. Patience, Rachel, and Ruth loved combing her hair and arranging it in different styles, each one disagreeing with the other about how she should wear it for the wedding day.

Patience loved organizing the wedding. She taught her charges in the morning and worked on the wedding plans every afternoon. Heather Flower was certain her love of planning every detail was a way to walk in her moccasins.

Joseph joined Barnabas, James, and Benjamin in the fields, working the soil and tending the tender shoots in the acres already planted. Heather Flower liked how Benjamin smelled of fresh earth when he came in, and she smiled as Mary shook her head at the mess they made and sent them back out to the barn to wash up.

She liked to think about the day they would have their own house, and she would welcome him into her arms at the end of a tiring day. They would stoke the fire if it was a cold night, or sit outside on a warm night and listen to the bullfrogs and crickets play their harmony while they enjoyed a light breeze.

Each day the happy plans folded into nights filled with dreams of the day she wed Keme. That memory made her heart squeeze and she prayed to God that this wedding would not be attacked.

The morning of her wedding dawned and she bathed at first light in the river and washed her long raven hair. She rinsed it with rosewater and dried it with the coarse linen towels Mary had given to her as a gift. The pair of eagles she loved soared high beyond the treetops. She watched them as long as she dared and finally returned to Winnie's wigwam, sat by the fire, and worked through her hair with the ivory comb Dirk had given her.

He'd saved her life in the wilds of Connecticut, and she'd thought he'd fallen in love with her. But he'd left her. She must forget him now, and be glad for a true friend like Benjamin. He was the steadfast one, always there, always wanting what was best for her.

Patience arrived and tied her hair in coils to set it with curls. "When we are done, we will go out and pick flowers from the meadow." She held Heather Flower at arm's length. "You are beautiful. Winnie would be so proud of you."

"Thank you, my friend. She was always good counsel to me. She was the strong one, the beautiful one. Your words, spoken like she would have spoken on this day, mean much to me."

They took stacks of deep baskets and

picked flowers to decorate her hair and Patience's dress, and for Abigail, Rachel, and Ruth too.

Later Mary came out with Lizzie to help her dress. The whalebone stays, laced with satin blue grosgrain ribbons, defined her already regal posture, and confined her ordinarily lithe movements. But she was willing to endure for her English friends and smiled at their "ooohs" and "ahhhs."

The embroidered blue bodice with creamy, billowing sleeves topped the full satin skirt with under-layers of pretty petticoats. Her beautiful high-top boots fit perfectly and completed her ensemble. She was a princess in every way.

Lizzie and Patience returned to the church and their final preparations. Abigail, Rachel, and Ruth joined them and untied the coils and arranged her hair in beautiful loose curls, scattering flowers through the strands. They decorated their own dresses and those of the littlest girls in the Corchaug fort with the blooms.

Patience helped her put the headdress with strings of shell beads on, lacing it through her hair.

The walk to the meetinghouse began with Heather Flower in front, flanked by Abigail, Rachel, Ruth, and Patience, with the little girls running circles around them. Benjamin would stand waiting with his family and hers, ready to welcome them, and it would be a day of feasting after their exchange of vows.

The path was alive this morning with a tempo of bird trill, waves of breeze moving gently through the young, tall grass, and tree limbs laden with green leaves and blossoms. Rabbits bounded out of the way as the procession came through, and squirrels chattered to each other like gossiping guests.

After the first hour the little dancing girls lagged behind, but their enthusiasm still bubbled. She half listened to her friend's cheerful banter, but her thoughts were elsewhere. How many times had she and Aunt Winnie walked this path? This was her wedding day, and as a breeze brushed past her cheek, she could almost feel her aunt's embrace.

Miss Button pushed hard and Dirk reined her back. "Whoa, missy, we've got women on those horses behind us. We won't be leaving them behind." Twelve native women came single file behind him, with Johnny following them all on a tall Dutch steed.

They'd been riding over a week, and tired as they were, they pushed on toward the

Montaukett village. They approached the pond near the Indian fort and dismounted to allow the horses to drink. The women chattered with joy. They were close to home.

Dirk took his hat off and rubbed his forehead as he and Johnny searched the eastern horizon. It was strangely deserted. "I don't like the looks of this. I'll be glad to get to the village and talk to Wyandanch."

Johnny nodded and walked to his horse. "Let's have the ladies eat and then head out. We'll be there in about one half hour."

"*Ja.*"

The women eagerly ate the biscuits and dried berries Dirk and Johnny offered to them. After some water, they helped the women onto their mounts, then swung up to their own and rode out north around the pond. As they approached the wigwams, a few wolf dogs came out to greet them, and as they dismounted, a young brave came out of the longhouse. His face lit up in recognition of the women who returned from their captivity at the hands of the Narragansett.

Dirk led Miss Button to the brave. "We are looking for your sachem, Wyandanch."

"He goes to the wedding across the bay."

"Wedding?" Dirk looked at Johnny, who shrugged his shoulders. "Across the bay?

Do you mean Southold, what you call Yennicott?"

"*Nuk.*"

"Who is getting married?"

The young brave glanced at the women. They nodded with curious looks. "Quashawam, daughter of Wyandanch."

Dirk's legs were unsteady, and it wasn't from the long ride. He turned to Johnny. "Heather Flower? Who would she marry?" He didn't need Johnny to answer. It would be Benjamin Horton. He'd been so determined to rescue the women, why did he think she would wait? What was he thinking? That she would fall in love with him when he was nowhere to be found?

That old jagged pain he'd felt when she rode off with the Horton men ripped through him again and he threw himself into the saddle. He reined Miss Button around with a nudge in her side. "I have to get there."

Johnny followed right behind. "What do you mean you have to get there?"

"*Ja,* just that. I can't let this happen. I love Heather Flower. Do you see? I've never loved anyone before. I can't let her marry the wrong man." He gave Miss Button one more kick and she took off at a gallop, with Johnny doing his best to keep up.

As they raced their horses toward the bay, Dirk thought it hadn't been easy, this rescue. It might not have happened at all if Johnny hadn't escaped from the *King Solomon* and run right into his camp. Two people who couldn't dislike each other more. Until they discovered a couple of things they agreed on. Their faith and getting these women back.

They'd both grown up hearing the gospel but tried to go their own way once they were grown. There was a Bible verse about training a child in the way of the Lord. It said something about when he was older he would not depart from it, but he figured it didn't mean they might not stray in the middle.

He and Johnny had some interesting talks at night on their way up to the wilds of Connecticut. They'd solved the problems of the Dutch and the English and everyone in between. And they'd plotted how to get twelve women out of the clutches of the Narragansett. Not bad for a couple of archenemies. Well, it'd taken some prayers too.

They rode the makeshift ferry across to Shelter Island. Jack rode with them to the opposite side and waved as they pushed off on the barge over to the north fork.

When they hit the small dock east of the Southold port, Dirk and Johnny led their horses off the ferry and began their race to Southold. The two Dutch horses stretched out, competing with each other until the riders brought them in.

They continued down Town Street until Dirk saw a beautiful woman walking up the flagstone to the meetinghouse like a princess, surrounded by big and little girls bedecked with flowers. Her blue and cream gown sparkled with beadwork and her glossy black hair flowed loosely about her shoulders in curls, studded with blossoms and coiled with strands of beads. His heart lurched to his throat.

Benjamin stood on the step waiting for her, a reverend on one side and a fellow who could only be another Horton on the other. Dirk surveyed the crowd. Obviously Heather Flower's family was present and half the Montauk village. He could see Barnabas and Joseph and what was most likely the rest of the Horton clan. They all turned as one as she walked toward them, surrounded by girls, big and little, bedecked with flowers.

But their gaze was drawn beyond her and the joy on their faces turned to utter confusion as he and Johnny approached. He

445

watched the princess step up to Benjamin, then slowly turn to follow his stare. Her eyes fell on his, and for a moment recognition lit the fire in those beautiful, dark opal eyes right before she fainted into the arms of Benjamin.

He watched Benjamin scoop her up, as he swung his leg over Miss Button's flank and jumped down. Everything happened in a blur. He saw the reverend rush to Johnny and Benjamin's parents help Heather Flower inside. But he didn't see Joseph's fist coming directly at his jaw until it hit and sent him flailing to the ground. He started to sit up, but as he opened his eyes to Joseph standing beside him, he saw Johnny lunge across him from the other side and land a punch on Joseph. He wrapped an arm around each of their legs and heaved them to the ground.

"Hey!" was all Johnny yelled as he hit the dirt next to Dirk.

Jeremy soon separated them and Reverend Youngs held Dirk with his arms behind his back. "Let's get him inside."

"Whoa, whoa, whoa, Father." Johnny stepped in front of them. "You can't treat him like this. I wouldn't be home except for Dirk."

Joseph's eyes were wild. "What do you

mean, Johnny? This man has been nothing but trouble."

"That's not true." He turned to Wyandanch. "Chief, he just brought home the women taken by the ones who took your daughter. I helped him, but it was his plan. He figured it all out." He turned back to Reverend Youngs and Dirk. "Father, you must release him and let's go inside and talk. We can tell you everything that happened."

The reverend looked at Dirk. "Is that true? You've brought back the Montaukett women?"

"*Ja.* I did. We did." He nodded toward Johnny.

Reverend Youngs let go of his arms. He dusted himself off and started for the meetinghouse as the reverend instructed the ladies and children to remain outside. The men trooped in and found Heather Flower surrounded by women. Benjamin and Barnabas hovered over them.

Dirk went directly to her. "Heather Flower, *hoe gaat het*? How are you? Are you all right?"

She looked up and blinked at the tears that sprang to her eyes. Dirk shot a look at Benjamin and was annoyed that he returned the same what-have-you-done look. Rivulets now traced her bronze cheeks and she made no effort to dry her eyes.

He went down on one knee. "I brought back the women for you. They are safe. You do not need to feel like you abandoned them."

Reverend Youngs tapped his gavel at the clerk's desk. "Men, we'll have a meeting now. Let the ladies take care of Heather Flower, if you will. I need a full report as to what occurred in New Amsterdam."

Dirk stood. He wanted everyone to leave, but it was obvious that they would have the meeting and it would be good to get some things cleared up. He took his seat next to Johnny. But he couldn't take his eyes off Heather Flower.

She cried and she didn't care who saw her tears. She loved Benjamin and his happiness meant so much to her. But when Dirk rode up, she knew she could not marry Benjamin. Her heart was not there.

She peered over at the group of men and listened to Dirk's account of the rescue. Though they'd been forced to marry Narragansett men, they were treated like captives in the beginning, and when the men left on hunting trips, they were bound together in a longhouse. But eventually, when the Narragansett knew the women did not know where to run or how they could escape, they were sent to the fields to work the crops. Dirk told how he and Johnny sneaked in and brought them out to the string of horses. He spoke of the dangerous ride through the very woods in which he'd taken Heather Flower, avoiding the North Sea where they would be open for attack.

After Johnny retold the story, Barnabas informed him that a bail awaited to be paid on his behalf and that he would need to turn himself in to the Dutch authority so the due process of law could be applied. He would then face a fine from the court in New Haven.

Heather Flower looked at Benjamin and found him watching her intently. His face held sadness, but there was kindness in those blue eyes too. She closed her eyes and said a prayer for him, and her, and Dirk. That God would somehow take care of them all.

Mary pulled her close and spoke low. "You must do what is right, Heather Flower. Follow your heart. We all love you. But it would not be right to try to tell you what to do. Go with your heart."

She looked at Mary. "You know that I've always loved Benjamin, *nuk*?"

"Yes, and you know how much I wanted this marriage — but only you know if it is the love of a sister or a wife."

She buried her face in her hands. "I feel lost without Dirk by my side. When he left, I had the ache in my heart I had felt for my Keme. It surprised me. It was strong. We are of one heart."

Wuchi patted her hand. "My daughter, you must go with your heart as Mary says."

Mary stood and faced the men, sympathetic tears in her eyes. "Perhaps 'tis time that we leave Heather Flower and Benjamin alone. They have much to talk about." She strode quickly and clasped Dirk's arm. "And please come with me — I need to talk with you."

Heather Flower watched Mary walk out with Dirk like she expected the group to do just as she bid. And they did.

41

May 27, 1654

Heather Flower sat in her beautiful blue gown. Serenity draped her like a gossamer shawl, not even the whalebone stays in her sides bothered her. Her hands were folded on her lap and she watched Benjamin as he sat next to her on the bench. He looked at peace too.

"I am so sorry, my paleface brother," she began. "I do not mean to cause you unhappiness or your family trouble. I would like for you and me to always be the friends we have been since we were little children. And I think I would have been very happy to have shared your home and raised your children." She took a breath.

"Don't cry for us, Heather Flower. We are all right, you and me. You are in my heart and that will never change. You love Dirk and it would not be right for you to marry me. He is here for you now. He loves you

— that I can see. And I think we both were trying to be happy, and we both knew our feelings were strong, but not the kind of love that two people should share when they marry. We were trying to make it something it wasn't."

She started to tremble and looked away. He must not see any more tears.

"Heather Flower, don't look away. I'm your friend — you can show me your hurt, your pain, and I expect you to share your joy with me also."

"Joy? How can there be joy now? Your people will make Dirk leave. They do not like him, they will not be happy until he is gone, leaving me again."

"I think the tide is changing there. Your father will be forever grateful that he brought not just you back, but the other women as well. Johnny certainly has accepted him, and you know something — I have too. I can't help but want to get to know the person you have fallen in love with."

Her eyes stung again, but these were tears of gladness threatening to fall. "But what about you, Benjamin? I thought you wanted to marry, and it cannot be Anna." She watched his reaction.

He smiled a slow smile, his dimples

emerging. "I want what God wants for me, and He's telling me it's not you. I don't know about me yet. I guess it isn't my time. But I think it's yours, and I think we should have a wedding. You look beautiful and we have the meeting hall, we have Uncle Jeremy, who would like nothing better than to officiate a wedding. You are the bride, Heather Flower. I think your groom awaits."

He bent over and placed a tender kiss on her cheek and stood. He removed a handkerchief from his belt, gently dried her eyes, and offered her his hand. "One last thing. I almost forgot. I got you a wedding present. I still want you to have it."

Her eyes teared once again.

"It's all right, Heather Flower. Look." He walked over and pulled a leather bag from behind the pulpit and placed it in her lap.

She untied the bag and pulled a pair of elk moccasins from it, beaded with blue flowers. The striking centers were of yellow jingle shell beads. Her breath caught. "I love these, Benjamin. I will always treasure them. *Ooneewey.* Thank you, my friend."

She wiggled her feet from the stiff pointy shoes and slipped the soft moccasins on. She clasped his hand as she rose and the two walked outside.

The whole town had gathered and the

people of Montauk and Shelter Island as well. Her parents waited nearby with Wyancombone. Barnabas and Mary stood to their right. The crowd parted as Dirk made his way to the front, his blue eyes on Heather Flower. He hesitated when he reached her, but Benjamin reached out and put Heather Flower's hand into Dirk's, then turned to Jeremy. "We are gathered here together for a wedding. If you will do the honor, I think the celebration can continue now." He stepped down to stand next to Joseph, with a smile for her that gave her courage.

Jeremy did not waste time coming forward, his Bible tucked under his arm.

A quiver pulled at her heart as Dirk's eyes, the color of the sunny bay, sought hers.

"I love you." He held her hand firmly like he'd never let go. "Will you marry me, Heather Flower?"

She cried happy tears, but all she could manage to say was, *"Nuk."*

Jeremy waved his hand to the crowd. "Ladies and Gentlemen, the custom for the banns is an English one. Since the two I am about to marry are not, I see no reason to wait." He turned to Dirk and Heather Flower and with the exchange of vows he pronounced them man and wife.

The little girls danced and flowers were

thrown as Dirk pulled Heather Flower close and swept her into his arms. His kiss was warm and reassuring. He pulled back and looked into her eyes. "*Hoe gaat het?* How are you?"

A pouty smile pulled at the corners of her mouth. "I am good, my friend. So very good."

The Indian braves pulled out their drums and began beating and singing in celebration like a *pau-wau.* Makeshift tables had been set up in the meetinghouse yard, and soon the women of Southold began bringing out the dishes they'd prepared.

Lizzie brought savory vegetables swimming in butter like the French recipes, and sugared plums and violets, and Patience brought tasty meat puddings. Mary brought platters of roasted venison and baked cod along with manchet bread. Barnabas's little ginger cakes surrounded a towering wedding cake as the beautiful centerpiece, and everyone laughed when they caught little Hannah hiding behind it with her finger in the frosting. Barnabas could not deliver a scolding when she looked up with her big green eyes and pronounced, "Good, Papa."

They feasted until the evening grew chilly, and as the festivities wound down they built a bonfire and gathered around. The ladies presented Heather Flower with the quilt they'd made for her from the scraps of the wedding dress. Lizzie had embroidered the date on the edge, but in what turned out to be a blessing, she did not have the time to embroider names.

Everyone wanted to hear the story of Johnny and the twelve Montaukett women. Heather Flower longed to hear the full story.

Dirk ran his fingers through his sandy blond hair, his eyes wide. "*Ja.* It just happened."

Benjamin and Joseph looked at each other, then at Dirk. Benjamin chuckled. "How could it just happen?"

Johnny walked over and sat down between his two friends. "It really did. It didn't take much to escape from the *King Solomon* — I just walked off and no one seemed to notice. But once I was free, I knew I needed to get to Flushing and find a place to hide. They wouldn't have thought twice about shooting an escapee."

Dirk nodded. "That is true. But Johnny wandered into my camp instead."

Heather Flower looked from Johnny to Dirk. "Why did you have a camp? You live at the fort. And I sent you a message. Why did you not answer me?"

He covered her hand with his. "I couldn't.

I'd been up north. I'd been sent on a mission with a mapmaker. We were in Narragansett territory and I knew we had to be close to their spring fishing grounds. We were practically right on them. While Visscher sketched his maps, I scouted and I stumbled on the women almost immediately. They were forced to work the fields and almost starving."

Heather Flower's eyes flashed as she remembered how Ninigret had forced them into the canoes and taunted them. "But you could not bring them back?"

"It would have been very dangerous. I needed to plan an escape for them and I needed to make sure the mapmaker was not in harm's way. So we returned, and when your runner appeared, I sent him on his way with no message, but a piece of wampum for his trouble. Then I requested a leave of absence. I needed time to figure out a plan, but I also knew I should act quickly. The women would either finish their work in the field or they would start dying. Either way it would not be good. So I set up a camp near Flushing. That's when Johnny walked in."

Johnny raised his hands like in a surrender. "I didn't have a choice but to hear him out. What else could I do?"

457

"I knew you would not hurt him, Dirk." Heather Flower's eyes stung and her throat ached, but it was joy behind her emotions.

Dirk continued. "There's a big farm out there where a fellow breeds horses, imported from Utrecht, Holland." He looked at Barnabas. "We felt like your English Robin Hood, but we stole thirteen horses. And rope. We linked the horses together and we started north."

Johnny nodded. "And we brought food. There's a woman who makes *poffertjes* for Dirk. She prepared a bushel full, no questions asked. We brought bacon and dried apples and tied all the provisions on the backs of the horses."

Mary leaned forward, close to the fire. "I am so thankful you two were able to save those women. I've been so troubled thinking about their fate. But how did you get them out? And were they not as frightened of you as they were of the Narragansett?"

"I had been there before and gave them a little food. I told them I would be back, but they must keep doing as their captors told them and work in the fields as they did each day. We watched and waited until the men were gone hunting. The women were ignored while they were in the fields. No one thought they would leave. Where would they go? So it was an easy thing for Johnny and me to go in and lead them out. We gave them food and water, then put them on the horses and single file led them away." He looked at Heather Flower. "We came almost the same way as we did when I rescued you."

Warmth flooded her cheeks that came not from the fire, and there was a patter in her heart as she looked into his bay-blue eyes. "You were my hero, Dirk. You saved me from death. You are my hero again today. Thank you for saving my friends, my sisters."

Benjamin stood and poked the logs with a stick, reviving the flames. "Yes, thank you, Dirk. I know we've had our differences, and certainly this will not solve the problems between your people and ours, but you have friends here in Southold. We are forever in your debt."

Mary and Lizzie looked at each other. Mary spoke their question. "Where will you and Heather Flower live?" All eyes turned toward Dirk.

He looked at his new bride. "I have much work to do as the Dutch government expands their trade west. If you will consent, we'll live at Fort Amsterdam. But I will make sure you have transportation to visit

Montauk, Fort Corchaug, and Southold as often as you like."

Heather Flower stood. Her eyes sought out Grissell and Patience as she took her husband's hand. "It is my hope that Long Island will not always be divided, that the people here may learn to live together as one. Until that day I will be by your side, my husband." She turned to Mary, Lizzie, and her parents. "But I will miss you all and Lizzie's Hatterie too. I'll come to visit you because you will always be in my thoughts and my heart. I cannot stay away."

With much hugging and kissing they said their goodbyes.

Dirk scooped her into his arms and carried her to Miss Button. He lifted her high onto the saddle's pommel. He climbed up behind her and with her blue satin gown flowing behind them and his arm around her waist, they rode off toward Flushing. It wasn't the end of the story. It was a beginning.

ACKNOWLEDGMENTS

I have much gratitude for those who have encouraged me, taught me, and prayed for me. I am blessed by you!

Thank you to my heavenly Father, the Author of dreams, my refuge and my strength.

Thank you to my family for their patience and support.

My father and my husband are the first readers I dare show my manuscripts, and I depend on their keen eye and words of advice laced with encouragement. My dad, Howard M. Worley, published his first novel, *The Stagecoach Murders,* in 2012 at age eighty-nine, despite an aortic valve replacement and followed two days later by a stroke suffered in the midst of completing his western romance, a la L'Amour and Zane Grey. He treated those setbacks as but a blip to his health and got back in the saddle to finish the book. Thank you, Dad, for your true grit. I love brainstorming with my husband, Tom — he gives me encouragement and fresh perspectives. Thank you for enduring with me to the deadlines and beyond.

I've been blessed with three supportive daughters and their husbands — Jennifer and Shane, Lisa and Jon, and Kelly and Cory — and eight grandchildren, Dylan, Emma, Abbey, Sophie, Olivia, Ashley, Caden, and Brody. Tom has brought more sweet family with his children, Sasha, Steve and his wife Michelle, and three grandchildren, Sarah, Vito, and Vincent — all who have shown me love and support and I thank you!

I have some pretty neat siblings too. Thank you to Linda Lohr, Cynthia Dort, and Mark Worley — each of you show your love and support in your own special way!

A big thank-you to the Southold Indian Museum. And to Lisa Cordani-Stevenson who so graciously kept the museum open for me when I arrived late on a Sunday afternoon. The museum is a treasure, and I'm so thankful for curators like Lisa who enjoy sharing their passion and knowledge!

And continued heartfelt thanks to the Southold Free Library and the Southold Historical Society for their support. I'm especially grateful to Melissa Andruski and Daniel McCarthy for their friendship, enthusiasm, and willingness to assist me.

A huge thank-you to the Revell team, who have become like family to me. A special thank-you to my editor, Vicki Crumpton, who makes my work stronger with her expertise, gentle advice, humor, and encouragement. A big thank-you to Barb Barnes, Twila Bennett, Lindsay Davis, Michelle Misiak, Claudia Marsh, Erin Bartels, Cheryl VanAndel. They and their staff — the talented group who work in editorial, marketing, publicity, cover art, and sales — strive to make my book the best it can be.

I'm forever grateful to Barbara Scott, Greg Johnson, and WordServe Literary Agency. Thank you so much for your belief in my story and continued support!

My thanks always to Bob Welch's Beachside Writers with Jane Kirkpatrick, the Mount Hermon Conference faculty and staff, and for the huge support of the American Christian Fiction Writers, Romance Writers of America, and Oregon Christian Writers.

And a warm thank-you to my readers — you have a special place in my heart. Thank you for joining me and the Hortons on our journey. Please visit me at www.rebeccade

marino.com to leave me a message or sign up for my newsletter. I love to connect on Facebook and Pinterest too!

A special thank-you to The BookLits, a group of readers dear to my heart, who encourage me, pray for me, and joyfully put a shout out for me. You are a dream of a team!

Dora Wagner
Lucy Reynolds
Debbie Curto
Angel Holland
Patricia Lee
Wanda McAnany
Courtney Clark
Kristine Morgan
Patty Mingus
Margi Dean
Iola Reneau
Kathy Jacob
Susan Strickland Grondin
Kelly O'Neil Hart
Lisa Landrum Henson
Lynne Young
Deb Stein
Cynthia Lovely
Cynthia Dort
Wilani Wahi
April Morris

Heather Tabors
Charlotte Dance
Rebecca Petersen
Bonnie Traher
Virginia Winfield
Kaytee Rodden-Beswick
Teresa Wade Sheroke
Betty Dean Newman
Cheryl Baranski
Laura Viol
Victor Gentile
Amy Putney

ABOUT THE AUTHOR

Rebecca DeMarino is the author of *A Place in His Heart,* a historical romance novel inspired by her ninth great-grandparents, Barnabas and Mary Horton. She lives in the Pacific Northwest with her husband. Learn more at www.rebeccade marino.com.